Float My Boat

Harri Beaumont

Contents

Prologue

Ten years ago

It had been three months, but it still felt like everyone was staring. Making jokes. Whispering. Every time I went to the rowing club, it felt the same, my presence no longer about hard work, training, and my efforts to get onto the national squad and go to the Olympics. Now all anyone cared about was—

'Hey, Miri!' called one of the juniors—an obnoxious seventeen-year-old who'd hit on me more than once. But today his tone put me on edge.

I turned, giving him a, *What the fuck do you want?* kind of glare.

'You know how you like *older men* ...?' he shouted for all to hear, his tone suggestive.

I turned away, closed my eyes for a beat, then climbed into my single scull without giving him the satisfaction of an answer.

It didn't deter him. 'Maybe you should pick Mac next!'

The kid and his friends all fell about laughing, seeing as Mac was the oldest member of the rowing club. He could barely walk, could barely hear, in short, was not long for this world ...

I pushed away from the pontoon, glad of the easy escape. I'd definitely found myself in worse predicaments in recent times, but something about being belittled by someone who could barely keep a boat afloat grated more than usual.

'You can run but you can't hide!' he shouted after me.

'How about Coach Jimmy?' one of the others hollered, emboldened by his idiot friend.

I gritted my teeth, telling myself to ignore them.

'That's the one!' laughed the first kid. 'Look! She's blushing!'

'Fuck it,' I whispered, raising my head to stare them down. 'I have never dated anyone at the rowing club,' I shouted, loud enough for everyone in the vicinity to hear, so very tired of the lies and bullshit and out and out bullying. 'And I damned well never will!'

The junior and his friends made ooo-noises, high-fiving for eliciting a reaction, and anger and frustration burned hot in my veins. I tried not to let it affect me, taking a half-stroke and focusing on maneuvering myself away from the moored boats in the marina, wanting only to get away, to lose myself in the rhythm and flow of exercise, and the feeling of flying up the river. But then the ooo-ing abruptly ceased, and my eyes flicked to the group of their own accord, where I found Andrew, a tall, blonde, new-ish member of the club standing over the kids, and he did not look impressed, his face scrunched into a dark scowl.

Andrew was intimidating, or so all my friends thought. Quietly brooding, divine to look at, and powerfully built. I wasn't sure what I thought of him, exactly, but intimidating didn't quite fit. Intrigue was more like it. He was so mysterious, keeping himself to himself.

I couldn't hear what he said to the juniors, but I could feel his fearsome energy from where I bobbed up and down on the water, openly watching.

The juniors ducked their heads, looking down at their feet while their mouths moved, then scuttled off into the boathouse. And then Andrew turned and looked up, our eyes meeting across the open space, and my stomach clenched at the warmth in his eyes. He gave the smallest of nods, and I returned the gesture, willing him to understand my gratitude, and realizing that maybe intrigue wasn't quite the right emotion after all.

Chapter 1

'Oh my good gracious, he is *such* a douchebag,' said Ottie, her curly, strawberry-blonde hair bouncing as she dropped into the chair opposite mine.

'*Such* a douchebag,' echoed Livia, leaning back and crossing her long legs, following Ottie's gaze to where Theo lounged against the bar, chatting up two women.

'Hmm,' I said noncommittally because although objectively I knew they had a point, a part of me wished I was one of those women, the object of his rapt attention.

Theo was tall and covered in lean, defined muscle, his brown hair, chocolate eyes, and high cheekbones making him devilishly attractive. We'd been on a couple of recent dates, and we'd kissed a few times, after he'd complimented me and looked at me like I was the only person in the room—just like he was looking at those women now—but when I'd refused to sleep with him ... curtains.

'Hell-ooooo,' said Livia, clicking her fingers in front of my face. 'Earth to Miri!'

I felt a deep blush creep across my skin but pretended they hadn't caught me ogling. 'Sorry, I was just wondering if the bar staff have enough limes.'

Ottie folded her arms across her chest. 'Uh-huh,' she said skeptically.

'We should drink elsewhere occasionally,' said Hazel, the fourth member of our crew, as she put down her empty G&T glass. 'It's not fair for us to always come here. You don't get to switch off.'

'It's so damned convenient, though,' said Livia, ever the practical project manager.

'And cheaper than anywhere else,' added Ottie, spoken like a true PHD student.

'Only because Miri gives us a discount,' said Hazel, furrowing her brow, her auburn fringe getting caught in the lines. She was a lawyer for a small law firm in town, and although we'd rowed in the same crew for years, I still felt like I didn't fully understand her. The other two, on the other hand, were open books.

'It's fine,' I said, waving a hand. 'It's close to the rowing club, and I'm glad for the business.'

My bar—named *Miri's* because creativity has never been my strongest suit—was a mere hundred meters from the club, upstairs from my café of the same name. Yes, I know I could have done better, and it's perhaps a tad egotistical, but I'm a competitive rower—it goes with the territory—and in my defense, as I've already pointed out, my imagination isn't anything to write home about.

Although I *was* genuinely happy everyone drank in my bar, it did get old, no one ever buying me a drink and always looking hopefully at me for freebies. It had got totally out of hand in the beginning, so I'd nipped it in the bud, offering club members a ten percent discount, and making it clear that was all they were ever going to get. It mostly worked, save for occasional puppy dog eyes from some of the younger members, but I'd learned to ignore them.

It had been a hard slog, setting the place up, and I'd even had to give up rowing for a couple of years to work evenings and weekends, and, well, all hours, really. But it had paid off, and now I had freedom and staff and fiscal security. What more could a woman want?

My eyes flicked back to Theo. *Sigh.*

The place was busy tonight, a Thursday, and not only was it packed with boaties, but a ton of young professionals had shown up, too. It was a warm, late spring evening, the first properly good weather of the year, and apparently the pre-programmed reaction of our species to those conditions was to run to the river and drink. Although that's hardly something for me to complain about.

We sat by the open doors out onto the terrace where the tables, chairs, and bench planters had all been lovingly handmade from reclaimed wood by Noah, another member of the club. The plants had come back to life, and a few patrons were snapping pictures of the fragrant wallflowers, something that always buoyed me.

'What's the session tomorrow?' asked Ottie.

We were all in the top women's squad of Dex Rowing Club, along with Belle, but she'd been absent for a few weeks because of work, something top secret apparently going on in her lab.

'Ummmm, sprints, I think,' said Hazel, prodding the lime at the bottom of her empty glass with her straw.

'Yep, sprints,' agreed Livia, who was always on top of such things.

The others started complaining about how much it was going to hurt, but I zoned them out, my gin and tonic having provided the perfect haze as Jack Johnson's voice came through the speakers, making me nostalgic for my youth.

My eyes drifted again to Theo, who was laughing loudly, the women still in his trance, and my guts wrenched. It was stupid because he was, objectively speaking, a douchebag, and much younger than me, but he was also hot, and arrogant, and right in front of me every freaking day. It wasn't like I wanted to marry him, but it wasn't like I had any other options ...

A hand squeezed my shoulder, a warm presence filling the space behind me, and I looked up to find Andrew placing a new G&T in front of me. He squeezed again, then moved away, taking his broad shoulders, stacked physique, and wavy blond hair out onto the terrace, where he joined the rest of the senior men's squad.

No one ever bought me drinks apart from Andrew, who also refused to take the ten percent discount. He said he could afford to pay full price and felt shitty about not paying it when he knew how hard I worked. It made me go gooey inside, which was unfortunate, seeing as he was off limits.

'Now that one is hot as the sun,' said Livia, already onto her third drink.

'Hot, but *terrifying*,' Ottie countered with a pout of her full lips.

'He's not terrifying!' I said on a laugh. He could be a little stern sometimes, it was true, but—

'Not to *you* because he *loves* you,' said Hazel, giving me a sly sideways glance.

I kicked her under the table. 'He does *not*.'

Livia grinned, clearly delighted at the prospect of a collective mobbing, then said loudly, 'Why don't you just date him? I would if I were you. I mean, *look* at him.'

I did, and found him looking right back, his lips quirking up a little at the corners. I quickly turned away, leaning closer to Livia. 'He heard you,' I hissed, 'and he's not interested. He's never made a move. He friend-zoned me—you know this!' My voice had become alarmingly high pitched, so I clamped my lips shut.

'Because you told him you never wanted to date anyone at the club,' Hazel said with an eyeroll.

She was right, I had said that, but I hadn't meant to say it to him! 'It would be too weird,' I said in a rush, my face flaming again. 'We're friends, and he doesn't see me that way.'

My eyes flicked back to Theo, who'd moved on, now flirting with a novice rower who was batting her pretty, fake eyelashes at him. She wouldn't last long. Rowing wasn't generally a sport for fake-eyelash-wearers because we had no time for such things.

A new woman, this one tall with long, silky, raven-black hair stepped up beside Theo, and my chest jumped with joyful recognition. 'Belle!' I shouted, leaping to my feet along with the rest of my crew and bundling her. 'You're here!'

She awkwardly returned our group embrace. 'Hey, guys.'

Theo leaned towards us, brushing my arm with his hand. 'Can I get in on that?' he asked, a glint in his eye.

Ottie gave him a dirty look as some drunk guy approached, barely able to walk straight. 'Can I get in on that, too?' he drawled. I froze, appraising him to assess what sort of drunk this one was. Over the years I'd seen them all, ranging from mildly lecherous to creepy to dangerous. One time it had been so bad, I'd had to use the panic button under the bar. I'd never closed alone again.

'I like big girls,' the drunk guy continued, stepping closer.

We were all tall, with muscular arms and powerful legs. Those features, along with our will to win, was why we were in the first crew. What made us the best.

'You like big girls?' he asked Theo, his half-raised eyebrow and thin smile saying, *am I right?*

Theo shrugged. 'Dude, I like all girls.'

The guy laughed as he pressed his chest to Ottie's arm, and she jerked away.

'Back up,' I said, holding up a hand to stop his advance, dread creeping low in my belly because this one was giving me bad vibes. At least tonight, I had an army at my back.

'Don't be like that! I'm only being friendly,' he said, angling towards me and looking me up and down. 'You want in on the action, is that it? I'm not usually a brunette kinda guy, but I could make an exception.'

'I'd like you to leave,' I said, my tone professional and firm, even if my insides were quaking just a little.

The man laughed, then looked to Theo for support. 'This girl! Who does she think she is?' He clapped a hand on my shoulder, and Theo cocked an eyebrow, looking from the man to me and back again as though this were entertainment, excited to see what would happen next.

I rolled my eyes as I removed the guy's hand. 'You're a dick, Theo,' I said to him before returning to the drunk. 'I'm the owner, and if you don't leave now, I'm calling the police.'

'Woah there, cowgirl,' said the guy. 'You're the big boss, huh? Then why don't I buy you a drink and we can get better acquainted?'

I gritted my teeth. 'Out. Now.'

For a moment, I thought he might object, but the rest of my crew were glaring, looking as though they would like nothing better than to kick his ass into the gutter, and over his shoulder, the men's crew had started taking an interest, too. My eyes connected with Andrew's for a split second, and the concern on his face warmed me from the inside out.

'Pft,' said the drunk guy, shoulder checking me as he passed. 'This place is a dump, anyway.'

I watched him leave, my heart hammering against my ribs, my hands starting to shake. The others squeezed my arm, then went back to squealing over Belle's appearance, but Theo leaned into my space. 'You're hot as fuck when you do shit like that,' he whispered.

My gaze connected with Andrew's once more, his features black as night, eyes throwing daggers our way, although whether it was on account of the drunk or his crew mate, I wasn't sure. I turned my attention back to Theo, sneering just a little. 'And you're a useless piece of shit. I'll be right back,' I said to my crew, then went to my office and closed out the world.

I sank into my leather desk chair and looked up at the ceiling, taking deep, steadying breaths. No matter how many times things like that happened, I never grew immune to them. And Theo was such an idiot ... *Fuck!* Why couldn't a nice, straightforward guy just appear in my life? Why did I have to find that arsehole attractive?

Because there's no one else, my mind whispered in reply.

Chapter 2

We all leaned back in our chairs, our legs like jelly after the eight five-hundred-meter sprints we'd just endured.

'Hell on Earth,' said Ottie.

'The worst,' agreed Livia.

'I think I'm going to be sick,' said Belle. 'I haven't done anything like that in a while.'

We sat on the terrace outside the clubhouse in the sunshine, watching as the men came in off the water, all of us unashamedly ogling their naked torsos from behind the safety of our sunglasses. Not that I looked at Pete or Noah. Only Theo, who, although dick-ish, was built like an Adonis. And if Andrew happened to be standing beside him, I could hardly be blamed for casting an eye over his broad shoulders, chiseled lats, and perfect six pack, too.

'Why do they have to walk around topless all the time?' said Hazel. She leaned her head against the back of her chair, looking up at the cloudless blue sky as though it might contain answers.

'Urgh, I don't know,' said Ottie, 'but I'm here for it. Like, more than usual.'

Belle nodded significantly. 'You're probably hitting peak fertility.'

We all swiveled our heads to look at her. She, being a scientist, was want to come out with all kinds of fascinating information we never knew we needed to know. And a good many things we could have done without knowing, too.

'Go on,' said Livia, always the one to dig for more.

'Well, when you're fertile, your body wants to have sex,' Belle said simply. 'You emit pheromones, walk differently, your temperature rises, and you're more interested in,'—she circled her hand in the direction of the men—'that whole situation over there.'

Hazel made an o shape with her mouth. 'Fascinating.'

'And are they more interested in us?' asked Livia.

I giggled at her tone, suspicious yet demanding.

'Of course!' said Belle. 'They can smell the fertility.'

Ottie gave a sharp, shocked inhale. 'They can ... what?'

Belle raised her eyebrows. 'Natural selection ... what a thing. And they probably notice when we bat our eyelashes more, although, it's not like they need much encouragement.'

'Well, I wish there was someone I wanted to smell my pheromones,' said Ottie. 'Everyone at the university is so *young*, and there's no one here at the club.'

'No hot professor?' I asked.

Ottie shook her head. 'Nope. They're all old and gross and arrogant; it's not like in the movies.'

'That sucks,' said Livia. 'But I feel your pain.'

'Urgh.' I joined Hazel in looking to the heavens. 'We all do.'

'Apart from Belle,' countered Hazel. 'How is your boyfriend?'

Belle waved a dismissive hand. 'Fine, I think. I haven't seen him in a couple of weeks.'

'Not at peak fertility, then?' joked Livia, raising a questioning eyebrow.

We snickered while Belle pondered the question. 'No, I guess not. I should arrange to see him next week.' She pulled out her phone, wasting no time, and he pinged her right back. 'I can let you know how he is after Thursday.'

'Wow,' said Ottie. 'You're a sniper.'

'It's always the quiet ones,' Livia agreed.

'She's not quiet,' I said. 'She's smart; there's a difference.'

Belle smiled as she shoved her phone into her pocket, and when I turned back to ogle the men, I found them approaching. My chest tightened as my eyes clocked first Theo and then Andrew.

'We've got to dash!' squeaked Hannah, their miniscule, blonde-haired cox, pulling her husband, Pete, behind her. 'See you tomorrow!'

'Bye!' we all chimed, as Andrew and Theo sat beside us on the step at the edge of the patio, leaning against the bollards. Andrew pulled a tee over his head while Noah lay back on the hard stone, draping his t-shirt over his eyes.

'Good outing?' I asked no one in particular.

'Yeah,' said Theo, but he wasn't looking at me. His eyes roamed across the rest of my crew, then inside, to where the novices sat together.

'It was good,' said Andrew, tapping my foot with his. 'How were your sprints?'

'*Abominable*,' Ottie said dramatically, drawing out the word as she leaned forward in her seat.

A smirk tugged at Theo's lips as he took her in. 'That bad, huh?'

'Worse,' I said, and then immediately wished I hadn't because Theo's features made it abundantly clear he couldn't care less what I thought.

'You're an arsehole,' said Ottie, getting up to refill her water bottle. 'Presumably that's why you have to date so many women, because as soon as you reveal your true self, they run for the hills.'

Theo laughed easily. 'If you want to date me, Ottie, you could just say so.'

If Ottie heard, she didn't show any signs, instead greeting Seb—the fifth member of the senior men's squad—as she stepped inside.

Theo shrugged it off and turned back to face me, but before Theo could get any words out, Andrew moved to crouch beside me and slid his hand into mine, lacing our fingers. 'Hey ...' he said quietly.

What the fuck? His hand. Into mine. His big, warm, callused hand, and his face was really quite close. The whole thing was entirely alarming.

He squeezed, and I looked from our joined fingers to his eyes and back again, glad my sunglasses must have been covering at least some of my shock.

'Can I borrow you?' he asked, his tone low and husky.

'Uhhhh, sure!' I said too brightly, aiming for something light and confusion free, but not quite nailing it. He stood and drew me to my feet, refusing to relinquish my hand, and I pasted a fixed smile on my lips and acted as though my heart hadn't stopped beating. At least, I tried, my brain working overtime, attempting to discern what in the name of the sweet goddess divine was going on.

He was, undoubtedly, putting on this show for some benign, friend-zone-related reason. Probably just being nice and rescuing me from Theo, and if that was the case, I wasn't going to look a gift horse in the mouth. Everyone knew Theo and I had gone out a few times. That was the problem with dating anyone at the club. As soon as you so much as scheduled a dinner, *everyone* knew about it, and then they could be relied upon to put two and two together and come up with a whole range of numbers that had nothing to do with four, complete with corresponding speculations as to the outcome.

I'd told my crew the truth—that when I'd refused to put out, Theo had dropped me like a stone—but they wouldn't have told anyone, so who knew what fiction the grapevine was spinning. Had Andrew heard something bad? Was that why he was doing this? I'd thought, given Theo's rampant womanizing, that our dates were old news, but maybe I'd missed something ...

Andrew still had hold of my hand, which was so *very* weird, and pulled me towards the boathouse, stopping out of earshot of the others—although still in their view—beside the open sliding doors.

I pulled off my sunglasses, and for a moment, all he did was look at me, standing too close. I looked back into his deep, green eyes, becoming twitchy, very conscious that if we gazed at each other for too long, we'd attract attention. Who was I kidding? We'd already attracted attention. I could practically feel the eyes of our crews burning holes in Andrew's back, no doubt watching with slack-jawed interest. But seeing as my own jaw was somewhere near the floor, I didn't have the wherewithal to check.

Andrew played with my fingers as he stared down into my eyes. The whole thing was bizarre. He knew it, I knew it, our crews certainly knew it, but only one of us knew what was going on, and it wasn't me.

'Andrew ...?' I said, my voice breathy, probably because my lungs seemed to have joined my heart in giving up the ghost.

'You like him, right?' he said quietly, swiping his thumb back and forth across my skin.

'Uh ...' My mouth went dry, and I wracked my brain as I tried to work out what he meant. 'Oh ...Theo?'

'Theo,' he confirmed in a voice that sounded almost disgusted.

What the actual fuck? Why would he ask that? And what was with the tone? 'Well, I ... We've been on maybe two or three dates?'

I faltered, sure a shadow had passed across Andrew's eyes, but he seemed to be waiting for more, so my brain sent signals to my voice box without consulting me about what should come out. 'He's hot, and has a certain charm, but ...'

Apparently I'd said the wrong thing because Andrew pulled back a little, but I didn't know what he wanted from me or what the hell was going on! Andrew and I never talked about dating. I'd seen him with women, and he knew I'd hooked up with guys, but nothing had ever lasted for either of us, and we'd always operated a strict don't ask, don't tell policy. I'm not sure why, really, but it felt awkward talking to him about men.

He raked a hand through his hair, looking tortured, hesitant, conflicted maybe? 'Theo's not a nice guy,' he said, some deep-seated emotion in his voice I couldn't decipher. 'Especially when it comes to women.'

They were in the same crew, meaning Andrew couldn't hate Theo *that* much, so I was surprised by the venom in his words.

He closed his eyes and exhaled. 'But if you want him to want you ...'

If I want him to—

'He needs to know there's competition.'

'I ... uh ...' I cast my eyes towards Theo, and he—along with everyone else—was taking a keen interest in our conversation, staring at our joined hands. And maybe it was because Theo's earlier slight still smarted, or maybe it was due to other reasons I steadfastly refused to acknowledge, but I leaned closer. 'You may have a point,' I breathed, inadvertently looking at his full lips before hastily returning my attention to his stormy eyes, 'but ... why did you bring me over here?'

My lungs finally remembered their job was to ingest air, and his musky scent became almost overwhelming, wrapping around me as he looked so deeply into my eyes, so unwaveringly—apparently not caring half the club was watching—that I very nearly went weak at the knees. *Must be the training session catching up with me,* I decided, as I tried and failed to extract myself from his gaze. Andrew was captivating, and I was desperate for more words to fall from his lips, to hear what he had to say, what this was all about ...

He half shrugged. 'So let's give him some.'

'I ... Andrew ... I don't ... wait ... what?' My eyes went wide, my lips parting on a gasp as I realized what he was suggesting. 'You want to ... um ... date me?' The words came out like spears, too sharp.

He leaned back—practically a recoil—his brow furrowing. 'Pretend to,' he clarified, his face shuttering, a barrier slamming shut between us, locking his tenderness up inside. 'It'll drive Theo crazy, not being able to have you.'

My brain was a haze of shock, not keeping up at all. 'I ... you ... want to *fake* date me?'

He smiled brightly, a plastic thing that didn't look right on his lips and certainly didn't meet his hardening eyes. 'It'll be fun,' he said, looking down at our joined fingers, 'don't you think?'

No! It wouldn't be fun at all! It would be torture of the most diabolical kind. 'Well, I ... guess?' Someone else seemed to have taken over my mind because his proposal was something I would surely never agree to. I *hated* lying. With the burning passion of ten thousand fiery suns.

He brought the heel of my hand to his lips, hovering it in front of his mouth for a moment, giving me a chance to pull away. I didn't, his touch winching my chest so tight I wondered if it was possible to crack one's own ribs, and then he kissed my skin, or, more accurately, nibbled it, his eyes still on mine.

'Andrew,' I said on a breathy exhale, my eyes fluttering shut because whatever he was doing was doing unspeakable things to me.

He moved closer, until his breath caressed my ear. 'Can I kiss you?' he murmured. 'Just a quick goodbye peck … Nothing showy.'

The sound I made in response was a cross between a whine and a groan and an almost hysterical laugh, and for a moment I wondered if I was in a dream. It *was* the kind of dream I'd been known to have.

'Please?' he said, and I felt the deep rumble of his voice low in my belly, so I leaned against him and hid my face in his t-shirt, smothering my blushing cheeks, clear evidence of the embarrassing effect he was having on me. He didn't want me. Not really. He was doing this to help me with Theo, but even so, my blood sang at the closeness, taking as much contact as I could get because my skin loved it but so rarely found it available.

I resisted the urge to purr like a creature possessed as his arms wrapped around me, and I slid mine around him, too, seconds ticking by as we just stood there, neither of us moving, the heat of our bodies merging, some dizzying chemical Belle would probably know the name of seeping into my blood. The steady thud of his heart beneath my ear lulled me, turning me languid and malleable, and I pressed myself closer still. It was totally inappropriate.

'Well?' he whispered.

I tipped my head back, peeling my face away so my words wouldn't be eaten by his chest, a thrill of excitement shooting through me as I met his insistent gaze. It was almost as though he *wanted* to kiss me, and that thought had my left eyebrow cocking of its own accord. 'Well,' I heard myself say in the most flirtatious of tones, 'we are dating, aren't we? So I'd be mad if you didn't.'

A wide, slow smile spread across his lips, and my stomach flipped. Actually freaking flipped. And then his lips were on mine, and his hand was on my neck, and I didn't know which way was up. And then the soft warmth of him was gone, and with a mischievous, victorious smile and a final squeeze of my hand, he stalked away, leaving me reeling, unsure if I could do vital things like pump blood around my body, let alone walk straight.

I watched his retreating back until it disappeared into the men's locker room and then donned my sunglasses and returned to the others, my heart hammering, my whole body feeling shaky—no doubt on account of the infernal training session. Sprints were the absolute worst for jelly legs.

My crew and Andrew's were all still staring as I returned to my seat, some of their mouths literally hanging open, and try as I might, I couldn't suppress my giddy smile.

'What?' I asked with an innocent half-laugh, trying and failing to force my lips into a neutral line.

Theo sprang to his feet and raced after Andrew, the door to the locker room slamming against the wall as he yanked it open.

Ottie dragged her chair closer. 'Spill,' she demanded in a low, conspiratorial tone.

Seb's lithe, dark-haired form joined our group, his eyes flashing delightedly as he took a seat and said salaciously, 'What did I miss?'

'You literally told us last night you would never be more than friends,' accused Livia, folding her arms and shuffling so close our knees touched.

I shrugged. *We're not. It's fake*. Something in my chest cratered at the thought. 'We *are* friends.'

'So that won't happen again?' asked Hazel, a knowing smile taking hold of her usually mild features.

The feel of Andrew's lips lingered on my skin, and every part of me hoped against hope it would happen again. It was likely, wasn't it? We would need to be convincing because ... why were we doing this again? Oh, yeah ... Theo. It made no sense. *I don't even* like *Theo!*

'Well?' Livia pressed.

'Um ... well ...'

'Oh my God, Miri!' Ottie squealed, clasping her hands to her chest in glee.

'Don't make it weird,' I hissed, trying to frown, but it was difficult, seeing as my brain was willfully disregarding my wishes, overridden by pesky endorphins, or some such thing.

'You're dating?' asked Livia, needing clarity in all things. 'Is that what's happening here?'

'I ... um ... think so?'

'You *think so*,' Livia said slowly, pursing her lips as though trying to piece together a puzzle that didn't quite fit.

'It's new,' I said. 'Really new. We're not at the label stage.'

'When did this even happen?' asked Ottie, her chin now resting on her joined hands as she leaned so far forward it was a miracle the laws of physics kept her in her seat.

'Are you at peak fertility?' said Belle, easily the calmest of my crew. She lounged on the grey paving slabs, her back against a bollard, legs crossed in front of her, observing us as though we were lab rats. 'That would explain his territorial behavior, and your openness to his so publicly staking his claim.'

'Jesus, guys!' said Noah, rolling to his feet. By the looks on my crew's faces, they'd all but forgotten he was there. 'Can't you just let them be happy?'

'Ha!' laughed Seb.

'Um ...' Ottie leaned back a fraction, looking as though she was genuinely considering it.

'No,' said Livia, dismissing the suggestion outright.

'It flies in the face of our group dynamic,' agreed Belle.

Hazel hummed. 'We could try, I suppose. For Miri's sake?'

But before they could reach a consensus, Andrew reappeared from the locker room, his kit bag slung over his shoulder, Theo a pace behind. We swung our gazes to gawk in a movement so synchronized it was as though we were controlled by a single brain.

'But are you?' demanded Theo, his tone edged with barely contained anger. 'Because we've been dating.'

Andrew turned to face Theo, looking down at him from his two-inch height advantage, appraising him for a beat before calmly asking, 'Is that what you call it?' But underneath the calm veneer, his tone promised violence, and of a kind entirely different to Theo's yappy dog variety.

'Fuck you,' spat Theo, squaring up to Andrew. My band of observers and I collectively inhaled.

It was absurd ... ridiculous, and the words, *it's all fake! Don't do it!* were only nano seconds from spilling from my lips.

But then Theo seemed to remember that along with his height advantage, Andrew also had a not-inconsiderable weight advantage, and instead of throwing a punch, he exhaled a sneer and pushed past his would-be adversary, throwing a dismissive, '*Whatever*,' back over his shoulder.

We observers exhaled, and my shoulders, which had crept up to my ears without my realizing, dropped back to their normal position, but before I could begin the inevitable debrief with my crew, Andrew's eyes found mine and held onto them for a moment, a triumphant gleam in his gaze. My chest ratcheted tight once more, then Andrew turned and followed Theo through the gate, and I sagged back into my seat, wondering what the fuck was going on.

Ottie grabbed my arm with an excited squeal. 'That,' she said, waving her hand in the general direction of Andrew's retreating back. 'Whatever just happened over there ... it was gold!'

'He's fucking terrifying,' said Livia.

'But hot,' said Hazel.

'And successful,' said Ottie.

'And clever,' said Livia. 'He convinced his company to sponsor all three of our new boats!'

'And he has the best ergo score in the club,' said Belle, ever the analyst.

'And he's Men's Captain,' said Hazel.

Livia nodded along. 'Mmm hmm, there's a lot to be said for a man with power.'

'Guys!' I protested, half-delighted and half-horrified.

'But goddamn is he easy on the eye,' said Ottie.

'Yep,' Seb agreed. 'Very, very much.'

Chapter 3

I was a ball of nerves out on the wind-swept water with my crew the following morning. Thank goodness we were doing a gentle, steady-state piece ahead of the regatta at the weekend, which didn't require much from my conscious brain.

The act of dipping my blades (known as oars to the non-rowing world) into the water, connecting with my legs, pulling through with my arms, then pressing the handles down to pop them out, had long ago become habitual. I was well past ten thousand hours, so all I had to do was set a decent pace for my crew behind me and remember to pay attention to my coach's occasional megaphone-enhanced commands from the narrow dirt towpath where she cycled beside us. Which meant I had plenty of time for my mind to process other things.

Like the text messages I'd exchanged with Andrew the previous evening.

Miri 21:15: OMG, Andrew!

Miri 21:16:

Yep, just one minute later.

Miri 21:16: Sorry. Probably no need for the exclamation mark.

And yes, I spelled out *exclamation mark* like the loser millennial I am. Then I freaked out because, why the hell had I sent that?

I put my phone down, then apparently immediately picked it up again, which I know because the time stamp on the next message was exactly the same as the one before. *How am I this tragic?*

Miri 21:16: I think I'm freaking out. How is this going to work? What are we going to tell everyone?

I'd then managed to put my phone down for longer than ten seconds, mainly because I'd had the longest shower of all time, and when I checked it again, Andrew had replied.

Andrew 22:01: Don't freak out. Breakfast after training?

His message was so calm. So assured. But it contained no hint as to why he was doing this, and none of it made any sense!

Miri 22:07: We need rules of engagement.

Andrew 22:07:

He messaged straight back – yay!

Andrew 22:07: Are we going to war?

Miri 22:07: You know what I mean.

Andrew 22:08: Go to sleep. We can plan our battle strategy in the morning.

Miri 22:08: Urgh, fine.

Miri 22:09: P.S. you're annoying.

Andrew 22:09: Night, Miri. Sleep tight. X

A smile spread across my lips at his use of my name, his equally dorky millennial punctuation, the X that, even in text message form, had made my insides squeeze. I'd tried to sleep, but sleep had evaded me, so instead I'd lain awake replaying our brief kiss, then imagining other things we might do ...

But in the pit of my stomach sat a weight so heavy even the endorphins couldn't lift it because fake dating Andrew also meant lying to everyone we knew. And I *hated* lying.

At the end of our morning training session, we put away our boat and blades, then headed to the locker room, my attention still half on Andrew.

'Breakfast?' Hazel asked, looking hopefully at us, her question finally snapping my brain into the moment.

'I've got an early meeting,' said Livia, disappearing into the showers.

Ottie shook her head mournfully. 'I'm trying to be financially responsible; this whole student thing really sucks.'

We nodded sympathetically, but I never went to university, so I wouldn't really know.

Hazel turned her puppy dog gaze on me—her last resort. 'I ... um ...' Embarrassment flushed my features as I pulled on sweatpants and a hoodie. 'I'm meeting Andrew for breakfast.'

They stared blankly at me for a long moment.

'You're really dating, then?' Hazel said eventually.

I coughed awkwardly as I picked up my bag, then gave them a half nod, even lying by gesture feeling horrible.

Ottie cocked her head to the side and narrowed her eyes, perhaps sensing my hesitation. 'Hmmm.'

'Breakfast tomorrow?' I suggested, my heart in my mouth, then I dove for the exit, not waiting for their answers.

I ducked through the pedestrian gate out onto the street and hurried towards my café. Andrew's crew had come off the water before us, and I didn't want to keep him waiting, but as I crossed the piazza, nervous energy balled in my stomach. What on Earth should I say to him? How should I greet him? What rules should I suggest? Did he think me overly dramatic for insisting on rules?

I pushed open the café door and spotted him at a table by the window overlooking the river. The café sat underneath the terrace of the bar above, and it was packed already, the clientele mostly professionals conducting breakfast meetings and people like us grabbing sustenance after a workout.

The comforting scent of freshly baked bread, coffee, and sweet pastries washed over me, and the familiarity calmed me a little as I waved warmly to my servers before joining Andrew. But the roiling in my stomach returned in full force as I sat, so I ran my hands over the rustic wooden tabletop, then turned my eyes to the wildflowers in the jam jar between us. Anything to delay looking into his eyes.

'You seem nervous,' Andrew said in a low, gentle voice, leaning forward and resting his arms on the table, ducking his head a little to try and snare me.

'I ...' I still couldn't meet his eyes, and realized I'd started playing with my napkin. I dropped it, then inhaled deeply. 'I guess I am.' As soon as I admitted it, some of my tension eased. 'It's so sudden and public and I'm not a natural liar.'

My eyes flicked up as my mouth ran away with me. 'And it's ... *you*!'

Disappointment flashed across his features. 'You want to call it off?'

'No!' The word was out so fast it took even me by surprise.

He raised his eyebrows and a smile ghosted his lips.

I flagged a server to cover my awkwardness. 'But we need rules, and a consistent story.'

He nodded, although I wondered if the quirk of his lips was teasing, and I wrinkled my nose.

'What can I get you?' asked my perky new hire.

We ordered lattes and scrambled eggs on sourdough, like the good little athletes we were, and then, once the server was firmly out of earshot, I took a deep, centering breath and folded my hands in front of me. 'Rules.'

Andrew inclined his head, then waited for me to continue.

'That's all you've got? This was your idea!'

He gave me an indulgent look, then reached forward and covered my hand with his. As our skin connected, a spell wove between us, around us, through me, the warmth and reassurance chasing my unease away. This wasn't so bad. Andrew and I had been friends for years. What was I even worried about?

A movement in my periphery caught my eye, and I glanced sideways to find Theo looking through the window, staring straight at us. Right. Theo. Guilt seeped through me at having been caught with Andrew, and then I realize that Theo being there was probably why Andrew had taken my hand. Theo stormed off, and as I turned back to Andrew, I saw him afresh, noticing that he'd showered, changed into a t-shirt and jeans, and smelled good enough to eat, while I, on the other hand, was a mess. I hadn't showered, my hair was wind-whipped, and my face was probably still red from the training session. Not that Andrew seemed to care. And why the hell did I care? He'd seen me looking this way six days a week for the last who knew how many years.

The server put our food in front of us, and Andrew began to pull away, but I caught hold for a beat, not wanting to lose his touch, and he stilled. His hand dwarfed mine—even though mine were big for a woman—and I loved the scratch of his calluses against my skin. All rowers had them, hard won after months of living with painful blisters.

I pulled away with a slight shake of my head, puffing out a breath as I picked up my fork, forcing myself to focus. 'Holding hands is fine,' I said, trying to sound businesslike, then hurrying on without giving him a chance to reply. 'Hugs ... I mean, we hug anyway, so that's fine. So long as that's okay with you?'

He nodded, his eyes watching me with an intense expression I'd never seen on him before. Warm but guarded.

'It goes without saying that we should keep this between ourselves—we'd never live it down if the others found out, especially after what happened with my coach ...'

A tinge of concern marred his features. 'Of course.'

'And pet names are a no,' I said quickly, not wanting to dwell on the past.

He cracked a smile. 'But I'd been so looking forward to calling you *Buttercup*.'

I reared back, the mere thought of him calling me that in front of our friends making me squirm. '*Buttercup*?'

The skin around his eyes crinkled as he picked up his cutlery. 'Buttercups are beautiful.'

I shook my head vigorously. 'Hard no, or I'll have to call you Sugarplum or Honeybun or … *Booboo!*'

His fork paused halfway to his mouth. 'Which would it be?'

I lifted a coquettish shoulder. 'I guess we'll never know.'

He put down his cutlery, rested his forearms against the table's edge, then watched me for a beat. 'What about kissing?' he said nonchalantly, and I nearly choked on my latte. 'I don't want it to be weird, but we should try to be convincing. Natural.'

Oh my God. My insides clenched in the most vicious way, and I wondered if every one of my organs was failing in synchrony, but then I realized the pulse pounding in my ears indicated things were still ticking over, if a little faster than average. 'Okay,' I breathed, and the word pulled the air tight between us, while the way he looked at me leeched all moisture from my mouth.

Fake. This. Is. Fake! And don't freaking forget it.

I coughed, then imagined we were discussing the weather as I said, 'Dates.'

Andrew nodded enthusiastically. 'We should go on them.'

'When?' I laughed.

'Good point. If the opportunity arises, then.'

I inclined my head, inwardly delighted. 'Dating other people?'

A frown dug deep furrows in his brow. 'Hard no.'

'Agreed.'

His frown lifted.

'When should it end?'

He flinched.

'I mean, I don't want to take advantage.' *Shit, that sounded sexual.* 'I mean ... what if you meet someone you *actually* want to date?'

His frown returned, and I panicked. Had the *taking advantage* thing offended him?

'Let's cross that bridge if we get to it,' he said a little curtly, then softened as he continued, 'and in the meantime, let's just be open with each other.'

I nodded dumbly because the word *if* was taking up all my brain power. *If* we get to it? *If*? Andrew and I had been friends for years, but nothing this intimate had ever taken place between us. We'd rarely even eaten alone together—more often surrounded by our crews—so that, by itself, would have been a little disorienting, but this ...?

I'd always been attracted to Andrew on some level, from the first moment I'd laid eyes on him, but he'd never made a move, had firmly friend-zoned me, and then he'd started dating someone else. Then I'd started dating someone else, and since then, we'd never really been single at the same time, although in my case, my relationships could more accurately be described as a string of flings with men who were very much not keepers.

Andrew, on the other hand, seemed to only date super humans. He'd split up with his latest girlfriend a month or so ago, some heiress to a financial fortune who'd set up a sea of charities. She wasn't a rower, so I'd only caught glimpses of her from a distance, but I got the feeling she'd wanted to spend more time with him, and he was *always* at the club. I couldn't blame her. If he were truly mine, I'd want to lock him in my bedroom and never let him out.

But he wasn't mine. He saw me as a friend, and was only doing this to make Theo jealous, which was *ridiculous* because I'd only dated Theo on account of a dry spell, my vanity had appreciated his attention, and there was no one else available.

I should tell Andrew, should end it, should release him from whatever this arrangement was, but as I finally re-solved to do it—at least the first part—he looked at his watch, then pushed back his chair. 'I have to get to work.'

'I'll walk you out,' I said, pushing back my own chair and deciding not to say anything. The moment had passed, so clearly the universe didn't want me to end it just yet.

Andrew pulled a couple of notes out of his wallet and dropped them on the table. 'Andrew!' I protested. 'Break-fast is on me.'

'Nope,' he said with a determined shake of his head, stepping to the side and ushering me in front of him. 'It's our first date; I'm not letting you pay, and it was delicious, as always.'

I smiled, a glow of warmth spreading out through my chest. It was always so gratifying when someone compli-mented my businesses because my businesses were a part of me, a reflection of my personality in some way. 'Oh, fine, but the next one is on me.'

He made a non-committal noise in the back of his throat, but I didn't push, too distracted by his holding the door open for me then wrapping his fingers around mine, my breath catching in my throat, part of me nervous we'd be seen. Which was silly, seeing as being seen together was exactly the point.

We headed towards the back of the building, to the external metal stairs that led to my apartment's front door, and the parking lot where Andrew had parked his truck. This side of the building was not scenic, but I'd done what I could, flower-filled planters lining the sidewalk and stairs.

We came to a stop beside Andrew's impossibly clean blue truck, and tension crackled between us. I bit my lip, looking down at his fingers, and then he drew me slowly towards him.

His expression was hopeful when I looked up into his eyes, and the edge of vulnerability tugged at my heart-strings. I'd rarely seen him look anything but the picture of quiet confidence.

He bowed his head, and my heartrate rocketed. Were we really doing this? My brain somehow gave my neck the instruction to angle my head up towards him, and then he put his hands on my waist and pulled me all the way against him, and then his soft, warm lips were on mine, and I sighed into his mouth and forgot about anything but him.

I expected it to be quick like the last time, but he lingered, so my hands lifted to his back and slid down the muscular ridges on either side of his spine. His lips played with mine, sucking gently, the feeling erotic enough to short circuit my brain, diverting all available blood south and making me moan just a little. And then I was deepening the kiss, opening my mouth to him, hungry for more, but he went rigid and pulled away with a cough, averting his gaze as hot, cruel shame rushed through my guts, embarrassment turning my face some shade of puce I was glad I couldn't see.

Familiar voices across the street drew my attention—the women's novice crew—and I wanted to cry. That was why he'd kissed me, to convince our audience, not because he'd *wanted* to.

Shit.

Shit. Shit. Shit.

What was *wrong* with me?

'Miri, I—' His voice was tight, uncomfortable.

'I'm so sorry,' I whispered, unable to look at him. And then I fled.

Chapter 4

I couldn't concentrate all day, replaying the disastrous kiss again and again, a wave of nausea rolling through me every time I recalled the way he'd tensed, his cough, how I'd practically tried to stick my tongue down his throat ...

I'd basically jumped the poor guy, who'd been doing nothing but nobly playing his part as agreed.

But it had felt so damned good for those one or two brief seconds before he'd pulled away. His lips against mine, his muscles under my fingers. I'd wanted to dive under his skin and never come out. But that's not what this was. And in half an hour, after the meeting to talk logistics for the regatta this weekend, he'd probably call it off. The thought made me want to scream, even if rationally I knew that would be the best possible outcome because this whole thing was utter madness!

I sat back in my chair and scrubbed my face with my hands as an automatic log-out screen popped up on my computer, covering the accounts I'd been pretending to reconcile for the last two hours. Apparently I no longer even possessed the ability to match up a few numbers, Andrew consuming my entire conscious mind.

Not that reconciling the same old accounts week after week was in any way interesting these days. I'd loved it at the beginning, not to mention seeing the fruits of all my hard work rolling in, but the shine had come off, and now it was just a boring task that was too easy to complete myself to justify palming off onto my accountant.

I'd been feeling out of sorts for weeks, and as I stared through my office window at the clouds, I finally admitted to myself that I was bored with my life. I'd been on the same work-rowing-work merry-go-round for a decade, and it was beginning to drag me down.

I hated being stagnant, and for the first time in my life, I was. Had been for a while, really. The café and bar were doing well, so much so they barely needed me anymore, and I did the same training week in, week out with the same people, then raced at the same regattas every year. I loved my crew and rowing and my businesses, but I needed something new. A challenge. *Anything* to get me out of this rut.

Like marriage and babies and a happily ever after, said a voice from the deepest recesses of my mind. I shut it down. I was in my thirties, yes, but I still had plenty of time. Although it had been years since I'd had anything resembling a stable boyfriend, and even he hadn't lasted long, mainly because I'd never had time to see him.

Andrew, said the voice.

'Fuck off,' I said aloud, then wondered if I was losing my mind because I was literally talking to myself.

I needed something else. Something new. Something for *me.* And a relationship wouldn't fix those problems, even if one would be nice. Andrew's face popped back into my mind's eye, the image of his intelligent eyes, pillowy lips, and mop of blond hair as he looked down at me from above. This time, I didn't fight the daydream of Andrew kissing me back this morning, a daydream that had been demanding airtime in my brain all day, and as I let it play, he didn't just kiss me, he shoved me against the side of his truck and ravaged me.

I closed my eyes and shook the reel away; I could not keep doing this to myself. We were just friends, albeit entering into an unconventional arrangement, but friends nonetheless. This was not a long-term thing. This was not marriage and babies. It wasn't even dating.

But he was reluctant to put an end date on it. Said we'd cross that bridge if we got to it ...

I growled at my self-destructive internal voice, then looked at my watch. *Shit.* I jumped to my feet, daydreams and existential crises would have to wait because I was somehow late for the meeting, and I *hated* being late.

I practically sprinted to the club, flying through the clubhouse doors, then pausing for several moments outside the small meeting room to catch my breath before pulling open the door as quietly as I could. Of course it squeaked, and the whole room, set up like an auditorium, turned to look at me.

'Sorry,' I mouthed, waving apologetically and scanning for a space to sit. There was none, and all the wall space was taken, too. Wherever I stood, I'd be blocking someone's view.

I was beginning to think I would have to sit on the floor at the front like a school kid, but then a hand closed around mine, and I looked down to find Andrew in the seat beside me.

He tapped his legs, and for a moment I didn't understand what he was suggesting. We would talk later, not now! I furrowed my brow and shook my head questioningly, but then he flicked his eyes to his lap and tapped his legs again, and understanding dawned. I froze, and my eyes flew wide. He couldn't mean ... I couldn't ... No.

He gave me a teasing look that turned into a dare, silently asking if I was chicken, and I narrowed my eyes, knowing full well he was using my competitive instincts against me. I was no fucking chicken. But I couldn't call him out because people were watching, and if I made an issue, it would lead to questions and suspicions and all kinds of attention I would be happier to avoid.

He released my wrist, seeming to know he'd won, and I gingerly lowered myself onto one of his legs. Luckily, our coach, Cassandra, started talking again, drawing the attention of the room back to her and making me marginally less awkward.

I tried to perch gently at first, taking some of my weight on my feet, worried I'd squash him. But it must have been as uncomfortable for him as it was for me because he pulled me to sit sideways across both legs, my feet off the floor, my side pressed to his chest, his arm around my waist.

'Sorry,' I breathed, briefly meeting his gaze, then turning my eyes forward. I tried to ignore all the places our bodies were pressed together and how his fingers loosely gripped my waist. I was stiff as a board, refusing to relax into him, the sting of his rejection too fresh in my memory, and I reminded myself, yet again, that this was fake for him. A way to mess with Theo. It meant nothing.

I tried to focus on Cassandra, but it wasn't easy, especially as his thumb seemed to have somehow slipped under my tee. How had that happened?

'We'll head up at 6am tomorrow morning,' said Cassandra. 'Neither crew is racing until the afternoon, so that should give us plenty of time to get there, register, and deal with the boats.'

Only the men's and women's first boats were going to our regatta, everyone else in the room—the less experienced crews—were heading to a smaller, more local regatta instead. Ours was a big two-day event to mark the beginning of the racing season, and it didn't do much to accommodate novices. That, at least, would make our logistics easy, as everyone going knew what they were doing, meaning faffing should be minimal.

Andrew's fingers squeezed my waist, and my whole being homed in on the zip of desire it sent to my core. I ignored it, and refused to turn my head to look at him lest my features betray the lust careening through my blood. It was just a squeeze of friendship, to reassure me, or—

'Relax, Miri,' he whispered, and then his thumb skirted gently back and forth across my skin. I squeezed my thighs together. *Friends.* We were just friends. This was platonic stroking. All entirely innocent. But somehow the side of my head had pressed itself against his forehead, and my eyes had closed, and my breathing had become ragged.

We'd never touched much as friends, the odd arm squeeze or hug all that was normal, aside from one party where he'd put his arm around me and I'd fallen asleep with my head on his shoulder. But that had been years ago.

'Any issues with getting there, or last-minute camping emergencies?' Cassandra continued, as Andrew circled his thumb once more.

My lips parted, and after a few more strokes, I was fighting hard against the temptation to touch him in return or rub my forehead back and forth against his. But this morning—

'Belle's work has quietened down, so she's coming along, too,' said Livia's voice from the front of the room. 'I'm assuming Miri's bunking in with Andrew, so Belle can share my tent?'

At the sound of my name, my eyes snapped open to find the attention of the room on us once more. My cheeks heated both from the weight of their collective gaze and because of what Livia had said. What the words meant.

'Uh ...' My mind raced. We hadn't covered camping in the rules, although we probably should have. We regularly travelled for regattas. Why hadn't I thought of that?

'Yep,' said Andrew. 'Miri can drive up with me, too, if you need a free seat in your car for Belle?'

'Yes! Thank you,' said Livia. 'Perfect.' She smiled in her slightly smug project manager-y way, no doubt because she'd checked not one, but two items off her list, then turned to face the front.

'If there's nothing else, then my crews, please load your boats,' said Cassandra. 'And then I'd encourage an early night.'

Andrew held me in place as our crews leapt to action, brushing his lips against my ear and murmuring, 'It's fine. Don't stress about it.'

'I'm not,' I said defensively, although I definitely was.

We were going to share a tent. Tomorrow night. Just the two of us. How the fuck had that happened? And what on Earth was Andrew playing at? This morning, he hadn't even wanted to kiss me. Yet now he was sticking his freaking fingers under my shirt. It made no sense.

'You two coming?' said Theo, who'd paused beside us on his way to the exit, his arms folded aggressively across his chest. I had to suppress a smile as I climbed off Andrew, but as he got up, he snagged my arms and pulled me back against his chest, so we walked together with an awkward gait. Theo huffed and stormed ahead, and I chuckled as Andrew released me, turning my head so we could share the childish victory.

By the time I got outside, my crew had already loaded our blades into the trailer and were waiting for me to lift our quad, *Em*, off the racks. 'Shit, sorry guys,' I said, jogging to the boat and taking my place.

'Ready, lift,' said Cassandra, and we slid *Em* off the rubber-covered metal struts, all of us on the same side, so we reached over and supported her awkwardly between us. When she was clear of the rack, Livia and Ottie ducked under, taking the far side, while Hazel and I shifted our grips so we only held our side.

'Shoulders, ready, go!' called Cassandra, and we lifted the boat to our shoulders, then carried her outside to where two slings awaited. At Cassandra's instruction, we lifted *Em* above our heads, and then gently rolled her down, the slings cradling the round underbelly of our carbon fiber beauty.

We all immediately set to work, my crew well practiced in detaching the wing-shaped riggers from the hull. We pulled out our *rigger jiggers*—spanners made with rowing boats in mind—and made short work of the task, so soon our riggers and seats had joined the blades in the trailer.

The men's four finished just after us, and we loaded and strapped down the boats in no time, then hitched the trailer to Noah's truck.

'See you tomorrow!' we called to the men's crew, and then we took off towards my apartment for our usual pre-race pasta party. I determinedly looked anywhere but at Andrew because I didn't know what the hell was going on, and I was too confused to be convincing in front of our overly interested audience. All day I'd thought we were headed for a fake break up, and now we were couple-camping? *What the actual fucking fuck?*

I closed my apartment door completely lost in thought, almost forgetting about the others, but as I turned, I found all three of them standing in a line, eying me with varying degrees of expectation. And then they launched their attack.

'Soooo,' said Ottie, cocking a hip as she leaned against my kitchen island.

'What a lovely evening,' I replied, walking to the wall of floor-to-ceiling windows that overlooked the river. 'Shall we sit on the balcony?'

'So you can use the excuse that someone might overhear us?' said Livia, her incredulity palpable.

My balcony was above and a little set back from the bar's terrace, and yes, that had been precisely my plan. *Damn her.*

'Nice try,' said Ottie, putting the kettle on. 'We're staying inside.'

'Can Belle join?' asked Hazel, looking up from her phone.

'Of course!' It was so nice to have her around again, and I was glad she was coming this weekend. Her work had stolen her from us recently, and I'd missed her quirky ways.

'Soooooooooo,' said Ottie again, leaning over the counter, her chin resting on her hands.

'Wait until Belle's here,' said Livia, pulling a bag of fresh pasta from her rucksack, 'then Miri won't have to repeat herself.'

'So considerate,' I said sarcastically, then I moved to the cupboard and pulled out a pan. I busied myself setting it on the stove and filling it with boiling water, then dumped the pasta in. Ottie was already chopping onions and garlic, and Hazel was picking fresh herbs from the planters on the windowsill behind the sink, while Livia got us all glasses of water, then laid the table, so by the time Belle arrived ten minutes later, we were almost ready to eat.

'I brought salad,' said Belle, holding up a bowl filled with green leaves, artichoke hearts, cherry tomatoes, pickled beetroot, and olives.

'Yes!' said Ottie, plucking it from her hands and plonking it on the wooden table, while Hazel found salad servers and slid those into the bowl.

I sprinkled parsley on top of the penne carbonara into which Livia had just stirred liberal quantities of parmesan cheese, inhaling deeply before Livia snatched up the bowl and took it to the table, my stomach rumbling as I followed, eager to tuck in.

'So,' Ottie said for a third time, this time accompanied by an expression that said she meant business. 'Are you finally going to tell us the story of how you ended up dating Andrew?'

They turned intrigued eyes on me, but I made them wait as I finished my mouthful of deliciousness, then said, 'No,' with a devious smile.

Ottie and Livia howled in outrage, and a laugh that sounded alarmingly close to a cackle sprang from my lips. I stifled it by taking a long sip of water, but as I returned my high ball to the table, it was clear they weren't going to let it go. Even Hazel looked expectant, and in fairness, I knew I'd be the same if our roles were reversed.

I looked down at my food, playing with a piece of pasta as guilt crammed into every empty space inside me. 'There's nothing much to tell.'

'Ha!' Ottie leaned in. 'Didn't look like nothing much when you were perched on his lap earlier.'

I rolled my eyes but couldn't help but smile along with them because yes, I had done that, and I still couldn't really believe it myself.

I shrugged. 'We're dating. It's new. And apparently we're staying in a tent together this weekend ...' I rounded on Livia, full of mock outrage.

Livia clamped her teeth together and pulled her lips wide. 'Sorry about that. I should have asked you first.'

'It's fine,' I said, waving her off, then loading my plate with salad. Although I wasn't in fact sure if it was fine. I wasn't sure if anything was fine at that particular moment.

'Have you shagged yet?' said Belle, making us all bark with laughter at her characteristically blunt question. Belle didn't say much, but when she did, she packed a punch. She dismissed our hysterics with a wave of her hand. 'You were all thinking it.'

They made various gestures of amused agreement, then shifted their attention back to me, and I froze.

'Hey,' said Hazel, by far the softest member of our crew. She rested a hand on my arm and squeezed. 'There's no pressure to tell us anything. Tell us to mind our own business if you want.'

'We haven't,' I said in a rush. Honesty was always the best policy, if one ignored the gaping lie, of course. 'It's so new, it's overwhelming. I wasn't planning on telling anyone yet—you know what the club's like—and after what happened ...'

'But you do like him?' said Livia, her skeptical frown telling me her spidey senses were tingling, knowing something about my story was off. I could never get a single thing past her.

'Of course!' I said, too brightly. My insides clenched just thinking about his thumb on my skin, and if a single thumb could do that ... 'But I don't know if it's serious, or what he wants, or what *I* even want.'

'I don't have to come this weekend,' said Belle. 'If you'd rather not share a tent with Andrew—'

'Or I'm sure we could find another tent,' added Ottie.

Hazel nodded, while Livia assessed me with slightly narrowed eyes.

'It's fine,' I said quickly. 'I'm more than happy to share a tent with Andrew. We are dating, after all.' I covered my discomfort with a salacious eyebrow raise, and they all laughed.

'Of course she is,' said Ottie. 'Have you seen the state of him?'

'Yes,' I confidently confirmed. Because *hell yes*, I'd seen the state of him. I'd gone one better than that. I'd felt the state of him. And I'd smelt the state of him. And tasted the state of him. And the state of his personality was top freaking notch too. The state of him was absolute perfection, now that I thought about it. But there was just one little problem. Our relationship was *fake*.

'Well,' said Livia, 'enjoy it because the rest of us are going through a dry spell.'

'I'm not,' said Belle.

'Rub it in, why don't you,' said Ottie, swirling the water in her glass.

Livia shook her head despondently. 'I fear dating apps are the only hope for me.'

Ottie scoffed. 'So use a dating app; that's what I do.'

'Do you?' said Hazel.

Ottie's head moved back a few inches. 'Don't you? Doesn't everyone?'

Hazel shook her head. 'I'm too scared of being trafficked or dumped over the side of a bridge somewhere or swindled.'

'You need to let loose!' said Ottie. 'Let your hair down! Untie those straight laces!'

'I'm happy with my laces just as they are, thank you very much,' Hazel said on a laugh. 'Although I wouldn't say no to a large, attractive man tugging them free.'

Livia saluted Hazel with her water glass. 'You and me both, sister.'

'What about Seb? Or Noah?' I asked, referring to the other members of the men's senior squad.

'Seb's gay,' said Livia, pushing the last of her food onto her fork.

'But is he *actually*?' said Ottie.

'Yes,' said Belle and Livia together, then Belle continued, her tone brooking no argument. 'My gaydar is never wrong.'

'And he's my best friend,' said Livia. 'Believe me when I say he's gay.' She widened her eyes meaningfully, and we all laughed.

'Noah, then?' I suggested. 'Although, did he and Seb have a thing?'

Belle whipped her head towards me. 'Did they?'

'Yes,' said Hazel, her voice quiet after our boisterous volume.

Ottie nodded enthusiastically. 'Pretty sure Noah's bi, but he's not for me.'

'Why?' demanded Livia.

'He's just so … nice.'

Livia doubled down. 'What's wrong with nice?'

'You want to date Noah?' said Hazel, gaining a little in intensity as she looked at Livia, and … had her cheeks just flushed?

Livia vehemently shook her head. 'Urgh, no. He's way too nice.'

We all laughed, then lapsed into our usual rowing chatter as we cleared up. Non-rowers always joked it was impossible to socialize with rowing types because all we ever wanted to talk about was rowing, and to be honest, they weren't too far off the mark.

With our early start looming, it was soon time to call it a night, and I waved goodbye to my crew, closed the door, then pulled my vibrating phone out of my pocket, my stomach tightening when I saw the name on the screen.

Andrew 21:03: I'll pick you up outside yours at 6AM?

Just a normal message from a friend. My heart sank a little as I typed my reply.

Miri 21:03: Sure. I'll bring coffee [steaming coffee cup emoji]

Andrew 21:04: You're the best. Pete and Hannah are riding with us. See you then. X

Relief warred with disappointment somewhere in the region of my stomach, while my eyes kept finding the word *us*. We were an *us*!

Of course we weren't an *us,* not really. Andrew only wanted to be friends, but the idea sent a thrill of excitement through me regardless. So I reminded myself of how he'd pulled away when, like a creep, I'd tried to deepen our fake kiss, told myself if I dreamed and hoped, it would lead only to disappointment or embarrassment or both. I had to remember this was fake, that he was doing me a favor and nothing more.

Miri 21:05: Sounds good. See you in the morning x

Chapter 5

Pete and Hannah were already in the truck when Andrew showed up at 6AM on the dot the following morning, and the same relieved disappointment gripped my chest.

'Hey!' I said through the open back window. Pete's enormous, dark-haired form dwarfed Hannah, her tiny frame childlike next to his hulking shoulders. They owned a gym in town, so both of them worked out all day long, him as a boxer and weight trainer, and her as a yoga instructor. They maintained a perfect Instagram existence, which seemed to be as good in real life as it was online. *Fuckers.* I wasn't totally bitter, maybe just like ten percent.

'Morning,' they said, him in his South African accent, her in her mid-Atlantic twang, as I passed coffees and breakfast sandwiches through the window.

'You are a *goddess*,' said Pete, inhaling deeply.

'Beats the protein bars I packed!' agreed Hannah, her high blonde ponytail bouncing as she gratefully accepted her breakfast.

Andrew grabbed my bags from where I'd piled them on the pavement, slung them in the back, then turned to face me. 'You truly are a goddess,' he said, echoing Pete's words with eyes so intense they held me hostage. And then he plucked his coffee from my hand, slammed the truck bed's cover shut, and headed for the driver's seat.

I stood completely still for a moment, entirely off kilter.

'Hurry up, Buttercup,' Andrew called with a mischievous smile, no hint of the sleepiness on his features that I knew dominated mine.

'No pet names,' I hissed as I yanked the passenger door open and scaled the great height to my seat. 'Remind me why you need this ridiculous gas-guzzler?' I wasn't as much of an eco-warrior as other members of my crew, but I did what I could, and Andrew was one of the more environmentally conscious members of the club, so the truck was jarring.

Andrew turned sheepish. 'Because I've always wanted one? I should probably trade it in for something electric, but—'

Hannah's head and shoulders appeared between us. 'How long have you two been dating?'

'Um ...' The abrupt question took me off guard, especially in my sleep-deprived state. I cast a sideways glance at Andrew as he gunned the engine, trying to read his reaction. 'A few days, I guess?'

'And she's already trying to change you,' Pete joked.

Hannah sat back and swiped her husband. 'She is not! She's trying to bring out the best in him, that's all.'

'Is that what you do to me, baby?'

Hannah took his enormous hand in hers. 'Exactly,' she said sweetly. 'Only some people need more help than others.'

Pete grabbed Hannah and locked his lips to hers, while Andrew caught my eye and smiled indulgently. I took a sip of my vanilla latte and turned my nervous gaze to look through the window. What if everyone saw right through us? What if our lie was exposed? Because let's face it, I was a terrible liar, and we weren't about to show even a fraction of the loved-up-ness Pete and Hannah were demonstrating in the back seat.

'And I agree,' said Hannah, when Pete finally put her down, 'pet names are gross.'

'You know *baby*'s a pet name, right?' Pete fired back.

'It is not! That's different. It's different! Isn't it, Miri?'

They bickered for a while, Andrew and I staying out of it, and as we left the city and headed into the lush green countryside on that perfect spring morning, we ate our breakfasts, drank our coffees, then lapsed into relative silence, only the odd question or comment punctuating the country music floating from the speakers for almost two hours.

I slid my sunglasses over my eyes and let my mind wander, trying to imagine what I would do if I really was Andrew's girlfriend. Would I reach across and take his hand? At what point would I start thinking of this as *our* truck? At what stage would I start leaving chap sticks and reusable shopping bags about the place?

Alas, I would never know … It was a painful thought and I quickly suppressed it.

I was in a happy middle ground between wakefulness and sleep, thinking about how pissed Theo had looked when he'd seen me on Andrew's lap, not that I cared about Theo any longer, but I was only human, so it was gratifying that he was finally getting a taste of his own medicine. And then my thoughts turned to how it had felt to be pressed against Andrew, the hard ridges of muscle, the way he'd stroked my skin, the—

'So,' Hannah said excitedly, slapping the back of my seat, invading my delicious daydream, 'how did you two finally get together?'

How was she this perky? Wait ... 'Finally?' I said, snapping my head round in surprise.

'Oh, pleeeeease. You two have been pining after each other for years. Coxes *see* things. Like longing looks across the water, or when an especially stern member of the men's crew repeatedly runs off to a certain member of the women's crew to be *overly* helpful.' She gave a delighted little laugh, vibrating with glee.

A slight flush colored Andrew's cheeks as I turned my head to look at him, but he kept his eyes on the road.

'Honey, don't embarrass them,' said Pete, although he seemed to be enjoying the inquisition just as much as his wife.

'Andrew helps everyone,' I said, trying not to sound hopeful or defensive.

'Uh-huh,' she said skeptically, turning her pointed gaze on Andrew.

We passed a sign for a service area, and Andrew grabbed the gift the universe had offered and deflected like a champ. 'Anyone want to stop?'

'Yes, please!' sang Hannah, clutching the back of Andrew's seat. 'I really need to pee.'

'Baby,' said Pete, squeezing her hand, 'you're so adorable.'

Hannah ignored him, her attention back on Andrew. 'What is it you do for work again, Andrew?' It was one of those questions people periodically asked him as no one ever really understood the answers he gave.

'I'm a data scientist,' he said quietly.

'But what's your job title?' she pressed.

'Hannah!' Pete interjected.

'What? It's a perfectly normal question! And when I looked him up on LinkedIn, I didn't get very far.'

'Oh my God,' Pete muttered, 'I'm sorry man.' And then he sat back and gave up trying to stop her. Personally, I was willing her to continue because I wanted answers too.

Silence descended as Hannah waited patiently for Andrew's response, and if she felt awkward like I did, she showed no sign.

'I'm Chief Data Scientist at DrewDox,' Andrew said eventually.

'Right,' said Hannah, 'the company that sponsored our boats. That was so nice of them! I guess that's why one of them is called *Dr. Dox*?'

Andrew shrugged noncommittally.

'No Drew, though,' said Pete.

Hannah tapped her pouting lips. 'Hmmm, no. Definitely no *Drew* in *Busy Livy* or *Em*.'

Andrew took the exit, and as the road curved, a stunned, 'Wow,' popped out of my mouth, an enormous lake opening up before us, encircled by indigenous trees and with swans paddling quietly across the millpond surface. It was the most picturesque service area I'd ever seen, and Hannah leapt out of the truck as soon as we were stationary, squealing with delight and snapping a few pictures for Instagram.

'It is *such* a drag having to do this stuff,' she whined, uploading them, then dropping her phone back into her pocket.

'Amen, sister,' I agreed, glad I had willing staff members to handle most of my social media now. It was relentless, and my mind wasn't well suited to the never-ending, repetitive task.

Hannah and Pete strode ahead, Pete slinging an arm around his wife as she chattered about engagement stats and follower counts.

'Do you think she ever stops talking?' asked Andrew, suddenly close. 'She's not like this in the boat.'

I threw him a conspiratorial smile. 'Doubtful. But she's nice. I like her.' I turned my head forward and found Hannah's phone pointed in our direction.

'Perfect!' she trilled. 'The look of love!'

'Do you think she's going to upload that to Instagram?' I asked, horrified.

Andrew chuckled. 'Undoubtedly.'

I groaned. 'Sorry. I can—'

'You know, I don't think there's a single photo of just the two of us together despite us having been friends for over a decade.'

Friends. Exactly. But ... 'You *want* a picture of us?' I asked, the words betraying my confusion.

He stopped abruptly, so I did too, a tortured look on his face. 'Miri ... Hey ... About yesterday ...'

Oh God, no. Not here. Not with Hannah and Pete watching our every move. 'It's fine, Andrew, you don't have to explain anything. We're friends. This is fake. We have rules!' My voice came out high-pitched and frenetic, betraying my alarm, and I turned away, planning to flee to the relative safety of the others.

But before I'd taken even one step, he wrapped his hand around mine and tugged me back to him, my panicked eyes not missing the apprehension marring his beautiful features. 'Miri ...' He seemed unsure, like he was searching for words that were difficult to find—words designed to let me down gently, no doubt.

'Hurry up, lovebirds!' Hannah called, and the interruption had Andrew shaking his head, snapping him out of it.

'Come on!' I said, exhaling the breath I hadn't realized I'd been holding, sagging a little in relief as we left the awkward moment by the truck. But as we strode towards the others across the sun-drenched parking lot, he didn't let go of my hand. Instead, he laced his fingers through mine and slowly traced his thumb across my palm.

Confusion did not even begin to describe how I felt as we put up the tents in the field beside the river, the distant, clipped voice from the regatta's loudspeaker our soundtrack. Andrew kept touching me and smiling at me and once even dropped a kiss on my temple, but it was always when other people were watching, so he was obviously just committing to the role, making sure we were convincing.

That was the only logical explanation because *he'd* been the one to suggest fake dating, *he'd* been the one to pull away from our kiss, and *he'd* tried to reenforce the boundaries earlier. He was trying to help me bag Theo like the good friend he was, but I didn't want to bag Theo! Never had, really. But Theo was the reason Andrew was doing this, and if I told him I was over Theo, he'd fake dump me in a flash, and I wasn't sure I could take that.

Oh, bloody hell, that's what I should do. I should tell him and put an end to this madness. It was the only rational course of action.

We'd friend-zoned each other a long time ago, but for me it had been an accidental friend-zoning. Andrew's friend-zoning had seemed more intentional, given he'd started dating someone else the next freaking day. It had felt like a rejection, even though that was ridiculous. I'd literally announced to all who cared to listen that I had no intention of dating anyone at the club. But why had Andrew had to hear it? *Stupid fucking mouth. Why, universe, why?*

'Hey,' said Andrew, sliding a hand across my shoulders and sending gooseflesh out across my skin. 'Everything okay?'

Turns out I'd frozen mid-way through putting out the camping chairs. 'Uh, yeah, sorry. Think the early start is catching up with me.' *Such a lie—I got up early every day.*

'Do you want to lie down for a bit?' he said, nodding towards the wing of his enormous tent filled with a king-sized camping mattress, pillows, and a duvet. It even had blackout material, so it was dark and cozy and so very appealing. But if I went in there, I would never come out again, let alone race later.

My eyes snagged on my sleeping bag, still stuffed in its sack at the base of the mattress. It made me wonder how things would work later because it looked very much like he planned for us to be tucked up in bed together.

'No,' I said breathily, then inhaled sharply, snapping myself out of it, 'there's loads still to do.'

Andrew squeezed my neck, making the muscles in my lower belly contract, then headed back to the truck, hauling out yet more kit, seeming oblivious to the effect he'd had on me.

'*That* is the camping equivalent of the Ritz,' Livia joked, nodding to Andrew's tent before heading to her car for the rest of her stuff.

Andrew was a camping pro, and every time we travelled, the whole club mooned over his setup. Today at least I could bask in the reflected glory. Silver linings ...

I looked over to Livia's no-frills three-man and chuckled, allowing myself to revel just a little in her good-natured envy.

'Enjoy it, won't you,' Livia said dryly on her way back, carrying her pillow and sleeping bag.

'Oh, I will,' I replied with far more confidence than I felt.

'Our camping experience will be wonderfully *rustic*,' countered Ottie, poking her head out of the next tent along, an exact replica of Livia's. '*Authentic*,' she added pointedly, crawling out and turning back to arrange her sleeping bag on her knees.

Belle looked longingly at Andrew's tent as she handed her own pillow and sleeping bag to Livia because there was only room for one arranger inside their tent. 'At least we get to dine at the Ritz.'

'Hopefully not dinner and drinks though,' said Hazel, striding past on her way to retrieve more stuff from the car.

'No,' I agreed because if we were drinking alcohol tonight, it meant our race had not gone well.

We finished putting up our tent village, Andrew's the social hub in the middle with its large, covered central area and separate shelter next door. He had a whole spare pod for storing food and chairs and coolers, and I was confident this would be my most comfortable camping trip to date.

Once everything was finally sorted, we tramped together across the field towards the river, the loudspeaker blaring louder with each passing step. It projected the voice of a man who was enthusiastically commentating on the current race, a race which was hotting up, if his mounting excitement was anything to go by.

Cheers went up as we used the rickety stile to climb over the fenced break in the hedge, popping out halfway between the start and finish lines. The course was relatively short, at only twelve hundred meters, and for each race, there was space for only two crews to battle side by side. It made the competition intimate and the supporters fierce, and adrenaline shot through my veins as I took it all in.

We headed right, towards the finish, to where the main hub of the regatta was situated. Bunting had been strung up on poles along the side of the river, the narrow dirt footpath busy with rowers in their colorful team kits and supporters strolling, jogging, or racing to keep up with the boats.

We passed screaming relatives, scowling coaches, excited juniors, and lightweights dressed up in many layers embarking on sweat jogs ahead of their weigh-ins. I thanked all my lucky stars that I would never have to worry about making weight before a race. It was stressful enough without having to manage that, too.

Eventually, we made it to the finish line and the horseshoe of tents that housed the regatta's organizers, along with food vendors, bars, and stalls selling all manner of clothes, jewelry, and even ceramics. The space there was deeper than along the rest of the path, and picnic tables were dotted around, already packed with bodies, most of the blue and white striped deck chairs lining the water's edge occupied, too.

Cassandra spotted us and waved us over in her usual no-nonsense way, then ushered us into the organizer's tent, handing out our racing licenses as we went. Like some overbearing kindergarten teacher, she refused to trust us to bring them ourselves. Although, to be fair, it was probably safer that way. All it took was one person to forget for the whole crew to be kept off the water.

We registered, pinned our race numbers onto our pink and green race suits, then headed for the boat trailer, which was parked with all the other trailers in a field behind the organizer's tent.

It was unseasonably hot considering it was only late spring, white heads of cow parsley bobbing at the edges of the field, the hedges still proudly displaying sprays of hawthorn blossom. Most wore only their strappy racing all in ones, caps, and sunglasses, while the spectators were clad in light, floaty summer outfits.

The rays of vitamin D merged with the regatta buzz, soaking into my soul, buoying me. I'd missed this over the winter. The exhilaration. The sense of purpose. The community. There were head races during the colder months, which took place over longer courses, where the participants set off one after another, but the weather was often atrocious, and the atmosphere was never the same as at a fully-fledged regatta.

We waved to members of other clubs we knew, identifiable at a distance by their club colors, occasionally stopping for a brief chat, although most were consumed by boat-building, registration, warmups, visualization, or pep talks. The bustle was ceaseless, as was the focus and commitment and general itch to get out on the water, at least for those of us whose races were later in the day. The bar was already filling with crews who'd been knocked out, whose only jobs now were to have a good time and cheer on the rest of us.

We made quick work of rigging our boats and then sank into our own pre-race routines, the first part of which was a briefing from our coach.

'Ladies,' said Cassandra, 'your race is at two, so if you want to eat, I'd do it now. The men's race isn't until an hour after that. We'll meet back here at one to recap the race plan and you can get straight on the water after that.'

We lounged in the shade by the trailer, pulling out our pre-race snacks and nibbling nervously while the men went off in search of a table by the finish line.

'Have we raced this Bridgeson crew before?' asked Ottie, between bites of her malt loaf.

I shook my head. 'They didn't have a crew in the open category last year.'

Belle hummed. 'I think one of the Telt crew moved to them, though?'

'Interesting,' I said, because Telt were reigning National Champions.

Hazel played with the tinfoil wrapping her flapjack. 'Then it won't be an easy race.'

'We'll be fine,' I said confidently, and I felt it because we'd always been fine before. We were an experienced crew, we knew the course, and we were fit, even if we hadn't had as much time on the water together in the last few weeks as we would have liked. But this would go our way. I'd never, in all my many years of rowing at this regatta, not got through to the second day.

Hazel gave me a tight nod. 'If you say so.'

At one o'clock, Cassandra had Ottie walk us through the race plan. Ottie sat in the bow seat at the front of the boat, so she would be the one making calls and adjusting our course using a sliding footplate attached to the rudder. Hazel was at two, Livia behind me at three, and I was in the stroke seat in the stern. We rowed a coxless quad, meaning we each had two blades and no cox, so there was no one to steer for us. Quads had become my favorite type of boat over the years, light, maneuverable, quick, and no nonsense.

We hadn't been rowing in this configuration for long, only since Belle had become too busy to commit to the crew full time. We'd had to rejig things when Ottie had become a permanent member, putting her in the bow and moving Hazel back a seat. It was working well as Ottie was great at multitasking and staying on top of the race, and Hazel had never liked it much in the bow anyway.

Once we'd visualized and warmed-up, we took our blades to the pontoon, then went back for our boat. The men's crew wished us luck as we pushed off, and I smiled at Andrew, my heart giving a little flip when I found his eyes glued to me ... which I told myself to ignore; I had more important things to worry about. I cast a quick glance Theo's way, and found him watching me, too, but aside from a small internal eye roll, his scrutiny didn't invoke anything in me at all.

I left my boy-drama on dry land and descended fully into our deeply familiar pre-race routine, everything else falling away.

We rowed down to the start line, and then past it, completing our usual warm-up, no chatter passing between us as we focused on the task in hand, Ottie making short, efficient calls to direct our movements.

We turned, chopping all eight of our blades up and down in perfect unison, the four stroke side blades pulling forward while the four bow side blades pushed back, and then we headed for the pre-race corral, where we sat alongside our competition. No one spoke, each crew in their own zone, waiting with a knot of nerves pulling tight in our stomachs. Or at least, I assumed that was how it was for everyone, it was certainly how it was for me. This part was the worst.

After what felt like an age, our race was finally called, and we paddled lightly to the start, adrenaline shooting into my blood as we lined up next to our competition, then backed up onto the temporary pontoon where a teenager leaned over the edge, ready to catch us. Our stern floated under, and he gently took hold, then looked to the umpire to make sure she was happy with our position.

I felt the familiar flutter of panic that I wouldn't be ready in time as I pulled off my long-sleeved top and dumped in in the footwell beyond my feet. I checked the screws on my footplate, then the ones keeping my blades in place at the top of the riggers, pulled my ponytail tight, and took a final sip of water.

Everything inside me went calm as I replayed our start plan one last time. I didn't look at the guy holding our stern or the other crew, paying attention only to the umpire's calls. We were here to race our own race, so my eyes rarely travelled beyond the edge of my own blades, which dipped into and out of the water in tiny movements, following Ottie's instructions until we were pointing straight down the course.

When both crews were more or less in position, we moved forward, sliding our seats halfway up the runners, our legs bent, arms straight, blades square and in the water, ready to lever backwards, pushing with our feet the moment the starter set us off.

My heart thundered, anticipation and trepidation swirling in my guts as we waited for the other crew to get straight. They seemed to take forever, and then Ottie had to make a correction to our own line, the light breeze pushing us slightly off course.

The other crew was finally happy, and the starter wasted no time. 'Attention! Go!' she bellowed, and my heart lurched as my legs pushed the boat away. We did two short half-strokes to get moving, followed by a three-quarter stroke, then full strokes after that. We went flat out for ten, ahead of our competition by a nose as we lengthened and settled into our race pace, still fast, but not so frantic as before.

We flew across the water, neck and neck with the Bridgeson crew, our blades so close that they clashed, the impact jarring, although all of us were experienced enough not to let it put us off, fighting hard to keep our own rhythm, refusing to give an inch to the other side. The umpire followed us in an antique wooden motorboat with a flag streaming out behind, and she shouted to the Bridgeson crew, telling them to move over. Ottie called for a push for twenty as they did, which meant we were somehow already halfway through the short race, and now was our moment to stamp our control.

We suspended off our blades for all we were worth, legs and lungs burning, and it worked, the boat leaping forward in the water, putting me level with the woman in their three seat. My heart leapt with glee. It was always easier to stay ahead than fight back from behind, mainly because when you were in front, you could see your competition behind you, and with every stroke it felt like you were pushing them away. It put you in control of the race.

Conversely, when a crew fights back from behind, it can destroy the leading crew mentally. People panic, feeling like there's nothing they can do to see off the threat, and then they get disjointed, not connecting together. Which is exactly what happened to us as we entered the last three hundred meters of the race. We put in another push, but it didn't gain us any ground, and then Bridgeson responded with a big push of their own, and all of a sudden they were coming back at us, moving steadily up our boat. And then we were level, and they were showing no signs of slowing down.

They kept moving up, inching ahead, and with only two hundred meters to go, we had to respond. Ottie called the wind-up a stroke later, and we started our final push for the line, but now Bridgeson had the mental advantage, and for every push we made, they pushed back, sitting on our shoulders, holding us off.

As we passed the hundred-meter marker, I knew we'd lost. I could feel Bridgeson's triumphant energy just as easily as I could feel our scrappy anguish, our frantic attempts to reel them in. But there was no way we could make up the distance in ten measly strokes. Unless they made the kind of mistake that senior crews very rarely did, we were done. Out. Our regatta was over.

We crossed the line, and the commentator announced we'd lost by half a length; it wasn't even close. We slumped forward over our blades, desperately sucking air into our lungs, made harder by the loss that squatted like a toad on our chests. Bridgeson barely seemed out of breath in comparison, smacking each other on the back and grinning victoriously, then heading for the pontoon.

I shut myself down, forcing all emotion from my body, numbly calling my congratulations to the other crew as they passed. Later, I would be disappointed and possibly even angry at myself, but in that moment, I had space for nothing but a stubborn, nagging feeling of disbelief. *How had this happened?*

We paddled slowly back to dry land, no one saying a word, and Noah and Theo pulled us in, helping to remove our blades and holding our riggers as we climbed out.

Everyone knew it was shit, that there was nothing they could say, so the men stayed silent, too, not even offering words of condolence.

We would dissect it in great detail later, but not then. Then we just wanted to get off the water, out of the lime-light, and away to somewhere we could lick our wounds.

Noah and Theo grabbed our blades while we lifted our boat up over our heads, then lowered it onto our shoulders. Andrew and Pete appeared with the blades for their own race, then followed us back to the trailer, where we rolled *Em* down onto a pair of waiting slings.

'It was a good race,' said Noah, sliding our seats off their runners because we wouldn't be needing them again.

'Really close,' Theo agreed.

'I don't think we could have done any more,' said Hazel. 'We were ahead at the start, but when they came back at us, there was nothing we could do.'

Bridgeson had been better, that was really all there was to it, aside from the fact we'd panicked. I'd felt it, a slight misalignment, someone throwing their hands away and rushing up the slide too fast, causing a check at the catch as they'd been forced to wait a fraction of a second for the rest of us. So there was *something* we could have done, but nobody needed to hear it at that moment. I probably shouldn't have even been thinking it ...

We finished de-rigging our boat as Cassandra rounded up the men's crew and gave them their pep-talk, then we lashed *Em* to the trailer, and called, 'Good luck!' as Hannah gave the order for the men to lift their boat, *Dr. Dox,* over their heads. They always made it look so easy, like *Dox* weighed nothing more than a cardboard box. But then, with muscles like theirs, it wasn't so surprising.

And you'll be sleeping next to one of those sets of muscles tonight. The thought took me by surprise, and I batted it away as Cassandra called us together.

'I have a few thoughts,' she said in her usual frank tone, 'but there are plenty of positives to take away. The start went well, and your first push put you up, and it was a close race. How did it feel?'

We went round in a circle, each giving our perspective, and the others agreed that we'd panicked towards the end. 'But ultimately, they were just better,' said Ottie, and it was hard to disagree.

We would have to train harder, and a veil of guilt encased my brain because I'd had to miss more sessions than anyone, and with Belle out, there had been no one to replace me. Our squad was small, and there weren't any obvious novices to bring on, but I'd thought it would be fine, that we'd be okay when it came to it. Clearly I'd been wrong.

We wrapped up, then grabbed a row of deckchairs next to the finish line and waited for the men's race. Livia detoured via the bar and handed us each a Pimms and lemonade complete with sprigs of mint and chunks of fruit and cucumber. The smell was summer in a plastic pint glass, and between that, the sun, the festival atmosphere, and the company of my crew, the sting of our loss was already starting to fade.

'Wait,' said Hazel, silencing us and concentrating on the commentator. 'It's the boys! This is their race!'

We jumped to our feet as they passed the halfway mark, leaning forward and looking down the course, finding them neck and neck with the other crew. 'Oh my God,' I said to no one in particular.

'Come on, boys!' Ottie breathed, gripping my arm. Then she shouted at the top of her lungs, 'Come on Dex!'

And then we were all shouting because they'd edged ahead with only a hundred meters to go.

'Come on Dex!' I screamed, jumping up and down, my heart in my mouth.

The whole place erupted into a roaring, stamping, clapping mass of humanity, even those with no allegiance joining in because it was just so tantalizingly close.

The other crew was coming back, the lead changing from stroke to stroke, and there was just no telling which crew would take it.

We all screamed our encouragement, frantic and delighted and full of belief. And then they crossed the line, and the crowd held its breath because no one knew who'd won.

'Well, wasn't that the race?' said the commentator. 'Closest we've seen this regatta ...'

He went silent, and we all stared expectantly at the nearest loudspeaker. And stared. And stared. And stared. The crowd grew impatient, people starting to mutter about the delay, and I looked at the two spent crews as they panted over their blades, the wait agonizing for us but abysmal for them.

'And you'll have to bear with me, I'm afraid, as I get final confirmation from ... yes ... thank you ... yes ... just as

I thought! Dex just pipped Calmarite to the post, taking it by a nose!'

We erupted into excited shrieks, then raced to the pontoon to congratulate them, our own defeat all but forgotten in the face of their nail-biting win.

Chapter 6

L ater that evening, we sat on blankets around a campfire Belle had insisted on being the one to construct—because she was a scientist—and basked in the warm early evening sunshine. I was onto my second glass of white wine and was feeling pleasantly buzzed as I chatted idly along with the others, glad to find it was dulling the sting of our loss, too.

Pete and Andrew were having a man-off by their matching mini barbeques, cooking sausages and steaks and haloumi skewers, the enticing smell making my stomach growl in famished anticipation. We'd all brought something for the meal, and bread rolls, salads, fruit, and a towering stack of delicious-looking rocky road sat on Andrew's camp table next to a bucket filled with ice and drinks—non-alcoholic ones for the men's crew, and hastily purchased booze for us.

'Oh my God, guys!' said Ottie, grabbing Theo's leg, then immediately snatching her hand away as though she'd touched something nasty. 'Your race was *incredible*.'

They all grinned like lunatics, including Pete and Andrew, who'd now put the lids on their barbeques and were discussing the oft-overlooked importance of the smoking stage of the process.

Their collective good mood was contagious, and we grinned along with them despite our defeat. Moments like this were why I loved rowing because even though my crew had lost, our club had won, meaning we all had something to celebrate.

'I thought they'd pipped us,' said Theo, leaning back against one of the long, sideways logs around the fire.

Livia clutched her drink to her chest. 'It was so freaking close! We had no idea.'

'Hannah cut the corner at the finish,' said Noah. 'If she hadn't done that ...'

Hannah blushed. 'I would never!' But the denial was accompanied by a gleeful flick of her eyes.

'Of course not,' said Theo, matching her overly innocent tone.

We went on like that for a while, dissecting every moment of their race, until Pete called, 'Grub's up!' as he carried a platter piled high with barbequed goods to the table where Andrew was already carving the steaks.

I helped myself to salad and a roll, then topped it with the perfectly pink meat, salivating as the scent of garlic wafted up my nose.

Andrew slid a piece of steak from his plate to mine. 'Best bit,' he said, leaning in so only I could hear. He moved to the other end of the table to load his plate, while I stood rooted to the spot, stunned, and surprised no one else had batted an eye at the casual intimacy.

When I regained power over my limbs, I joined the others at Andrew's second camping table and took the seat he'd saved for me. I was acutely aware of how our legs brushed as I sat, and I froze, sure Andrew would shift away, but he didn't, and when I relaxed, even more of my thigh slid against his, the contact sending sparks of electricity shooting through my blood.

Hazel and Noah volunteered for washing up duty, and the rest of us moved back to the blankets by the fire, grabbing jumpers and coats on the way because now the sun was setting, a chill had seeped into the air.

Hannah used Pete as a human blanket, sitting between his legs as he leaned back against a log. Everyone else was single and sat alone, aside from Belle, whose boyfriend was about as likely to turn up to a regatta as Elon Musk.

It was usually fun to see who migrated towards whom at such moments, but all my brain had space for was Andrew, who'd disappeared with the trash, presumably taking it to the dumpster near the office. When he finally rejoined us, instead of dropping down beside me as I'd expected, he urged me away from the log I was resting against, his hands on my shoulders. I did as he bade and shuffled away from the log, and then he slid into the space behind me, cocooning me in his arms just like Pete was doing to Hannah.

I stiffened as a host of curious eyes roamed over us, but eventually their interest waned, and I gingerly eased back into him, finding him warm and comforting, his sweet, musky scent engulfing me.

The drunk part of me wanted to rub myself against him like a cat, marking him as mine, but luckily my sane sober brain was still in charge. At least, mostly, because somehow my hand had found his bicep and was stroking up and down.

'I'm sorry about your race,' he whispered, pulling me even closer.

I shifted so I could see his face in the flickering firelight. He understood what the loss meant to me—the first time I hadn't made it to the second day of this regatta, and I'd been coming for over ten years. 'I'm happy you won,' I said, meaning every word.

He gave my arm a squeeze. 'Your opposition had a ringer.'

I huffed a laugh. 'She's a fully-fledged member of their club!'

He hummed skeptically, and I rested my temple against his chest, doing what felt natural. He didn't seem to mind.

'It's okay,' I said, realizing I wasn't as devastated as I should be. I was embarrassed and a little shocked, but mostly I couldn't help feeling it was all my fault, and shame filled me.

He hugged me tighter, as though sensing my spiraling thoughts, and then Theo's voice pierced our private bubble. 'Miri's never at training, so you should start there if you ask me ... It's not okay.'

I lifted my head from Andrew's chest as Ottie said, 'Theo! Shut the fuck up! Miri's amazing.'

He tried to counter, but only got as far as, 'I'm just saying—' before the rest of my crew buried him under a barrage of vitriol.

'She has the best ergo score in the club,' said Belle.

'She's got more race experience than you could ever dream of,' said Livia.

'She's the linchpin that holds our crew together!' said Hazel.

Andrew pulled me towards him so my back pressed flush against his chest, his arms closing possessively around me. 'And she's right fucking here,' he growled, the sound vibrating through him and into me in a way that had my eyes falling closed. He kissed my temple, then left his cheek pressed against my skin, and some combination of the alcohol, his musky scent, and his words had me almost forgetting the others existed.

'Jesus ...' Theo laughed. 'Get a fucking room! Am I right?'

This time, I didn't even bother to look at him. I didn't care what he thought, seeing as I was entirely wrapped up in the delight-for-all-the-senses that was Andrew.

'No,' said Noah. 'As usual, you're not right.'

'Dude!' Theo sounded indignant, but all I cared about was the press of Andrew's skin and whether I could reasonably get away with kissing him, my tongue tingling at the idea of undulating against his.

'Urgh, why do men always think with their fucking dicks?' spat Ottie, the venom in her tone finally grabbing my attention. My eyes flew open just in time to see her jump up and storm off into the darkness.

Theo laughed it off, or at least tried to. 'What was *that* about?' he joked, looking around for supporters, but finding none.

'You need to apologize,' said Pete, his features set into a hard line.

'Dude!'

'Now,' Pete pressed. 'She's had a few drinks, and if she hurts herself out there ...'

'Come *on*! She's a big girl.'

'Don't make me kick your punk ass,' said Pete, in a tone I'd never heard from him before. 'Get the fuck up and go after her.'

Theo shook his head like a petulant teen, and Pete shifted as though about to get up.

'I'm going!' said Theo, scrambling to his feet. *Jesus*, you people!'

'There's a torch on the table,' said Andrew, and as I turned to chastise him for his inflammatory tone, I found his eyes locked on me, dark and captivating.

I barely heard the *pfft* noise Theo made, or Hannah calling, 'Be nice!' after him.

How could I have ever thought dating Theo was a good idea? He was a child, immature and lost, in need of the older men to show him the way, while the one whose arms I inexplicably found myself in had his shit well and truly together. He was the kind of man who thought about torches, and was undoubtedly good at DIY, and had a very sensible job none of the rest of us understood, and could, I was sure, were it ever required, bring down a deer in the woods with only his bare hands and a pocketknife. Fuck, that was such a turn on. He was such a catch, and in my slightly tipsy state, I wanted him more than I'd ever wanted anyone before. More than I thought possible.

I turned and brushed my lips against his, little more than a featherlight touch, and he kissed me back for a heartbeat, then gently pulled away, exhaling as he pressed his forehead to mine.

'Are you okay?' he whispered. 'You know you're an asset to any crew, right?'

What the ... He wanted to talk about rowing at a moment like this? 'We're not gelling as a crew,' I heard myself say, keeping my voice low while trying to work out if he'd just rejected me again.

He pushed a wayward lock of hair behind my ear. 'You guys haven't been together long. Sometimes it takes a while.'

'And sometimes it's never going to work, but Theo's right, it is my fault. I haven't been around as much as I should have. We haven't had the consistency we need.'

'Where have you been?' he asked, sliding his thumb across my cheek, then trailing his fingers down my neck.

I shivered, leaning into his touch and suppressing a moan. 'It's just ...' I hesitated because I hadn't told anyone. It felt stupid, given how lucky I was. I puffed out a breath. 'I think I'm in a rut.'

The stern face he used when he was thinking appeared—the face I'd long suspected to be the reason so many at the club thought him scary, when in fact it was just that he did a lot of thinking.

'It's stupid,' I continued, when he didn't say anything. 'I have everything—two businesses, a great social life, rowing ... I shouldn't be feeling this way.'

'Don't diminish your feelings,' he said with a gentle shake of his head. 'Do you know what's causing it?'

I lifted my eyebrows, then looked up at the stars as I considered his question. 'I think I'm bored of my life, of work, and even rowing doesn't motivate me the way it used to.'

'I'm sorry.'

'It's fine.'

He paused for a beat. 'Is it?'

I looked away. 'I'll figure something out.'

He ran his hand across my back and pressed his mouth against my hair. 'Can I help?'

I shook my head. 'I don't know how you could.'

'Do you need to speak to someone?'

I turned back to face him. 'Like a therapist?'

He lifted one shoulder. 'Or a business advisor or life coach or ... Do you need a mentor?'

'Fucking hell, Andrew.' How was he so perfect?

His face shuttered and he started to withdraw. 'Sorry, I'll—'

'No,' I said quickly, cutting him off, halting his retreat, desperate to keep him with me in our private little world. 'I didn't mean it that way.'

He looked into one of my eyes, then the other, and then his watch vibrated, intruding on the moment. He glanced at the message on the screen, and his shoulders sagged, some underlying tension seeming to seep out of him. 'Thank fuck,' he breathed, more to himself than to me.

My stomach leapt with worry at the look on his face. 'Everything okay?'

He turned off the screen, plunging us into a new kind of darkness now the light from his watch had ruined my night vision, then surprised me by kissing my temple. 'My sister's finally coming home.'

Andrew was the oldest of three children. He had two sisters, Dorothy, who was close to him in age, and Beth, who'd been a surprise to his parents more than ten years later. She'd taken off to travel the world almost two years ago and hadn't been home since, and although Andrew rarely talked about his family, I'd got the sense there was some kind of rift going on that pained him.

'She's agreed to come to our annual work party,' he said, and I would have pressed him for details about the slightly bizarre statement, but Pete's loud fitness instructor tone grabbed our attention.

'Bedtime,' he said, helping Hannah to her feet. 'We want to be in tip top shape for the morning.'

'You're such a personal trainer!' laughed Livia, several drinks tipsy.

'And what exactly is wrong with that?' Hannah asked in mock outrage.

Livia barked an even louder laugh. 'You really have to ask?'

'He's right,' Andrew grumbled in my ear. 'You should have fun with your crew, though, don't feel like you have to go to bed just because I am.'

My stomach pulled tight at the mention of our shared bed, but as he urged me forward so he could stand, I stood with him. 'I'm tired,' I said by way of explanation when he hesitated just a little, and more to the point, I wasn't in the mood for a public grilling from my crew. Yep, that was it, those were the only reasons I was going to bed.

I grabbed my toiletries and headed to the facilities block, hurrying past where Livia, Belle, and Hazel still sat chatting by the fire.

'Oh no you don't!' called Livia, spotting me and jumping to her feet. I raced for the facilities block, but they followed, hot on my heels, Hazel's giggling betraying just how close they were. My heart leapt, and I squealed as my flight reflex kicked in, running and diving into a stall the second I got inside, my heart beating frantically as a triumphant giggle burst from my lips.

'You can't hide from us, Miri!' called Livia.

'We have you cornered!' agreed Belle.

'And unlike you, we have nowhere better to be!' added Hazel, followed by a fit of giggles.

'Oh my God, what's going on?' said Ottie's voice, as I leaned against the door.

'You're back!' squealed Hazel.

'What happened?' demanded Livia, and I could have hugged Ottie for her distraction, giving me a moment of respite to pee before I had to face them.

'Nothing happened,' Ottie said defensively, then added more slowly, 'Theo apologized for being a dick, I sort of forgave him, and then we walked back, which is when I saw you lunatics hurtling across the field like a pack of wolves after prey.'

'The prey being Miri,' said Belle, 'in case you didn't see that bit.'

I flushed, then unlocked the door, and all four of them turned to face me, their expressions gleeful in the harsh light of the fluorescent strip bulbs.

'Soooo,' said Ottie, leaning against the counter beside me as I washed my hands.

I gave her a questioning look.

'Oh, don't play dumb with us,' said Livia, hip checking me out of the way, even though there were plenty more sinks.

'Do you have contraception?' asked Belle.

I choked on thin air, then busied myself with my tooth-brush.

'Well?' said Ottie.

'It's a good thought,' agreed Hazel.

I spun to face them, waving my toothbrush through the air. 'We're not sleeping together in a field with only canvas between us and all of you!' I hissed, keeping my voice low because there was bound to be a hole somewhere between the men's and women's sides.

'Oh, please,' said Ottie. 'You were practically climbing him out there.'

'I was not,' I said indignantly. Had I been? I'd thought I was being subtle, but then, I was three glasses in ...

'Don't listen to them,' said Hazel. 'We're happy for you really.'

'And jealous,' said Livia, folding her arms. 'Don't forget the jealousy.'

Ottie nodded vigorously. 'You should totally do it.'

'I would,' agreed Hazel, shocking us all, making us laugh.

Belle shrugged as we calmed down. 'It's just biology.'

My stomach dipped both because I hated lying to my crew, and because I didn't have any of what they thought I did with Andrew. What I was coming to realize I very much wanted with Andrew, a stable, healthy relationship. But that wasn't what this was. It never would be. He'd made that clear.

'But have you got contraception?' Belle asked again. 'Just in case?'

'No,' I said. 'But I don't ...'

Belle pulled a couple of condoms from her pocket and tucked them into my wash bag. 'Better to be safe, don't you think?'

'Wait,' Livia said incredulously, 'do you just carry those around with you at all times?'

Belle shrugged as though surprised Livia didn't, and I shook my head a little at the general ridiculousness, but I knew it was pointless to argue.

Hazel folded me into a hug. 'Are you okay?' she said in my ear. 'You seem ... well ... something seems ...' She pulled back and held me at arm's length, staring me straight in the eye. 'Funny.'

'I'm fine,' I replied, then stuck my toothbrush into my mouth and turned back to the mirror, but apparently I wasn't convincing because they were still fixated on me. I spat, then repeated, 'I'm fine!' accompanied by a robust wave of my arms. 'Go get your toothbrushes!'

They didn't, but, small mercies, Ottie started spouting hate about Theo, so I took full advantage of the reprieve, grabbed my washbag, and fled. Luckily, they didn't follow.

By the time I got back to the tent, my heart was hammering hard against my ribcage, and as I unzipped the outer door, the sound overwhelmingly loud in the near silent campsite, it became hard to breathe.

I kicked off my shoes, abandoned my washbag on the table, then swallowed hard as I approached the bedroom, guided by dim lantern light, Andrew already inside.

I paused before entering, wondering if I was really doing this, but the night air was cold, and Andrew would wonder what on Earth I was doing if I hesitated any longer, so I stepped over the threshold and zipped up the bedroom door behind me, enclosing us in the small, intimate space, the air thick with possibility.

I turned to find Andrew watching me from under the duvet, and as I took in his naked arms, chest, and shoulders, my pulse ratcheted higher. I grabbed my PJs and turned my back on him as I stripped off my top half, then pulled on the long-sleeved top.

As I replaced my leggings with the pajamas, my chest tightened, wondering if his gaze was on my naked flesh, thinking how hot that would be ... But when I turned around, his eyes were angled towards the ceiling, and a sinking feeling sank through my stomach. But although it was disappointing in a way, it did give me the chance to study his big, well-defined form, the smooth, curved lines of his biceps, the alluring hollow at the base of his neck.

How was he topless? The temperature had dropped to something a long way south of pleasant, and yet there he was, skin exposed to the elements, as though it were positively balmy. I grabbed my sleeping bag from the base of the air mattress, thinking I'd sleep on top of the very cozy-looking duvet, when Andrew's low, deep voice stopped me in my tracks.

'Don't even think about it. I can hear your teeth chattering from all the way over here.'

I paused. 'You want me to ...'

He moved to the other side of the bed and flicked open the duvet where he'd been lying, revealing a brushed cotton sheet that looked oh-so-tempting. 'I want you to be warm, Miri.'

My face flamed. *How about hot? Because, mission accomplished!*

'It's cooling down,' he murmured in a cajoling tone.

I abandoned the sleeping bag and slipped in beside him, almost purring in delight as I luxuriated in the warmth he'd left behind, but also nervous in a way I hadn't been in years. He was careful not to touch me as I settled my head on the pillow that smelled of him, and I trained my eyes on the canvas above.

He turned a little towards me. 'Does this make you uncomfortable?' he asked, concern laced through his words.

'No,' I whispered, both hyperaware of all the ears around us, and of him, only inches away. 'You?' I added as an afterthought, swiveling my head so I could gauge his response.

He smiled as though I'd said something amusing. 'No.' He reached out and brushed his thumb across my cheekbone, and my eyes closed involuntarily, savoring his touch as I tried to stay afloat amid the frothing tide of confusion swirling in my brain. It tried to force me under, tried to throw my lips against his, but I fought its currents, knowing exactly where they led ... to disappointment and rejection.

'You're tired?' he asked, pushing my hair behind my ear, and I clenched my thighs against the sensation his touch elicited in my core.

I slowly opened my eyelids, and as I met his gaze in the barely there light of the lantern, I wasn't sure what I saw. I examined one of his dark orbs, then the other, trying to decipher the silent messages they were sending, but it was no good because what looked like longing couldn't be, and what I might have taken for lust wasn't something we should act on, even if that was the truth of what lurked in his deep green depths.

But I reached out a hand and skimmed his solid pec with my fingers anyway, and his breath hitched. Encouraged, I slowly shuffled forward, watching him as I went, giving him time to pull away, to stop me if this wasn't what he wanted. Then I replaced my fingers with my cheek, sighing as his hand slid into my hair, cupping my head, holding me to him. His heartbeat under my skin was soothing and evocative, and I couldn't help but brush my lips against his almost hairless chest.

'Miri ...' he said in a tight voice.

'Friends snuggle, right?' I breathed, scared to let him voice whatever protest he'd been about to make. He tensed, and I pulled back, needing to see his eyes. 'For heat-related purposes?' I added quickly because his face had morphed into something entirely unreadable. 'I know this is fake,' I clarified. 'I just ...' I trailed off, looking hopefully up at him, but his features were not encouraging. 'Sorry,' I whispered, as the weight of his rejection crashed over me. I turned away, trying to hide the tears stinging my eyes. *Damned alcohol.* I would never have been so bold if I was sober. And now he would fake dump me, and that would be that.

The tears tried to force their way free, but I drove them back. I would not cry. It had been an emotional day, I'd had too much to drink, and I was in a tent with a half-naked demi-god. Could anyone really blame me for wanting to snuggle? To not be alone at a time like this, when my crew had lost, I was unhappy with my perfectly fulfilling life, and I was fake-dating one of my oldest friends for no good reason? But he'd already made it clear what this was. He'd rejected me once already, twice if I counted the kiss by the campfire ... I covered my face with my hand. What the fuck was I doing? What had I been thinking? Of course he didn't want to—

He brushed his fingers down my spine, and I arched, the unexpected intensity of it so great I had to stifle a gasp. 'I don't know if friends snuggle, Miri,' he said, his voice little more than a murmur, 'but I want to if you do.'

I almost cried in relief, only just holding it together as his strong arm closed around me and pulled my back to his chest. Warmth seeped from his skin into mine, and my heart raced, my insides tight with longing, my body screaming at me to kiss him. But I couldn't because friends definitely didn't do that, and if I tried, he would push me away, and then I wouldn't even have his arms and chest and thighs as consolation.

So I settled for skimming my mouth gently across his bicep and forcing myself to resist the temptation to do more.

Andrew's watch buzzed, and he pulled away to look at it, saying, 'Sorry, I'll put it on silent.' I didn't care about the watch, only that he hugged me some more, so when he switched off the lantern and returned, I couldn't help the hum of relief that slipped through my lips.

He tensed, so I spat out the first words that came into my head, terrified he'd put space between us. 'So what's this work party?' I asked, his watch having reminded me of the earlier message from his sister. It seemed strange for their reunion to take place there, especially when she'd been away for so long.

'DrewDox invites everyone's families,' he said. 'It's a small company, but we do this big bash every year ... It's fun, and my sister used to love it. There's live music and good food and ... everyone feels valued.'

'Hmmm,' I murmured, 'that does sound nice.'

'It is.' I felt his low, rumbling words all the way down to my toes and found myself pressing back against him a little harder, a sudden flood of desire making me want to do so much more.

He grunted and shifted his lower body away, and shame rushed through me, the damnable word *friends* stabbing a hot dagger into my heart. When would I learn? How many rejections would it take? But he didn't roll away. Instead, he kissed my hair and whispered, 'Sleep, M,' in my ear, and to my eternal surprise, I did.

Chapter 7

I did little but daydream about Andrew for the whole following week, but the only time I saw him was when our boats passed on the water. Our eyes occasionally met, but I was never sure what to read in his blank expression, and he hadn't texted me once.

As I stood behind the bar at work, emptying the till after a busy night, my mind filled for the umpteenth time with the memory of that morning in the tent. I shuddered, wishing I'd done something differently, wishing I'd said something to convince him to stay because for a single, glorious second, it had been everything I wanted.

I watched the scene replay in my mind, shards of sunlight piercing through chinks in the zip as I came back to consciousness. I heard the others unzipping their own tents, asking each other how they'd slept, Ottie complaining because she'd left her trainers outside and they were covered in dew.

Andrew and I were still pressed together, his naked torso flush against my skin where my top had ridden up, his lower half pressed to mine, too, I realized, at which point my mind had cranked into sharp focus, banishing all vestiges of sleep. His hand was a hair's breadth from my breast, and it had sent want trickling low in my belly. I'd wished the circumstances were different, that it was real, that I could act on my desires.

I'd shifted and felt something hard between my thighs, realizing with a jolt that only the fabric of Andrew's boxers and my thin PJs separated our flesh, and that he was as turned on as I was.

I froze, scared to move, half hoping he would pull away and half hoping he wouldn't. 'Andrew?' I said quietly, then a second time when he didn't answer. 'Andrew?' He started muttering incongruent words, and I realized his mind was still asleep, even if his body was not.

He started rocking against me, and it felt so freaking good, I let him do it for a few furious heartbeats, knowing I shouldn't, that I should wake him, that it was wrong on so many levels. But I wanted more. Wanted everything. Wanted his hands to slide over my breasts, to squeeze my rock-hard nipples. I wanted to rip off our clothes and feel him against my core, for him to push me down and slide inside me. But I forced myself to do the right thing, shaking his arm until I felt him start awake, then immediately wishing I hadn't because as confusion turned to realization on his features, he jerked away as though I burned like lava.

'I'm ... I'm so sorry,' he'd breathed, mortified, running a hand through his hair, then rolling away and reaching for a pair of sweats. 'I'm sorry. I mean ... I ... I didn't want ...'

'Andrew!' I said, sitting, trying to process, trying to slow things down as he headed for the tent flap. 'Andrew?' But it was like he couldn't hear me, and he bolted, leaving me in a confused, frustrated heap on the blow-up bed.

I snapped back to the present and put the meager cash takings in the safe—everyone paid on card these days—then joined the servers on clean up, clearing dishes, wiping down tables, and sweeping the floor.

A rap came from the door, and I looked up to find Hazel waving hopefully on the other side of the glass. Guilt sliced through me because I'd had to miss training again tonight. One of my servers had called in sick and no one else could cover, so I'd had little choice.

Luckily, Belle had been available at the last minute, so my crew had trained without me, but I hated letting them down.

'Hey!' I said, pulling open the door. 'I'm so sorry I couldn't make it.'

Hazel stepped inside. 'We understand. Have you got a minute?'

Uh oh. That didn't sound good. 'Sure!' I said with an over-the-top smile, then led her to my office. 'What's up?'

Hazel looked awkward, like she didn't want to say whatever it was that had brought her here. 'Well ...' she started, and I got the horrible feeling she was about to kick me out of the squad.

'I'm really sorry I've been such a shitty crewmate recently,' I said. 'I've had a lot going on with this place, and Andr-ew ...' My voice cracked on his name, and Hazel's features crumpled. She pulled me in for a hug.

'I'm here to see if you're okay,' she said softly, stroking my back. 'Ever since the regatta, you've seemed distant.'

I nodded, then pulled back. 'I've just got a lot on, and Andrew and I had a ... fight. I haven't seen him since the regatta.'

Hazel perched on the edge of the desk. 'Want to talk about it?'

I tipped my head, resigned to my fate. 'I don't think there's much to talk about. I think it's over.'

Hazel blanched. 'No,' she breathed. 'I can't believe ... The way he looks at you ... and it's so new!' She paused, collecting her thoughts. 'Do *you* want it to be over?'

I kept imagining all the ways that morning in the tent could have gone differently. What if I'd moved away and not woken him? What if I'd rolled over and kissed him? I didn't want to fake date Andrew, I wanted to *real* date him, I knew that for certain now. Preferably forever, complete with little Andrew shaped babies and—*Oh Lord, get a grip, Miri!*

'No,' I told Hazel, shaking my head as the word burst free, 'I don't want it to be over, but it's not that simple.' A tug of regret pulled at my heart because I so wanted to tell her the truth, but Andrew and I had agreed to keep the fake part of our relationship between us. At least if it did end, I wouldn't have to lie to my crew any longer. And what was I expecting, anyway? It was *fake*. It was always going to end, so better now than later, when Andrew found the woman of his dreams and cut me loose.

A knock came from the door, and one of the servers poked her head in. 'There's a man here to see you.'

'Thanks,' I said reflexively, not really taking in her words until she stepped aside and revealed the tall, blond-haired man of my dreams.

'Hey Hazel,' Andrew said evenly, his eyes flitting over her, then finding me.

Hazel jumped hastily to her feet. 'I was just leaving. You know where I am if you need me, M.'

I nodded but barely noticed as she left and pulled the door closed behind her, unable to look away from Andrew's sea green eyes.

'Are you okay?' he said, taking another step into the room.

I folded my arms across my chest, needing a physical barrier between us, needing to protect myself. 'I'm fine.'

'You weren't at training.'

'I'm fine,' I repeated, a cool edge to my tone because of course I wasn't *fine!* He'd run from me, then ghosted me all week. 'One of my servers called in sick.'

'Oh,' he said, finally turning his intense gaze away.

Silence descended, and I squeezed my arms so hard I left finger marks. 'Why are you here, Andrew?'

He turned wary under my harsh scrutiny, becoming guarded, his eyes boring into me as though trying to read the truths etched into my soul. 'I came to make sure you didn't need anything,' he said quietly, 'and to apologize for ... in the tent ... I really didn't mean for that to happen.' He looked positively ashamed, a slight flush staining the tops of his cheeks, but he didn't look away.

'You were asleep,' I said, my tone cutting. 'Of course you didn't *mean* for it to happen.'

He hesitated, his mouth opening then closing, then his forehead pursed a little as turmoil appeared in his eyes. 'But I don't want you to think—'

'I get it, it's *fine*,' I snapped. 'This is fake. You didn't want to touch me like that, and you've been feeling bad about it all week. Honestly, don't worry about it. In fact, we should probably just call it a day; it's too messy, anyway.'

He went very still, looking like I'd slapped him. 'You want to ... break up?'

I froze. 'Don't you?' My heart thundered as I waited, searching his face for some clue about what he truly wanted.

'I ...' He seemed to be searching for something, inspiration, maybe. 'I ... What about Theo?'

Fuck Theo! How could he care about Theo when it was just him and I in the room? I retreated into myself and built a brick wall in front of me, stuffing any feelings I had towards him in a bomb-proof chest and throwing away the key. He didn't see me like I saw him. He saw me as a friend, nothing more.

'He's already been sniffing around, so mission accomplished,' I said, throwing projectiles from the safety of my freshly minted battlements, refusing to let him see any glimmer of what really lay inside. Andrew's jaw worked, and I was delighted to have successfully hit my target, not really sure why I wanted to hurt him, but knowing it was safer than lowering the drawbridge and risking rejection another time.

'Oh. Right. That's ...'

I could feel him withdrawing, closing down just as I had, and I knew any second he would leave. But I wasn't done. I couldn't bear the thought of this conversation being over ... of us being over. 'Why are you even doing this?' I demanded, lifting my hands in frustrated question. 'What's in it for you?'

He exhaled a long breath, then swallowed hard. 'I enjoy spending time with you, Miri. We've been friends for a long time, and ...' He trailed off when he saw the scowl that had taken my face hostage because I didn't believe a single one of his bland words.

I leaned against my desk and refolded my arms. 'That's not enough.'

He looked away and gave a slow, pensive nod, agonizing beats of silence stretching between us. When he turned back, there seemed to be some new determination in the set of his shoulders. 'I came to ask a favor.'

Our eyes locked in an intense, captivating hold. 'What is it?' I breathed, desperate to know.

'The work party I told you about.'

I frowned, not catching his meaning. 'The one your sister loves?'

'I was hoping you'd come with me.'

Holy ... 'As your girlfriend?'

'As my girlfriend,' he confirmed in a husky tone, watching me closely.

The idea of turning up at his work party, talking to his sister, and meeting his colleagues was all utterly terrifying, and yet an electric thrill of excitement ran through me, too. What would it be like, being on his arm, in his world, away from the safety of the rowing club? How did his colleagues see him? Would he kiss me in front of them? Hold my hand? Wrap his arm around me?

But it would still be fake ... *Oh, God, I should tell him I don't like Theo.* The thought repeated over and over in my mind. *I should be honest. I should—*

He ran a hand across his stubble-covered jaw. 'Please.'

The word tugged at my heartstrings, melting my fragile resolve. 'Why?' I whispered.

He said nothing for a beat, just stared at me in a way that made my breath catch. 'It would mean a lot to me, Miri.'

Something about the way he said my name pulled my belly tight every single time. Perhaps the deep timbre of his voice or the way his eyes seemed to darken or because whenever he said it, it was easy to imagine he was really mine.

I studied him for a moment, then nodded once, and he sagged a little, seemingly in relief, his shoulders falling, his head tipping back, and later that night, while the moment replayed for the umpteenth time in my mind, I still couldn't help but wonder why on Earth he wanted me there at all.

Chapter 8

My phone vibrated in my clutch as I waited in the parking lot for Andrew to pick me up, nervously excited in a floaty green dress I'd bought especially for the occasion. I fished out the phone and rolled my eyes when I read the message.

Theo 10:38: Andrew is a liar.

I sneered at the screen, then angry-typed.

Miri 10:38: You're the liar.

Theo 10:39: [crying laughy face] You're going to his party ... you'll see.

I didn't reply, but he sent me another one thirty seconds later.

Theo 10:40: Come find me when you know.

I shoved my phone back into my bag and tried my best to forget all about Theo. Andrew wasn't a liar ... at least, not usually. Our fake dating was a special case. He was dependable and trustworthy and sometimes a little scary, but entirely dedicated. To the club, his crew, his family, and apparently his job, too, if he cared so much about what people thought he was willing to bring a fake date to their annual party.

A black truck pulled into the parking lot, and my mouth dropped open when I realized it was Andrew behind the wheel.

'What the fuck is this?' I demanded as I yanked open the passenger door. 'Did you buy a new truck?' My words were light and jokey, but underneath, my heart fell a little. He'd said he felt guilty about his gas-guzzling ways.

Andrew grinned. 'Like it?'

'I ...' I faltered. He'd seemed sheepish about his last truck, but now he was almost proud of himself.

'It's electric!' he exclaimed as I climbed in and slammed the door behind me. It made a pleasingly deep *thunk*. Andrew started gushing about the truck's many advanced features, but I didn't hear the individual words, too distracted by how good he looked in his shirt and chinos, how, over the smell of new car, I caught notes of his musky scent, and how his whole face lit up when he smiled.

Then he was looking at me expectantly, as though he might have asked me a question. 'Uh ... it's ... Wow, Andrew!'

It seemed to be an appropriate response because he beamed, then spun the truck and got us on the road.

'I've been thinking of doing it for a while, but then I was driving past the showroom, and, well ... here we are.' He looked a little guilty, perhaps because he'd just admitted to buying a truck on a whim, but I couldn't help but smile at his infectious enthusiasm. And data science was lucrative, apparently.

'So,' I said, no desire to discuss four wheeled objects for the entire journey, 'tell me more about this party. Actually, no, tell me why you need a fake date for this party; that's what I really want to know.' I flashed my eyes, and Andrew shook his head indulgently, tapping the steering wheel with his thumb a few times as we waited at a junction.

Part of me wondered if he would refuse to tell me, the silence stretching beyond the point of comfort, his features contemplative, but as we drove on, he said, 'I realized you'd never met my family.'

I barked a laugh. 'This is a work party though, right?'

He nodded slowly. 'Sort of. Work and family are pretty much the same thing for me.'

I felt like I was missing something, something big, and unease undulated through me. He made it sound almost like he was a drugs baron!

'I want to show you.'

'Show me what?' I asked, my eyebrows raising a little.

Another long silence followed, and I wanted to shake the answer out of him. 'The other side of my life. The side I keep private.'

My mind went blank. What the hell did that mean? But I'd run out of time to ask because we turned onto a long, tree-lined drive, where all the way to the grand, Georgian house at the top, flags sporting the same *DrewDox* logo that adorned our boats fluttered in the breeze.

He pulled right up to the generous turning circle by the front door, waited for me to jump down and walk around to his side, then handed his keys to a valet.

He put his hand on my lower back, guiding me to the top of the flag-lined entrance steps where a dark-haired woman with a severe bob in a black linen jumpsuit waited, a broad smile on her ruby red lips.

'Andrew!' She wrapped him in an energetic hug, then pinned me with intense energy. 'And you must be Miri! It's so nice to finally meet you.' She pulled me in for a tight squeeze. 'I've heard so much about you.'

'This is my sister, Dorothy,' said Andrew, when the woman finally released me.

She waved a dismissive hand. 'Call me Dox, everyone does.'

'As in the boat?' I blurted. 'And the ... company?' I added as an afterthought.

She faltered, her eyes flicking to her big, silent brother, then back to me. 'Sure, like the boat.' She handed Andrew a badge that said, *Chief Data Scientist*, and I realized she had a badge on, too, one which read, *CEO*.

'Wait, this is your company?' My gaze swung to Andrew, but his expression was unreadable as he watched my reaction.

Dox let out a tinkling laugh, higher and brighter than I'd expected. 'It's Andrew's company; I just run the place. He got the techy brains, I got the organizational ones. Works like a charm, actually.'

Before I could question her further, she raised an eyebrow at her brother, then spun and headed deeper into the beautiful old building. I glanced up at Andrew, silently asking for an explanation, but he just shrugged as though it wasn't a big deal, then snagged my hand and pulled me after her, my mind reeling.

What was this? Andrew owned a company? He owned a company that made the kind of money where he could sponsor boats and hold swanky parties in big country houses? *What the fuck?* My heart raced as I followed numbly, not really noticing where we were headed until we came out in a large reception room filled with people, and every single one of them turned to look at us. Or more accurately, at me.

Their eyes raked me up and down, no doubt wondering who I was and what I was to Andrew.

'Hey, boss!' called a young guy with an elaborate pink drink in his hand from across the room.

'Hey, Pete,' Andrew called back, then said in a low voice to Dox, 'there are curly freaking straws?'

She squealed. 'Aren't they divine?'

Andrew rolled his eyes, while I felt like I'd been dropped into another dimension, only then realizing there were kitsch decorations all over the place, from flamingo sculptures to sparkly pineapples. Dox leaned towards me and laughed in the same tinkling way. 'Andrew *hates* shit like this.' She waved her arm around triumphantly, motioning to the many and varied questionable decorations.

'And yet she does it anyway ...' said Andrew, in a resigned tone.

'That's the reason *why* I do it, brother.'

'Will you ever grow up?'

She gave a shrug, then flitted off to the bar, leaving us alone. But not for long because a crowd descended, introducing themselves and asking an endless stream of questions. I barely heard any of it, completely disoriented because none of this made any sense. I mean, I knew Andrew was successful and intelligent and that everyone else thought he was scary in a boss-man kinda way, but he'd never been like that with *me*. Why hadn't he told me? Why hadn't he told anyone?

'Drink?' Andrew asked, leaning close, and I nodded, then followed him to the bar. Alcohol was a marvelous idea. The very best. I ordered a cocktail aptly named *Oh My God, I Can't Believe It*, and waited patiently for my drink as Andrew was pulled into a conversation with a short, grey-haired man and a tall, beautiful Spanish woman who was unashamedly batting her eyelashes at him.

From what I could hear, they were talking about something technical. Something to do with algorithms and databases and clouds. Something I couldn't contribute to, but that Miss Spain was enthusiastically gesticulating about. Maybe she was why Andrew wanted me here ... to make her jealous.

An older woman with a matronly air stepped up beside me. 'She's a marvel, isn't she?'

'Um ... sorry?' I turned my confused expression on her.

'Sophia? Legs like a gazelle, hair to die for, and a brain like a ... oh I don't know. A computer? That doesn't sound right though, does it? And,' she leaned in close and whispered, 'she's a *princess* ... or something like that, I forget the specifics.' She looked wistfully over at the woman and sighed. 'But if she can't bag him with a figure like that, what hope is there for the rest of you?' She laughed, and I smiled weakly, not wanting to be rude. 'And believe me, she's tried!'

Andrew thankfully chose that moment to return, wrapping his arm around my waist and pulling me into his side. I slid gratefully into the warm, comforting space and wrapped my arm around him, too, fitting perfectly under his arm. He kissed my temple, the brush of his lips sending an electric shiver down my spine, and the older woman's mouth fell open. 'Oh ...' Her eyes flicked to my lower half, then ran back up to my face. 'Um ...'

The bartender handed me my drink, and the woman made her excuses, presumably off to spread the news that by some miracle a woman with actual thighs had bagged their most eligible bachelor. If only she knew the truth ... that would really give her something to gossip about.

I downed half my drink as the bartender handed Andrew a crystal tumbler filled with gin and tonic garnished with cucumber, and then I headed for the back of the room, not waiting to see if he was following because curious eyes were already tracking me, and I hated it. I wished to be anonymous, to blend in, especially because I didn't fit in here, and the whole room knew it just as well as I did.

'Miri ...' said Andrew, catching up with me in the clear space at the back of the room, a mere ten paces from the door. I took a breath, then turned and plastered a bright smile on my face. 'Is everything okay?' he asked in a gentle, soothing tone, stepping into my space so I had to tilt my head to look up at him.

'I ... uh ...' *No! Everything is not freaking okay! You own a company! This is* your *party. You're a celebrity to these people.*

Dox took to the temporary stage at the front of the room, and as the crowd shifted their attention to her, I exhaled in relief, letting Andrew's green, green eyes ground me. It was curious how they could do that, especially when all my brain wanted to know was, 'Why, Andrew? Why did you never tell me?' *Why did you never tell anyone? Why did you bring me here? Why didn't you warn me?*

Dox's voice filled the room, talking about numbers and projections and a big deal they had in the works, and then, before he'd answered my question, she introduced Andrew, who kissed me on the temple and murmured, 'Two ticks,' then squeezed my arm before heading to the stage.

I shrank back, feeling vulnerable without him in this room full of strangers, feeling entirely like a fish out of water. I wasn't a social beast, which people often found strange, given I ran a café and bar, but there, I always had an excuse to leave an awkward conversation, and I was removed, on the other side of a literal barrier most of the time, where everyone—or at least most people—understood the social contract. It was simple and straightforward and easy. Practical. Never with long stretches where I had to converse with people I had nothing in common with. Even at the bar, I always had an office to escape to. But this, here ...

My back hit the wall, and I exhaled long and hard, giving myself a pep talk as Andrew began his speech. This was fine. I didn't have to talk to anyone. I didn't have to do anything other than listen to Andrew. And breathe. I should probably keep doing that. This was not a crisis situation, and now I was at the back, no one could even look at me. In fact, I could look at them, just like a crew with the upper hand in a race.

But there wasn't much to see, other than a sea of adoring faces turned on Andrew, hanging off his every self-depreciating joke, some of them even issuing little sighs as he thanked them for their hard work.

And then it hit me. Properly. Andrew had built this. This whole company. And no one at the club knew anything about it. It was utterly, completely amazing. It made my businesses look like craft club at the library in comparison, but why didn't he want anyone to know? The thought sent a flutter of panic through me.

'And finally, I want to thank my very special guest. Someone who's inspired me since the beginning,' said Andrew in a warm, low tone, the words only registering because he was looking right at me. Into me. A slight line of concern on his brow, perhaps because I was pressed up against the back wall like I was facing a firing squad. 'Her work ethic, persistence, and determination make me and Dox look like slackers.' The crowd chuckled, a few of them following his gaze, glancing at me. 'And if she hadn't set the bar so high, if she hadn't been so focused yet good-humored about all the challenges she faced, I wouldn't have had to work so hard to keep up!' Another laugh. Andrew lifted his tumbler. 'To Miri, my endless inspiration.'

I felt more than saw the skeptical eyes turn on me, asking if it could possibly be true that *I* had inspired *him*.

Of course it wasn't true. It was fake! All of this was. Why he'd said those things, I couldn't even begin to imagine. Although, it was the first time anyone had publicly celebrated my business successes, which was nice, objectively speaking. My national rowing titles were the only achievements anyone usually cared about, and he hadn't mentioned my rowing prowess once.

'To Miri!' the crowd echoed, lifting their own glasses, and I wanted the wall to open up and swallow me whole, so many faces now turned my way.

My eyes flitted back and forth across the room, my weak smile fixed and plastic, my chest strangely tight. Andrew jumped down from the stage and made a beeline for me, brushing off everyone who tried to intercept him. He snagged my hand and peeled me off the wall, a faint smile on his lips. 'Everything okay?' he asked, leaning close.

Without the wall holding me up, I realized how not okay I was. And now he was here, practically *everyone* was looking at us, or at least, that's what it felt like. I could feel them scrutinizing me with judgmental eyes. Wondering what we were to each other. Wondering if I'd truly bagged their boss ... impossible, surely, given my legs were probably as un-gazelle-like as legs could be, nor was I a genius data scientist.

I couldn't breathe. Too many eyes. Too much scrutiny. I couldn't speak. I couldn't do anything. I looked up at him with what I was sure was my best rabbit-in-headlights expression, willing my lungs to work, vaguely wondering if I might pass out there and then. Would he catch me? Or would I hit the floor, my dress flying up, displaying my underwear to the room. What underwear did I even have on? Either way, it would be embarrassing.

'Shit,' he breathed, then tugged me away from the prying eyes and into a smaller side room that was blissfully devoid of life, but I didn't have enough breath. I barely had time to notice the open floor-to-ceiling windows and the billowing fabric being buffeted by the breeze before my head started rushing, blackness collecting at the edges of my vision, my chest crying out for air. I crouched, my legs buckling, standing apparently too difficult, too disorienting.

'Miri ...' he crouched at my side, his hand rubbing circles on my back, but my chest was so tight ... terrifyingly tight. Like, call an ambulance, I think there's something seriously wrong tight.

'Andrew,' I gasped, grabbing hold of his hands.

'It's okay, Miri. It's a panic attack,' he said in a quiet but commanding voice.

A panic attack? A what? I'd never had a panic attack. Was this really what one felt like? This was what I imagined a heart attack to feel like, my chest locked, everything sort of tingling and constricted, like a snake had wrapped around my ribs and was squeezing me from the inside out.

'Andrew,' I spluttered again, gripping his hands with everything I had. 'I don't ... I ...'

'It's okay, M. It's just us, just you and me, and we can stay in here for as long as you need. All day if you want. Just try to breathe. To relax.'

A panic attack. Okay. This was okay. I wasn't going to die, even though it felt like it. The tight feeling lessened a little, and I managed to get a bit of air in. It would be okay. It would. I wasn't going to pass out from oxygen starvation. I could breathe. I could do this. I did this every day!

Andrew's soothing, calming words continued, anchoring me, and so did his stroking, until eventually I'd got a hold of myself enough that he led me to a padded bench by the window. We sat side by side, Andrew rubbing my back as I leaned forward, my head between my legs, and I found I was crying, big, fat, silent drops falling from my eyes, marring my dress as they fell near the hem.

My mascara had probably run halfway down my face by now. I probably resembled a wayward teenager after a long night of sweaty dancing on a slightly sticky dancefloor.

Nothing Andrew hadn't seen on me before, but still, it was mortifying considering this was his company's annual party, and I was his fake special guest.

I felt like a fool and a failure, and embarrassment crept in as the panic receded. I had to get it together, to buck up, to get back out there and be the best fake date I could be. I wiped at the tears, then lifted my head, refusing to look at Andrew as I searched hopefully for tissues.

'Here,' he said, snagging a box from the sideboard behind him and handing it to me.

'I'm so sorry,' I whispered, grabbing a handful and using them to mop up the fresh river of tears. *Damn it.*

'No, Miri, *I'm* sorry. This is all my fault. I thought ... I wanted ...' He looked away, as though the enormous mirror over the fireplace might contain answers.

What? What had he thought? What had he wanted? I was filled with a deep desperation to know.

He shook his head slowly. 'I didn't mean to upset you; that's the last thing I wanted.'

'Why?'

He turned wide, alarmed eyes on me.

'Why did you lie about DrewDox? Why didn't you tell me this is your company?' Is this what Theo had meant?

He shook his head again, this time a little frantically. 'It's not like that!'

'It is like that!'

'It's not ... I'm not ... I'm just the data scientist.'

'Andrew ...' My tone was harsher than I'd intended, but he was downplaying a massive achievement. Did that mean my company was a joke to him? If all he'd built wasn't worth telling anyone about, then what did that make my businesses? My *life?*

'Dox runs the company, and I ... I'm good at what I do. That's all that matters to me.'

I didn't understand, not one bit. 'Then why did you get up on stage and make a speech? Why did you say all that stuff about me?'

He faltered. 'That you inspire me?'

'Yes,' I breathed, my heart stuttering, hoping for something it shouldn't.

'Because it's true,' he said in a quiet, intense voice.

I laughed cruelly, mostly at myself—not that he knew that—and got to my feet, taking a step away. 'Andrew, if you don't think what you've done is noteworthy, then you can't possibly have any respect for what I've achieved. And the idea that I somehow inspired all this ...?' I laughed again as I threw up my hands, another bout of tears threatening.

'That's not ... no!' He sprang after me, only stopping when he was so close I could feel the heat from his chest. 'Miri, you did inspire me. *Do* inspire me! Every day. Like when you changed the layout of your café to make the customer flow better, and the way you dealt with that sleazebag the other night, and the way you stopped those arseholes at the club from taking advantage of you.'

I shook my head. 'You built DrewDox! And according to your sister's speech, you're *buying* another company ...' It was a world I couldn't relate to; I'd worried about expanding from the café to the bar, I couldn't imagine what it would take to buy a company like his with important clients and HR departments and no-doubt endless regulations.

He stepped closer still, lifting his hands and placing them on my arms, his eyes tender as he looked down at me, and I let him, apparently possessing no self-preservation. 'What we did is the same, Miri.'

I scowled. 'How could you think that?'

'If anything, what you did was harder. It needed up-front investment and rigorous planning and long hours. I started from my apartment and scaled up as the work came in. Very little risk. Very little outlay.'

Frustration bubbled up inside me and I shrugged him off, lifting my hands in an almost violent movement. 'No, Andrew, it's not.'

He stepped back, hurt in his eyes. 'I'm sorry. I'm so sorry, Miri. I never meant—'

'I want to go home, Andrew.' I didn't know why I was so upset. Why his saying nice things made me hate myself and feel like a fraud. Why I cared so much that he hadn't told me about DrewDox. If he wanted to keep it private, wasn't that up to him? It's not like we'd ever been BFFs, and we weren't really dating, he didn't owe me anything.

But Theo had set me on edge, calling Andrew a liar, and I wasn't good in social situations, especially when I was put under a surprise spotlight. It had been a shock, all of it, since the moment I'd got out of his truck. It had felt like an ambush.

'Of course, anything you want.' He looked ... I wasn't sure how he looked. Maybe like he'd shoved his feelings down so deep that his face didn't know what was going on, either.

I tried to compose myself, dabbing at the tears with a tissue and taking a few deep breaths, as though that would do anything to un-puff my red, blotchy skin. I stepped up to the mirror and wiped away the black rings of smudged mascara. Luckily the rest of my makeup had held up fairly well, so my face wasn't a complete disaster, only a partial one.

But as I looked at my less-than-ideal reflection, I started to feel foolish and angry at myself. I'd had a full-scale breakdown over a few curious people and some nice words. And why did I care so much about whether Andrew really meant them?

I turned and looked at Andrew, whose guarded expression I still couldn't read, and guilt joined the growing self-loathing rolling around in the pit of my stomach. 'I'm sorry, Andrew. I don't know what came over me. I guess … I just …' I shook my head as I thought about it some more, trying to sort through my feelings, to understand what they meant. 'What I've done is nothing special, you know? Nothing to brag about. Loads of people do it, and have a far more difficult time of it than I've had.' The words spilled free before I'd had a chance to really consider them, but they seemed right, and certainly they made me feel better, like in the light of them my actions had been, if not justified, then not totally unhinged.

His head cocked to one side, a curious look crossing his features as he watched me.

'What?' I said. 'Why are you looking at me like that?'

He took a step closer. 'That's what that piece of shit used to say.'

Huh? 'Who?'

'Your coach. When you were in the national squad.' Andrew was looking at me as though something profound had just slotted into place in his mind. 'I overheard him saying things like that so many times ...'

'*No*. No, I—' That couldn't be right, could it? That man was gone from my life; I'd made sure not a single trace of him remained. Panic fluttered in my chest as I tried to suppress the memories Andrew was dredging to the surface.

Andrew shook his head, as though shaking away his own memories. 'It made me want to punch things, but I never realized his bullshit had burrowed so deep.'

And then it was like I was back there, my old coach before me. *Be humble, Miri. You have nothing to brag about until you win gold. Until then, you're nothing special. Just do the work, keep your head down, and remember you still have a long way to go.* The voice from my past rang through my skull. Words my old coach would say when someone at the club bigged me up or congratulated me on a win.

I froze, flinching as though my past had reached out and slapped me. '*Fuck*,' I whispered, realizing Andrew was right. 'Oh my God.'

He was suddenly at my side, running his hands down my arms and then tugging me into a hug so all-consuming I momentarily forgot everything but him. It was safe and warm and smelled sweet and woodsy and while it lasted, I could almost believe the fantasy we'd spun, that we'd been in love for years but never acted on our feelings. That he wanted me.

But as Andrew pulled back and stroked my cheek, I reminded myself that he didn't want me, not really, that he'd suggested a fake relationship, not a real one. 'Why did you invite me here as your date, Andrew? Why not just bring me as your friend?' Would I have had this freak out if he'd done that?

'I …' His thumb worked back and forth across my cheek, and his green eyes dipped to my lips, which parted under his scrutiny. 'It's not important,' he breathed, shaking his head.

It was important to me! Very important. Possibly the most important—

The door crashed open, and Dox clattered into the room. 'Thank fuck, there you are,' she panted. 'Our mother needs to be diverted. She just arrived and she's making a beeline for—'

'Beth,' Andrew finished, instantly understanding the direction of his sister's thoughts. 'Shit.' He made to move, then stopped himself, looking back at me.

'Go,' I said, meaning it. It sounded serious, whatever was going on.

He slid his hand into mine and linked our fingers. 'Come with us,' he said, his eyes imploring, his palm so big and warm and right against mine.

I let him tug me along, following him out of the room, and we rapidly retraced our earlier steps, exiting through the front door.

'Shit,' said Dox, casting her eyes around the gravel turning circle. 'She's gone. I told her to wait!'

'And when has she ever done anything she was told to?' said Andrew. He and Dox looked at each other for a long beat before saying together, 'The hut.'

They took off in perfect synchrony, hurtling towards a lavender-lined path that led around the side of the building and deposited us in the beautiful, mature gardens at the back.

'There,' said Dox, pointing to where a tall, grey-haired woman who looked to be in her late sixties was marching purposefully towards a small hut on the edge of the lawn. In front of the hut, which I could now see housed a bar, stood several tables and padded wire chairs, on which lounged a group of young, trendy-looking twenty-some-things.

It was an intimidating group I wouldn't have ordinarily approached, with their multi-colored hair, large earrings, and clumpy black boots. But neither Dox, Andrew, nor their mother seemed to have such qualms, all of them rushing for the tables—me meekly in tow—to where a young woman with long dark hair and many piercings watched our approach with wide-eyes.

The young woman jumped to her feet, putting space between herself and the group, presumably trying to keep whatever altercation might follow to a limited audience. 'Uh ... Mum?' she stammered, her stance uncertain and a little defensive, as though not sure what to expect but preparing to be bulldozed just in case.

The older woman enfolded her into a tight hug, then launched into a tirade that sounded angry but with words that didn't match. 'Don't you let something like that come between us again, Beth ... he's a silly boy, and you—'

'Mum!'

Andrew and Dox exhaled in relief, then Dox inserted herself like a wedge between the two. 'Alright, alright, our turn!' She hugged first the older woman, and then her sister.

'I already said hi to you!' complained Beth.

'Can't I hug my sister two times in one day?' Dox shot back.

'I'd rather you didn't.'

'Beth,' said Andrew, releasing my hand as he stepped forward and hugged her tight. 'It's so good to see you.'

Beth seemed uncertain as they pulled apart, and perhaps a little bashful, but then Andrew was introducing me, and I was being yanked into a hug so hard, my teeth rattled. 'It's so nice to meet you,' Beth gushed. 'We've heard so much about you over the years.'

'Uh ...' I would have said the same, but the truth was, Andrew rarely talked about anything personal, so I'd barely known they existed ... just like his company.

Their mother stuck out her hand, and I returned her firm handshake. 'It's so nice to meet you, Mrs. Delacour.'

'And you,' she said, sizing me up with formidable grey eyes. 'Finally.'

'Mother!' Dox cried, then pulled out her vibrating phone, her eyes sparkling with delight when she looked down. 'Claire's here.'

'Chocolate!' squealed Beth, and then took off at a run, Dox hot on her heels.

Andrew chuckled. 'Claire's a chocolatier,' he explained.

'Claire's a *marvel*,' Mrs. Delacour corrected, watching her daughters disappear. 'Beth looks well, doesn't she?'

'She does,' Andrew agreed, smiling as he, too, watched them go.

Mrs. Delacour looked up at her son, so much passing between them that I couldn't even begin to decipher. 'All's well that ends well, then,' she said, then went after them, albeit at a more sedate pace.

Andrew came close and slipped his arm around my shoulders, and I leaned into his touch. 'Shall we go?' he asked, and when I looked up at him, he seemed not even the tiniest bit resentful at the idea of leaving early.

My eyes roamed over the croquet set, shaded seating areas, and canapé trays crammed with delicious morsels, and whether it was because we were outside, away from the crowd or because the initial shock had passed or because I wanted to spend more time with the people who mattered to him, I realized I no longer wanted to go. 'Let's stay,' I said, looking deep into his eyes, showing him I meant it.

He squeezed my arm and shook his head. 'No. You said you wanted to leave.'

'I did,' I agreed, 'but now I want to stay.'

'You ... Miri ...' He seemed conflicted.

'Really, Andrew. I'm not just saying it.'

He pulled me around to face him. 'You don't have to do this. I will happily take you home or we could go for a walk or to the movies? I'm sure there's some terrible romcom you could force me to sit through.'

'Hey! Romcoms are not terrible.'

'Precisely my point.'

I swayed closer. 'I want to stay,' I said in a low voice.

He appraised me for a moment, then took a deep breath, visibly relenting on the exhale. 'You had better not be putting on a brave face.'

I smiled mischievously up at him. 'You're the one who'll need a brave face after I whoop your ass at croquet.'

I pushed off him, his unyielding body giving not an inch, then headed for the mallets, accompanied by the tune of his laughter. 'We'll see, Buttercup,' he called after me. 'We'll see.'

We played croquet—he won, much to my deep consternation—then took plates piled high with sushi and salad slathered in carrot and ginger dressing, and lounged the afternoon away under a shade on the reclining chairs down by the pond.

Waiters occasionally brought us new drinks, and Andrew's colleagues occasionally stopped by, but for the most part, it was just me and him, chatting, laughing, or sitting in companionable silence and watching the ducks.

'Thank you,' he said as he drove me home, the stars twinkling in the inky blue sky through the windshield.

Even his side profile took my breath away. 'For what?'

'For coming with me today. For staying.'

'I had fun!' In truth, it had been so good it hurt. 'And you must admit, it was nice of me to let you win at croquet.'

He barked a laugh. 'By all means, tell yourself that if it makes you feel better.'

'Don't make me call witnesses.'

'Witnesses? Which witnesses do you think will come to your aid? I literally paid them all to be there.'

My heart gave a dangerous squeeze. 'Beth. She'd definitely side with me.'

'Hmm.' I took the sound as reluctant agreement.

'And your mother.'

'Ha! My mother ... Good luck with that one.'

'She seems nice.'

'She'd bite your head off if she ever heard you saying that. She detests the word *nice*. Says it's for wimps and wigwams.'

'Wigwams?' I laughed in bewilderment.

He shrugged. 'Don't ask me.'

Silence settled for a beat, my heart full and heavy. 'Can I ask you something?'

He threw a sideways glance my way. 'Always.'

'Why did you take me as your date?'

His shoulders lifted half an inch, and he didn't answer right away. 'I ... How do you mean?'

'It's a simple question, Andrew.' He knew exactly what I meant.

He glanced at me again, but didn't say anything for a while, not until we'd pulled into my parking lot and he'd killed the engine. An apology was on the tip of my tongue, but I chastised myself for it. Didn't I have a right to know, seeing as I was the fake date in question?

He exhaled and drummed his thumbs on the steering wheel. 'I don't know, exactly.' He continued to look straight through the windshield, to where moonlight bounced off the rippling water of the river. 'I guess I just wanted you there. It felt like you should be there.'

'Why? Why as your date?'

'Because what I said in my speech was true.'

'Andrew—'

He turned his body, angling himself towards me. 'I don't want to upset you—that's the last thing I would ever want—but you *are* amazing. I want you to know that.' He covered my hand with his. 'I want you to *believe* that.'

His words made my cheeks flush hot in the darkness, his proximity so overwhelming, I was worried what I might do if I stayed a second longer. I yanked the door open and half fell out of his truck, my feet thankfully finding the pavement while I clutched the door to steady myself.

'Miri! Are you—'

The sound of him unbuckling his seatbelt had me turning back around, pinning him in place with my eyes, worried if he got out and stood before me, I would do something foolish under the false cover of the moon-lit darkness. And then he'd reject me again, and I wasn't sure I could take it. 'I'm fine, I'm ... I just ... I don't understand *why*?'

His forehead pinched.

'*Why* invite me as your date not your friend?'

He ran a hand through his hair. 'Because otherwise I wasn't sure you would have come.'

Oh. What did that mean? 'We're friends, Andrew. Of course I would.' *Probably. I think ... Wait, would I?*

'Would you?' he said in a low, quiet tone that sent a very strange sensation skittering down my spine.

'Yes!' But for some reason I couldn't look at him.

'Miri—'

'It's late,' I blurted, 'you should go.'

He recoiled as though I'd slapped him, looking through the windshield for a beat before returning his gaze to me, his face having morphed into a careful, unreadable mask of nothingness. 'Is that really what you want?'

'Yes,' I whispered, too quickly, 'and I don't think we should do this again.'

A dark look crossed his features, but it was gone before I had a chance to study it. 'You—'

'It's messy, and ...' *I so desperately want it to be real.*

His eyes searched mine. 'What about Theo?'

I grunted as a bolt of pain hit my chest, my brain shutting down as it dealt with the verbal wound, the reminder that Theo was the real reason he was doing this. 'I don't care about Theo.' My words were more to myself than to him, and barely even audible to me, but they were all I could manage. 'Goodnight, Andrew.'

'Miri, I'm sorry.' He leaned towards me, reaching out a hand. 'I—' But I slammed the truck door, unable to bear any more, and half ran for the stairs.

Chapter 9

I spent the following week feeling sorry for myself. I hadn't had many break-ups in my life, but of the few I'd gone through, none had felt anything like this. This made all of them look like a walk in the park, which was telling, wasn't it? I cried a lot, trained a lot, and slept and ate little. I also brainstormed endless ways to get myself out of my life rut because it was something I really had to figure out, and it helped to fill my mind with things that weren't Andrew.

I didn't see Andrew for the entire week, and he'd given up texting when I hadn't replied to his first three messages. But what could I say? They'd all asked me if I was alright, and I certainly wasn't that. I'd hoped to see him at the regatta the next weekend, just to lay eyes on him, to see if he'd been affected like I had ... a ridiculous thing to wish for, I knew, but it didn't stop my stupid heart from hoping anyway. And then Livia had reminded me the men's crew were racing elsewhere, and my stomach had sunk and filled with relief at the same time, the sensation so odd it had made me nauseous.

I was such an idiot. Andrew had made it clear our relationship was fake, yet I'd jumped in with both feet anyway, somehow surprised to find the water too deep, too fast flowing. So now I was clawing my way back to the safety of the shallows before I drowned, and even though it hurt, I knew it was the right thing to do. Andrew would find some high-flying business mogul to marry, and I would … well, anyway. I had enough to occupy my mind with work and training and my friends.

But as I sat on the start line of our race that weekend, the sky overcast and grey, the air damp and heavy, raindrops surely only moments away, it wasn't our rival crew that had my stomach tied in knots, but thoughts of Andrew, his eyes, his hands, his throat … He'd almost looked disappointed when I'd called off the fake dating, hadn't he? Wishful thinking, no doubt. *Urgh*, why did I keep doing this to myself? If he wanted to date me, he'd just ask me out. But he didn't want that. He'd rejected me many times. *For fuck's sake, Miri, get a grip!*

'Attention!' the umpire called, and I inhaled, the earthy scent of riverbank filling my nose as the familiar flood of adrenaline poured through my veins. But as it did, an unwelcome thought speared its way into my mind. Theo's words: *Andrew is a liar*. Was Andrew's company what he'd meant? And If so, how had Theo known when no one else had? But then the umpire yelled, 'GO!' and everything but our starting sequence was forced from my mind.

———ele———

'Miri … everything alright?' said Livia, snapping me out of my thoughts. We were on the pontoon after a training session, and the others were waiting for me to pay attention so we could lift the boat out of the water.

'Yes, sorry, not getting much sleep.'

'Why?' asked Ottie.

I searched around for a reason that didn't involve spilling my guts about Andrew. 'My family are having a reunion this weekend? It's all a big drama, and as usual I'm going to turn up alone, and I don't know if my aunt will be there—she's the only sane member of my family.' The guilt of having to miss another outing was making me ramble, so I clamped my mouth shut before I accidently said anything I'd regret. My crew knew things were tricky between Andrew and me, as I'd bitten their heads off, telling them I didn't want to talk about him, and since then they'd let it lie, mostly ...

'This weekend?' said Livia, a heated look turning her features fearsome. '*After* training?'

'Uh, no,' I said, guilt and shame eating me alive. 'I thought I'd mentioned it?'

'Nope,' said Livia, popping the *p*.

'Sorry, guys, I ...'

'We'll ask Belle to fill in,' said Hazel, sending Livia a dark look. 'You've got loads on your plate right now. We understand.'

'I'm sorry, I know I've been terrible recently. Maybe I should take a step back?' I said the words without really thinking, but to my surprise, I didn't hate the idea.

'No!' said Hazel. 'You're the best we have. We can't lose you!'

Livia didn't look like she agreed, and Ottie was non-committal, and that, on top of everything else, had tears pooling in my eyes. I quickly blinked them away, and as soon as we'd put the boat back on its rack, I made an excuse to leave, barely looking where I was going in my haste to escape, which was how I ran headlong into a solid wall of muscle as I hurtled through the gate.

'Shit, sorry,' I breathed, then froze when I realized the sculpted torso my hands were pressed against belonged to Andrew. I screwed my hands into fists, not moving away, butterflies taking flight in my stomach, spreading out and brushing their wings against every nerve in my body.

For a second, we just stared at each other, tension I didn't understand hovering in the air between us. 'I ... uh ...'

'I heard your conversation earlier,' he said, his features carefully casual.

'Oh?' I said, trying to think which conversation he meant. Had I said anything about him? I didn't think I had ...

'About your family's reunion.'

'Oh ... right ...' My stomach sank. 'You want to talk to me about missing training, too? As Club Captain?'

'No! I want to come with you.' He paused, scrunching his forehead. 'I mean, you shouldn't have to go alone.'

I laughed. Literally laughed in his face. 'Very funny.'

I tried to push past him, but he reached out and touched my arm, stopping me in my tracks before snatching back his hand and looking mortified by what he'd done. 'Sorry ... I ... But I'm not joking, Miri. I know your family can be hard to take, and you shouldn't have to deal with that alone.'

I vehemently shook my head. 'I don't want to explain to my entire family how I'm so tragic I had to bring a friend. I couldn't deal with their gleeful pity.'

'Then we'll tell them we're together.'

'After it went so well last time?'

'It ...' He frowned as though he disagreed with something I'd said, but whatever it was, he didn't voice it. 'It'll be a onetime thing.'

'Andrew ...'

'Please,' he said, putting his hands on my shoulders, then sliding them down to hold my upper arms, 'let me do this for you.'

I knew I should say no, to keep him as far away from my trying family as was humanly possible, to spare him the burden, but I really didn't want to go alone. And he did look like a demi-god. If I was going to turn up with anyone, he wasn't a bad choice.

'Why?' I breathed, searching his eyes for answers. 'Why subject yourself to the outer circles of hell?' *Why do we have to pretend at all?*

He did nothing for a beat but look back into my eyes, indecision lurking in his irises.

Say it, I silently urged. *Say whatever it is you're holding back because this whole thing is killing me.*

His thumbs swiped back and forth across my biceps. 'I want to be there for you.' A clear hedge.

'Why?' I pressed, needing answers. Needing something concrete and real, not half-truths and vagaries.

'Because you deserve it.'

I tutted. 'Andrew ...'

He took my hands, and I didn't fight him, happy to have his skin on mine, even though I knew it would just hurt even more when he let go. 'I don't have all the answers,' he admitted, and then we just stood there, seconds ticking by, looking at each other. 'Please let me do this for you.'

I inhaled deeply, trying to get my brain to think his offer through, to weigh it carefully, but all it would supply was a whirling nothingness. I gave a small nod, my thoughts too scrambled to take the sensible route.

He exhaled in a rush. 'Okay, good. I'll pick you up. Text me the details.' And then he squeezed my fingers and quickly made for his truck as though not wanting to give me a chance to change my mind, my head spinning as fast as a senior crew late for the start line.

A cough sounded behind me, and when I looked over my shoulder, I found my whole crew watching. *Fucking boat club.*

Ottie stepped forward. 'I thought you'd split up?'

'We did,' I snapped, wondering how much they'd heard.

Hazel scowled at the other two, warning them to be nice. 'Are you okay?'

'I'm fine,' I snapped. 'I have a shift.'

'We're heading there, too,' said Hazel, ignoring my tone and falling in beside me, linking her arm through mine. She held on tight, giving me no chance of escape, but she didn't probe further as we walked, the other two trailing us, discussing the kit order Livia—in her capacity as Women's Captain—planned to place for the club in the next few days.

I zoned them out, my mind full, not of thoughts, exactly, but of a reeling sensation, and when I looked up what felt like seconds later we were already outside my café. How had we got there so quickly? We'd only just set out from the club ...

'I'm here if you need me,' said Hazel, squeezing my arm, then stepping inside. She didn't wait for an answer, which was good because I didn't want to give one, but her words only added to the empty feeling in my chest.

As I climbed the stairs to my flat, needing to shower before work, a message appeared in our crew's group chat. Belle could fill in for me on Saturday morning, thank goodness, meaning my crew would be able to train without me. A small weight lifted from my mind. At least there was that.

Chapter 10

On Saturday morning, as I waited inside the café for Andrew to pick me up, I stared at the picture Hannah had just posted to Instagram of Andrew and I on the way to the first regatta of the season. I'd forgotten all about it, but I screenshotted it in a heartbeat, and had already reached for it at least twenty times, the part of me that liked torturing myself obsessing over the way Andrew looked down at me, and the way I looked back at him. The intensity of it. The purity. The way his whole being focused on me like there was no one else in the world. Why Hannah had posted it now, I had no idea. Perhaps low on social media content or maybe she was meddling in our love lives ...

'Hey,' said Andrew's voice, startling me to such an extent I almost dropped my phone.

'Hey,' I said, flushing as I hastily shoved it inside my black leather clutch.

He looked me up and down. 'You look beautiful,' he said in that deep, intense way of his.

I wore a knee-length silk day dress with elbow-length sleeves. It was sage green, was covered in large, dusky pink flowers, and cinched in at the waist. I'd swept my long dark hair back, with loose plaits on either side of my head which I'd tied up in an artful bun. And of course, I'd applied make-up, which almost never happened.

'Thanks,' I said. 'You too.' Because he looked like his usual demi-god self, enhanced by a perfectly tailored blue suit.

His lips twitched. 'I'm so glad. I always aim for beautiful.'

I rolled my eyes, then headed outside to where his truck waited. He opened the passenger door for me, then closed it when I was safely inside, which always gave me weird vibes because my hands felt like spare parts, and the door felt like a weapon, ready to strike, even though I knew he was only being nice.

Silence gripped us in its firm clutches as we got going, pressing in on us, making me consider that taking Andrew to the reunion after everything that had happened might be a terrible idea. *Too late now.*

I repeatedly pinched my thumb and forefinger together as I sought solace through the window, but solace never came.

'Why so quiet?' Andrew said eventually.

For a moment I didn't answer. *My family. My mother. My successful cousins who look down their noses at me, lording their highfalutin careers and perfect marriages.* But that wasn't the truth, at least not the whole truth.

I sighed. 'Lots of reasons.' *Not least of which, you.*

'Want to talk about it?'

'No.'

'Are you embarrassed to introduce me to your family?' he teased. He'd met my mother before, not to mention, how could anyone ever be embarrassed of him?

'I will be when I have to tell them you broke up with me.'

'Then tell them it was you or that it was mutual. Or … we don't have to do this if you don't want to.'

I waved a hand. 'It's fine. I just want to get it over with, and I already told them you're coming.'

'Okay, then tell me what's going on with Hazel and Noah.'

I rounded on him so fast, I almost gave myself whiplash. 'Um … what?'

Andrew laughed as I leaned across the space between us. 'They spend an awful lot of time together, that's all I'm saying.'

'Andrew! You never gossip!'

He chuckled. 'Just a friendly enquiry.'

'Hmm,' I said skeptically, as I considered Hazel and Noah as a couple for the first time. 'I mean … maybe? Honestly, Hazel keeps her cards so close to her chest, I never know what's going on with her.'

'Sounds like someone else I know …' He cocked an eyebrow as he glanced at me.

'Hey!' I scowled. 'I'm an open book.'

'Oh yeah? Then why won't you tell me what's really getting you down?'

I sat back in my seat and stared through the windshield. *Because it's you, Andrew, you're getting me down.*

'Besides our fake dating complications and your family reunion, of course.'

Our fake dating complications? Is that what he was calling this? I huffed out a breath as I watched the hedgerows whip by, vibrant and full of early summer color. 'I'm thinking of buying another business,' I said quietly, hardly believing I'd voiced it, especially to him.

'No way!'

'Maybe a club, or a deli and gift shop. I don't know.'

'That's incredible!' he said, snatching glances at me between monitoring the road.

'No one knows, and if I do it, it'll take up a ton of time. The financial projections are already keeping me up at night, and it's bad for my crew.'

'But it would get you out of your rut. You said you wanted something new, and you're so good at knowing what'll work. Your café and bar have both done so well.'

Why were compliments always so awkward? 'I mean, it'll be small, nothing like your expansion, but hopefully it will be different enough from the bar and café to make it interesting.'

'It sounds amazing, Miri. And I can help with the financial projections ... if that's ... if it's helpful.'

My heart gave a sharp thud. 'Thank you. I'm just worried how my crew will take it. I won't have time for anything else for a while, and Hazel understands, but Ottie and Livia ...'

He gave a relaxed shrug. 'They have Belle, and your crew don't own you. You don't owe them anything, especially if you feel like you need a new challenge. They'll understand.'

I nodded, hoping he was right. 'I just don't like letting people down.'

'Even if they're disappointed, your crew will get over it. They want what's best for you ... We all do.' My heart lurched, and oh, God, why did he have to be so perfect?

'Ready?' I said brightly, checking my makeup in the mirror and plastering on my game face as we pulled into the hotel's parking lot.

Andrew sent me a cavalier smile that had my heart singing. 'Buttercup, I was born ready.'

I clutched his arm a little too tightly as we entered the grand hotel my second cousin twice removed had graciously footed the bill for. He'd done well in finance and liked everyone to know it, so every email relating to the event had contained a thank you note to our sponsor at the bottom, and as we sailed through the glass doors into the opulent, minimalist entrance hall, even the welcome banners sported the same message.

The hotel wouldn't have been my first choice, all clean lines and popping colors. I was more into old world charm and rustic chic, but hey, if modern was what my rich cousin wanted, who was I to argue? And as we entered the large, open event space, the view across the moorland beyond the wall of glass literally stopped me in my tracks.

'Wow,' I said, scanning the barren beauty. 'I wasn't expecting that.'

'Me neither,' said Andrew, stopping close behind me, his hand resting on my lower back. For a moment, I pretended it was just the two of us and the stunning vista, that we were here for a romantic couple's retreat, that my entire extended family weren't lurking around every corner. Alas, my make believe did not last long.

'Darling!' said my mother's shrill voice, shattering our moment of tranquility. She was using the clipped tone she reserved for family occasions when the *good* relatives were in attendance, and I inwardly cringed.

'Mum,' I said, fighting with my face to make a smile appear.

She pulled me in for a hug, then planted a sloppy kiss on my cheek, and this time I couldn't fully cover my shudder.

'Lovely dress,' she gushed, pulling back. 'Although I never liked you in green.'

Yes, well, there are many things we all think about others, Mother, but most of us have the good grace to keep them to ourselves. 'You remember Andrew?' I said with a bright smile.

He dutifully stepped forward and kissed my mother's cheek before returning to my side. 'Lovely to see you again, Mrs. Murdock.'

'Cadence, please! How many times do I have to tell you? And you and Miri are ...' Her intent gaze flicked to where Andrew's arm disappeared behind my back.

'Dating,' he supplied.

'But I thought ...'

'Yes?' I asked, the word a challenge, my eyes sharp. It was amazing how a few simple words from my mother, said in *that* voice, could turn me back into the teenaged version of myself. Perhaps more alarmingly, I didn't immediately want to return to the adult realm.

She gave a shake of her head, losing some of her bustle, and I relaxed a little. 'Well, Andrew was there, I suppose, during that difficult time. Perhaps *he* can help you find solace where others have failed.'

Andrew's features pinched. He seemed to be genuinely confused, and perhaps a tiny bit frustrated, presumably because the rest of the world had long ago forgotten that I once was on the cusp of an illustrious Olympic career ... at least if my mother's version of the past was anything to go by. In truth, that dream had been a lot more precarious than she liked to remember.

'I'm sorry, Cadence,' said Andrew. 'I'm not sure I follow.'

'Rowing, of course! Miriette's never having reached her full potential!' Yes, my mother called me Miriette. I have never forgiven her. 'She could have been *famous*, if only she hadn't thrown it all away for that *café*.'

'I think Miri's café is incredible,' said Andrew, who still seemed a little lost.

'Oh,' said my mother, 'well ... yes, I suppose ... not that it matters now of course.' She leaned towards me and grasped my arm. 'Did you hear? Your cousin, Ariana, is getting a divorce!' She raised her eyebrows and bit her lips in a comical display of delighted mock compassion.

'No,' I said, glaring at her. 'I hadn't heard. Is she okay?' I happened to like Ariana.

'Oh, don't worry about her. She'll get stacks of money in the divorce. Not like me ...'

'She did earn at least half of it,' I fired back, 'so that would be fair. But that's not what I meant, Mum. Emotionally, how's she holding up?'

'Oh, I don't know. I haven't actually *seen* her yet. Her sister told me. Wait, there's Bea. Maybe she'll know more.'

I breathed a sigh of relief when my mother hustled away in search of superior gossip, but didn't miss the look my aunt Bea flashed my way when she saw my mother inbound. My parents had divorced around the time I'd failed to realize my potential, and although Bea, my dad's sister, would have liked to be Switzerland, Mum wouldn't allow it, so instead she'd had to be the shoulder for both of them to cry on, at least, she did until my dad died.

I sent Bea an expression that said, *I've done my time, you're on your own*, then looked around in search of safer pastures.

'I don't remember her being quite like that,' said Andrew, flagging down a passing server and selecting two mimosas, one of which he handed to me.

'Ha! Maybe she's getting worse with age. She conveniently forgets that I probably wouldn't have been good enough to be an Olympian anyway. She put all her eggs in a basket that wasn't even there.' It was sad when I thought about it like that. 'But thanks for sticking up for me. Most people just smile and nod.'

Andrew steered me to the refuge of an alcove near the windows. 'I get the impression she's less devastated for you and more for herself.'

I looked up at him dumfounded. 'Yes, exactly! No one ever understands that.' Only my aunt Bea, and my dad, before he died. It's not like the Olympics were ever my dream. I love rowing for the community, not the glory, although it's always fun when we see a bit of that, too. I can't deny my competitive streak.

'But you're wrong, you know. You were good enough.'

His eyes watched me with an intensity that had my breath catching in my throat. I bit my lip, then shook my head. 'Well, we'll never know, but I don't care. It's in the past. I moved on a long time ago, and I just wish my mother would put it behind her, too.'

'But what about your cousin's divorce?' he said salaciously.

I covered my face with my free hand. 'Please, spare me from this torture!'

He bumped my shoulder with his, and as I scanned the room, I found the place had filled up with distant cousins I only vaguely recognized, and let's face it, had little intention of talking to. Most of them were pleasant enough, but my family had a way of putting me on edge, and I dreaded the predictable questions.

I turned my back on the room, but that, alas, did nothing to deter my more persistent relatives, and we fielded an endless barrage of queries, plastering fixed smiles on our faces and supplying nebulous answers before making polite inquiries of our own. People asked how we met, when Andrew was planning to propose, if we'd discussed babies because, according to my great aunt, *one couldn't leave it too long*, and even whether we had a joint bank account.

Andrew navigated the treacherous waters without breaking a sweat, taking the brunt of the question-answering responsibilities and deflecting the more personal probes. I relaxed into it, Andrew's family-gathering competence taking the edge off—or maybe that was the mimosa—and by the time the droning, high-pitched whine of bagpipes filled the air, I was even starting to enjoy myself.

'You are *really* good at this,' I whispered into his ear, just as a piper appeared in the doorway. I groaned inwardly as our sponsor and his family processed into the room, smiling and waving as though they were royalty. Andrew watched wide eyed, a faint smile on his lips. I was never going to live this down.

'We have Scottish ancestry,' I murmured, as though that somehow justified my cousin acting like our chieftain.

'Very nice,' said Andrew, with a gently mocking incline of his head. I poked him in the ribs, and he squirmed, grabbing my finger and holding it down by his side to prevent further attack, not letting go as our sponsor stepped onto a raised platform.

'Family!' said my cousin, spreading his arms wide and giving us all a view of his very white teeth. 'I am so delighted to sponsor this, our tenth annual reunion! For what matters more in this world than family?'

He let silence descend for a beat, his features solemn. 'And we—*my* family and I—look forward to chatting with each and every one of you. To hearing the highs and lows, mysteries and surprises, achievements and struggles you have faced since last we met. But first, we dance!'

My cousin lifted his arms so fast he almost staggered backwards off the podium, but he caught himself just in time and jumped down, almost styling it out.

'In the name of all that is holy,' I breathed. Andrew smirked and squeezed my finger.

The piper started up again, processing out as a group of musicians took their places at the far end of the room, where a drum kit and microphones already waited. They made noises for a few moments on their fiddles, drums, and panpipes—warming up as musicians always do—while the caller pulled one of the microphones from its stand and tapped it to check it was on.

'Hello, Murdock family!' she called in her Scottish lilt, and a cheer went up from some of my more exuberant relatives. 'I'm delighted to be back with you all again, especially in this lovely new hotel!' She'd led the dancing every year since the inaugural celebration. 'Now, I know most of you donnae need me anymore, but for those who cannae remember the steps, never fear, I'll walk you through each and every one.'

Andrew took my hand and led me to the dancefloor, where others were already eagerly congregating. I pulled back a little. 'Andrew, you don't have to ...'

He grinned down at me. 'I've been to my share of Ceilidhs, Miss Murdock.'

The band launched into a Scottish jig, and the caller raised her voice. 'We'll start with the Gay Gordons to ease us in gently!' And with that, we and the other dancers formed a circle, and away we went.

We spun and clapped and hopped along with the others, and after we'd Stripped the Willow and Dashed the White Sergeant, the caller announced a break. I was glad of the reprieve, and we grabbed glasses of water before heading out onto the balcony to cool down.

We moved away from the crowd, stopping on the boundary to the next-door function room, which was blissfully empty. I leaned my arms on the railing, glad of the breeze cooling my skin, then tried—and failed—to ignore how Andrew's arm settled against mine as he took the space beside me.

'You're a good dancer,' he said, nudging me so the full length of his arm rubbed against mine.

'I had a good partner.' He hadn't been lying when he'd said he knew what he was doing. How could one person be so unreasonably good at so many things? My gaze flicked up to his, and at the look in his eyes, I became a fly caught in a web, but unlike a fly, I had no interest in breaking free. I didn't even struggle, quite the opposite, I willed him to glide across his delicate creation and wrap me in his silk.

His eyes dilated, and I was sure mine had too, our bodies like disobedient pets, conversing in ways we had no control over and without our permission. Although, if my eyes had asked, I probably would have told them to dilate some more, and if whatever part of me produced such things had asked about pheromones, I would have enthusiastically thrown some of those in his direction, too.

He leaned so close, he blocked out the world, and I lost myself in him. In his green eyes, the warmth of his imposing body, his sweet, earthy smell. I tipped my head back a little, enough to encourage him, but not so much as to beg because I was sure he would reject me again if I tried to kiss him. Especially here, in front of so many interested eyes.

My phone buzzed in my bag, rattling the railing through the leather, but I ignored it because Andrew crept closer still, so close we shared the same breath, so close I could think of no other explanation for it aside from his intention to kiss me. My lips parted on an exhale, and Andrew's gaze flicked to my mouth. He swallowed, his throat bobbing, my heart fluttering wildly, and then a small child shrieked behind us, knocking us apart a second later and breaking the spell.

'Sorry!' the little toad threw over his shoulder as he hared off without a care in the world, chasing his older cousins.

I huffed out a breath, then pulled my phone from my clutch and unlocked it. Andrew's eyes flicked to the screen, to where ... *Shit*. Heat rose up through my chest, scalding my cheeks as I snatched my phone away. I closed my eyes, wondering how I'd been so stupid. Why did he have to see that?

'You should make it your background,' he said, his lips beside my ear, his voice a low growl. 'You know, to really sell the lie.' He slid the phone from my grasp, then presented it back to me so I could unlock it with my thumb. I dutifully did as he asked, then watched in fascination as he set the picture Hannah had taken of us as both my background and my lock screen.

'Then you should, too,' I said, cocking an eyebrow. 'Or I seem more committed than you.'

He pulled out his phone, a dangerous look on his features. 'I can do one better than that,' he said, placing his water on the wide railing. He slid his free hand to my neck, and he met my gaze as he held out his arm and snapped a selfie.

Then he lowered his head, pressing his forehead to mine, his lips so tantalizingly close. He pulled me the last inch towards him, and my eyes slid shut as I became lost in the thrill of him, of relinquishing control. And then his lips were on mine, and he was pressing a deep, claiming kiss to my very willing mouth.

He pulled away too soon and looked at his phone. 'Perfect,' he said, showing me the pictures. Pictures that made me go weak at the knees. Andrew looking at me as though he wanted to consume me. Andrew kissing me. He set the first photo as his lock screen and the kiss as his background, and my whole being seemed to liquify. 'Satisfied, Buttercup?'

I shook my head, then took hold of his phone, our fingers brushing as I slid it from his grip. It was intimate, having access to another person's phone, and a thrill shot through me as I sent the photos to myself. 'If we were dating, I would make you send me these,' I explained, then looked up at him from under my lashes. 'And I'd probably scroll through your messages and photos, too.'

A new light danced in his eyes. 'By all means, be my guest.' But I wasn't brave enough to do it, so I dropped the phone into his pocket instead. My lips tingled from the kiss, and I caught my bottom lip between my teeth. His eyes darkened as he took in the movement, and he lifted his hand as though about to tug it free.

'Miri! Darling!' said an exuberant voice emanating from my aunt, a tall, short-haired, stick-like woman with a cigarette between her fingers.

'People still smoke those things?' I asked, irritated by her terrible timing.

'It's nice to see you, too,' Bea quipped. 'And this must be the delicious Theo you've told me so much about! It is *so* nice to finally meet you. And I must say, you're even more delectable in the flesh than I imagined.'

'Uh ... Bea,' I said, sending an apologetic look at Andrew while wishing the ground would open up and swallow me. 'This is my boyfriend, *Andrew*.'

She paused mid arm wave. 'Oh, shit, sorry. Well, anyway, as I said, you look far better than that Theo waster! So, tell me, what do you do?'

Andrew shook her proffered hand, seeming to take her eccentricity in his stride, and I breathed a sigh of relief. 'I'm a data scientist, and it's nice to meet you, too.' He leaned in conspiratorially. 'I hear you're the only sane one in the family.'

I gasped, rounding on Andrew, but Bea barked a delighted laugh. 'You're not wrong there! Don't look so shocked, Miri, it's hardly a secret.'

Andrew chuckled, but there was something different about him, something more aloof, professional maybe? And was there more space between us now?

'I used to run to Bea when my mother got too much,' I said, sliding my hand into the crook of Andrew's arm, needing to eliminate the physical gap. 'Her house was a wild, free place, and Mum hated it!' I was rambling, desperate to ease the discomfort caused by Bea's careless words.

Bea nodded and waved her cigarette around, swathing us all in smoke. 'I don't like to speak badly of my sister-in-law, but her parenting style is not what mine would have been. But then again, I never had the misfortune of popping out a mini-me or two, so we'll never really know. I probably would have turned into a full-blown alcoholic by now. God, can you imagine having to look after little people all the time? Every single day? For twenty-four hours straight? Let me tell you, I was *not* cut out for that.'

I suspected a part of Bea had wanted kids, and that an even larger part of her was resentful that Mum had had one but had never seemed all that interested in winning a parent of the year award. But the whole thing had worked out well, actually, because although they complained mercilessly about one another, Bea was always there for Mum, as Mum was for her. Whatever happened, at least they had each other.

'Excuse me,' said Andrew, pulling away, his body too stiff. 'I'll be right back.'

As soon as Andrew was out of earshot, Bea screwed up her features. 'Sorry, darling. I really cocked that up.'

I gave her a disbelieving look on account of her cavalier apology, my head beginning to rush with worry. 'Yes, Bea, you really fucking did.'

'I am so sorry about my relatives,' I said as soon as we closed the doors to Andrew's truck. It was late, following hours of eating and dancing and chatting, but Andrew had been a shadow of his former self after the conversation with Bea. I mourned the loss of him and was desperate to make amends, to bring him back.

'Don't be,' he said. 'I've always wished I had a big family like yours. I think that's why we have the DrewDox party every year.'

'Oh. Well, you're welcome at my family events any time! Everyone loved you.' The words sounded forced, and worry gnawed at me when he didn't say anything in reply.

He gave me nothing but silence for the whole ride home, my fingers hurting when we got there from all the clenching and unclenching I'd done on the way. I wracked my brain for words to undo the damage, for anything that might bring down the walls he'd put up between us, but I came up blank. What could I say?

Maybe I should have just told him how I felt. Maybe he felt the same. Maybe that's why he'd reacted so badly to Bea's words. It was a terrifying hope, and telling him was perilous, fraught with danger and embarrassment, and what if he rejected me again?

He parked, but didn't move to get out.

'Thank you for coming, Andrew. Really—'

'You were right when you said this was a bad idea,' he said, cutting across me. He looked through the windshield, refusing to meet my eyes. 'I'm sorry I forced you to take me today.'

'You didn't force me. I ... it was—'

'Theo's who you want. You were clear about that from the start. My crew messaged. They're in your bar, and if you want that little punk ...'

His words made everything inside me rush backwards, and my brain ceased to know how to form words. 'Andrew ...'

He got out and opened my door, and I dutifully stepped down, Andrew careful not to touch me, still avoiding my gaze. 'See you at training, Miri,' he said, shutting my door with a controlled slam, then moving back to the driver's side.

'Andrew ... wait!'

His truck was halfway across the parking lot before my brain regained function, and it took several long moments before I remembered where I was, that I should go inside.

I trudged up the stairs to my apartment, let myself in, then stood leaning back against the closed door for long minutes, staring at the lights beyond the windows. It had been like a dream, having Andrew at the reunion. Everyone had loved him, and he'd been so at home, so willing to join in, so fun ...

I wanted to pull out my phone and call one of my crew, but I couldn't. What would I tell them? That I'd just fake split up with Andrew for a second time? And this time, I didn't even have tears for comfort, just brutal, harrowing emptiness. Pure desolation because for a few fleeting heartbeats, it had felt like the real thing, and it had been perfect.

So what the fuck was I supposed to do now?

Chapter 11

I avoided everyone for days, not wanting to run into Andrew at the rowing club, and not wanting to face questions from my crew about what was going on because, hell if I knew.

Andrew had taken a selfie of us kissing, had lavished his full attention on me, but one mention of Theo by my aunt and he'd shut down, seeming upset. What did that mean, exactly?

I'd messaged him to say thank you, to tell him how nice it had been to have him at the reunion, how much it had meant to me, but he'd replied with only a thumbs up, and then a minute later, a picture of a wigwam. It had taken me a minute to remember what his mother said about the word *nice*—that it was for wimps and wigwams—and the inside joke had made me want to cry. Then I'd wondered if he'd been mocking me somehow, and that tiny triangular image occupied my thoughts for endless hours.

My phone buzzed, and I picked it up from where it lay on my desk, dwelling for a moment on the photo of Andrew and I on my lock screen—no, I hadn't changed it because apparently I was a masochist. I opened the new message from Hazel, which told me my crew was in the café, and they wanted me to join them for breakfast.

I'd pretended to be sick to explain my week-long absence, and I was dreading seeing Ottie and Livia, who would undoubtedly give me shit, and would probably make some remark about how I looked perfectly fine. But I couldn't avoid them forever, and anyway, the last few days had given me space to think, and I had something I wanted to say to them, too.

I pushed back from my desk and went out to find them, but hesitated as I entered the café because at the table beside my friends were the four hulking forms of the men's first boat, including the two people in the world I most wanted to avoid.

I squared my shoulders, and after a cursory appraisal, forced myself not to look at Andrew, then selected the seat facing away from him because I could not be trusted not to stare. But I should have sat on the opposite side because now we were close, our chairs back-to-back, and I was aware of every millimeter between us.

'You look like shit,' Livia said by way of a greeting, eyeing me warily.

The smile died on Ottie's lips as she took me in. 'I thought you were lying, but … wow …' She scooted her chair away.

'It's not contagious,' I said quietly, hunching low in my chair.

'How do you know?' demanded Belle.

'I've just got a lot on, that's all,' I said, making it clear the subject was closed. 'Good outing?'

Hazel examined me with concerned eyes, her fingers wrapped around her coffee mug. 'It was fine.'

I nodded, silence settling for a beat. 'There's something I wanted to talk to you about.'

'Oh?' said Livia.

'What?' said Ottie, leaning forward, her elbows resting on either side of her plate of steaming eggs.

I sat up a little straighter, steeling myself. 'I need to take a step back from the crew.'

'Oh,' said Ottie, leaning back.

'What?' said Hazel, her eyes flicking over my shoulder towards the men. 'No!'

'I can't give rowing the time it needs right now because ...'

'Because?' prompted Ottie, when I'd paused for less than half a second.

'I'm starting a new business.'

'What?' Ottie squealed.

'That's awesome!' said Livia. 'What kind of business?'

'A gift shop and deli. I haven't found a premises yet, but I want to do it, which means it's going to eat up all my time. I don't want to keep letting you guys down, and now Belle's back, you don't need me, so—'

'We'll never not need you,' said Hazel, putting her hand over mine. 'But I'm so happy for you, and I can't wait to shop there.'

'And if you need a manager, I'm your woman,' said Ottie, her tone containing its usual frivolous tone, but with a hint of something more serious, and perhaps a little desperate.

'I, uh ... I'll bear that in mind,' I said hesitantly. I'd never taken on anyone from the boat club, as it had always felt too close, too likely to go wrong, but if she really needed a job ...

Hazel pushed her chia porridge around with her spoon, her lips forming a hint of a pout. 'What about the National Championships? Don't you want to race at those?'

I sat back, her words taking me by surprise; I hadn't considered that as a possibility. 'Of course I'd love to, but it wouldn't be ...' I was going to say *fair*, but that wasn't exactly right.

'So long as you train,' said Hazel, 'we can select a final crew closer to the time, just like we always do.'

'Well ...' I said, looking at the faces of each of the others in turn, trying to gauge their reactions. 'I was planning to keep training, although I can't promise to come to regular sessions. I'll need to fit it in when I can, and only if everyone is okay with the idea, otherwise I'm happy to just bow out now.'

'Of course we're okay with it,' said Hazel, surprising me with her uncharacteristically forthright display. 'Having you in our squad makes us stronger, and the lingering threat that you might take one of our seats will make us train harder.'

'She's got a point there,' said Belle. 'Nothing like a bit of competition ...'

I looked around the table and found them all smiling and nodding, and I knew them well enough to know they weren't lying—Livia especially would have said something if she disagreed. 'Okay, then. If you're sure.'

'Good,' said Hazel, as a server approached to take my order. When she left, Theo leaned between Ottie and me, irritatingly close.

'When's it going to open?' he asked.

'What?' I said, frowning in confusion, then I realized they must have overheard everything. 'The shop?'

'Yeah.'

'I don't know.'

He shuffled his chair between mine and Ottie's, half joining our table, and wrapped his arm around the back of my chair. 'What are you going to stock?'

'Lots of things,' I said curtly, leaning as far away from him as I could.

'Will we get the same discount?' He pressed his face against my shoulder, literally cozying up to me to get what he wanted. It was a joke, but I didn't want him to touch me.

'Fuck off, Theo,' I snapped, out of damns to give after the week I'd had, mourning the probable loss of Andrew because of my supposed pining for this irritating child. Or maybe Andrew would never see me the way I saw him. Maybe he only wanted me as a friend, but either way, I was happy to take my vitriol out on Theo—someone really had to take him down a peg or two if he thought it was okay to act this way.

'Ooo,' he said, not moving away. 'You're feisty this morning.'

'Take your fucking hands off me, or I swear to God, I will throw you out and revoke your discount.'

Theo reared back as though I'd shocked him with ten thousand volts, then turned to his crew, trying to laugh it off, but his crew had gone very still, all of them looking about ready to punch him, including Andrew whose jaw was clenched tight, a muscle ticking in his cheek.

'Jesussss. No need to get your knickers in a twist!' Theo stood, spun his chair back around, and pushed it under the table. 'We should get going, anyway. We have a second session.'

The men murmured their general agreement, then stood and headed for the cash register, Theo leading the way, seemingly unaffected by our altercation.

Andrew hung back, and I turned to look at him, worried what he might say, but after briefly meeting my gaze, he followed his crew, and I could have sworn I felt the faintest ghost of a touch across the nape of my neck as he went.

'*What* is going on there?' said Ottie, her voice hushed.

I looked down and shook my head. 'When I work it out,' I said dryly, 'I'll be sure to let you know.'

Chapter 12

It was freeing, not being beholden to a six day a week training schedule, and to start, I wasn't sure what to do with myself. I hadn't had a break from rowing since I'd set up the café, and I'd already found the venue back then, so the moment I stepped away from training, I'd jumped straight into setup.

This time was different. I spent a week just scouring the internet for premises suitable for a shop with a deli. Ideally it would be close to the café, but the area around the river was sought after and expensive, and it was unlikely something would come up that ticked all my boxes. So I expanded my search area, looking specifically at the more affluent parts of town with good footfall and easy parking.

I wandered around the areas, getting a feel for them, people watching in coffee shops and striking up conversations with shop owners until I had a solid shortlist of options. And then I doubled down on the internet searches and called a few commercial property agents. No one had anything that fit, but they all promised to keep a lookout.

I still had to run my existing businesses, and I was training every day, but now I didn't feel like I was letting my crew down, I felt lighter, happier, liberated. Whereas before I'd dreaded going to the rowing club because I hadn't wanted to see my crew, now it was only Andrew I wanted to avoid, even if I did stare longingly at the picture of us on my phone a hundred or so times a day.

I hadn't seen or heard from Andrew since I'd told Theo to fuck off, and I'd filled the silence with all kinds of irrational thoughts. Maybe our friendship was over. Maybe he'd already found a new girlfriend—perhaps the Spanish, gazelle-legged woman from his party, or the chocolatier his family loved so much. Or maybe he'd discovered just how much time I spent fantasizing about him, and was even then enlisting the help of a lawyer to take out a restraining order against me.

To stop myself dwelling on Andrew every waking moment of every day, I'd taken to making lists, and today it was the turn of the kind of suppliers I wanted in the shop, followed by a Pinterest board of interior inspiration, then a list of similar shops across the country to check out online.

I was feeling highly productive by the time I closed my laptop and headed out to help with the café's lunchtime rush, where I lost myself in the rhythm of taking orders and making drinks.

Two hours passed before I came up for air. It had been a fun lunch shift with plenty of regulars and even a bit of harmless flirting with the hot guy from the butchers farther along the street. I hung up my apron, feeling more content than I had in weeks, and was contemplating a run before the evening rush when my phone rang. It was a number I didn't recognize, and I picked it up just as Andrew pushed open the café door. I shrank back into the corridor to my office, silently thanking the universe for the excuse to avoid him.

'Hello?' I said, picking up the call.

'Hi, Miri. It's Paul from *Hudson and Stoker*. We spoke a few days ago about commercial premises for a shop?'

'Yes!' Paul's words grabbed ninety five percent of my attention, the other five preoccupied with tracking Andrew's progress through the line. 'Do you have something?'

'A brilliant little place has just come up in Portico. It's currently split. Half's a hair salon, and the other half's a café and bookshop. It has amazing potential.'

'Why's the owner selling?' Portico was a great area, not too far from the river, and near the top of my short list.

'The guy who owns the building wants to retire, and the owner of the hair salon is his wife. I think they're off to the continent as soon as they find a buyer.'

'What about the café? The person who runs that doesn't want to take on the salon?'

'She can't afford the whole premises, and I get the impression it's more of a hobby. The opening hours are erratic, and she's retirement age, too, and is best friends with the owner of the hair salon.'

'Right,' I said. 'When can I see it? And what's their timeline?'

'They're keen to sell ASAP, and you're welcome to see it now if you can slip away? You'll be the first through the door.'

'Yes!' I breathed, the word out so fast I surprised even myself. 'Text me the address and I'll be right there.'

'Good news?' said Andrew, who'd picked up a chicken and pickled red onion focaccia from the counter.

I quickly hid my phone, or more accurately, the picture covering the background, and said, 'A property agent thinks he's found a good option for my shop in Portico.'

He smiled warmly. 'That's amazing, Miri.'

'I'm heading out to see it now.'

'Good luck!' he called after me, as I high tailed it out of there, no idea what to say to him.

But when I reached the parking lot, I found my van had been blocked in by not one, but two cars. 'Shit,' I said aloud, pulling out my phone and swiping to find my taxi app.

Andrew appeared over my shoulder, his takeaway lunch in hand. 'I can give you a ride.'

I jumped and spun around, nearly dropping my phone. 'Oh, don't worry. I'll grab a cab. You're busy.'

'Miri, I'm going that way. My office is in Portico.'

'Oh ... um ... well ... if you're sure you don't mind?'

His face morphed into a look that said, *stop it and get in the damn truck,* so that's what I did, but as soon as our doors closed, the air turned thick and charged, as though one little spark might make the whole cab explode.

I looked out of the window as Andrew pulled into the slow-moving traffic, feeling his eyes roam over me as we stopped at a red light.

'Are we going to talk about it?' he asked, his tone gravelly.

I turned to him with a blank expression, my heart skipping a beat at how good he looked in his open-necked shirt, the sleeves rolled up to his elbows, showing off his muscular forearms. 'About what?'

He huffed a laugh as he turned his eyes back to the road, the light now green.

'About how you told Theo to fuck off in front of half the rowing club?' He sounded pleased, and when he glanced back at me a smile tugged at his lips.

'He's an arsehole,' I said with a shrug. 'Someone needed to.'

'Glad you finally noticed.'

I scowled hard. 'I've always noticed,' I spat. 'Do I think he's attractive? Yes. But I was only ever interested because there was no one else. I haven't had a steady boyfriend in years, Andrew. I work all the time, and when I'm not working, I'm at the rowing club. Theo has the personality of a horny dog, but my options are limited.'

Andrew stopped at another red light and this time when he turned to look at me, my words had wiped the smile from his perfect lips, his eyes stormy.

'And it's not like *you* want to date me.'

His eyebrows shot up, but I was done walking on eggshells around him, something about my newfound freedom, or maybe the excitement of going to see a potential property, making me throw caution to the wind. 'This is me,' I said, opening the door and jumping out. 'Thanks for the lift.' I slammed the door behind me and didn't let myself look back as I headed along the street to the hair salon.

Andrew's truck drove past, but I refused to look at him, busying myself with scanning for the property agent, who was climbing out of the tiniest car I'd ever seen.

'Paul!' I called, as he turned around.

'Miri! Good to meet you in the flesh.' He shook my hand. 'This one's an absolute gem; it'll get snapped up in no time, mark my words. Details ...' He thrust a folder at me but didn't give me time to even glance inside before ushering me into the salon, which was empty, save for a woman in her late fifties wearing a snakeskin patterned shirt, her hair a platinum blond perm.

The woman jumped up from her seat and clip-clopped around the counter on her impossibly high heels. 'Hello! Miri, isn't it? Paul says you want to start a shop.'

'Uh ... yes.' I gave her a warm smile. 'He said you're relocating?'

'Sun!' she squealed. 'All year round! Can you even imagine such a thing?'

I laughed, then gave her the answer she so clearly wanted. 'Sounds divine,' I said, even though it didn't sound divine to me at all. I liked seasons, enjoying the constant changes and how there was something different to appreciate at every stage of the year.

'I was thinking you could put the shop in this section,' said the woman, walking to the back. 'With the counter over there by the door, and then knock through to the café—you'll want that space, too, I'm sure, and Sue's happy to pack it all in. We put the wall up when we bought the place. Nothing structural to worry about. Of course it'll need a refit, but I'm sure you'll have ideas about that. Paul said you own Miri's café down by the river?'

I nodded, but she was already speaking again.

'Such a lovely, stylish place. But cozy, too. We've been many times.'

'Yes, it's wonderful,' said Paul, cutting in at the first available moment. 'Feel free to take a look around, Miri. I need to run Mrs. Banns through a few things. We'll just be a minute.'

'Thanks,' I said, hurriedly turning my back, grateful for the reprieve.

'And of course you should go next door,' Mrs. Banns added. 'Sue's expecting you!'

'Will do!' I pulled out my phone to take some photos, and my heart lurched when I saw a message from Andrew waiting to be read. I ignored it and started snapping because who knew how long I would have before Mrs. Banns relaunched her attack, and what if the message was bad? What if he made me feel foolish for the tentative fly I'd placed on the water? Yeah, right, it was probably more accurate to describe what I'd done as hurling a stone into a millpond ... but I couldn't think about that now.

I forced him from my mind and was soon lost in my task, imagining where I would put counters and stands and what would work best in terms of customer flow. When I'd given the salon a thorough once over, I headed out onto the street, then into the café next door, which was quaint but rundown, with peeling paint and dated everything.

'Hi!' said the plump, grey-haired woman behind the counter, her long, knitted cardigan a little dowdy, such a contrast to Mrs. Banns. 'You must be Miri?' she asked in a gentle tone.

'Yes,' I said tentatively. 'Nice to meet you.' A couple of the tables were occupied, but the customers mostly ignored us, too involved in their conversations.

'I'm Sue. Nice to meet you, too.' She looked at me appraisingly, and then a knowing gleam appeared in her eyes. 'Did Shelly pounce on you? I'm afraid she's got a bit of a habit of that.'

'She seems ... lovely,' I said diplomatically, wondering what about my body language had given it away.

Sue chuckled. 'She is, but she's also a tornado. Don't worry, I won't keep you. You have a good rummage around. Rest rooms and kitchen are out the back. Want a coffee?'

I smile gratefully. 'No, thank you, but I appreciate the offer.'

She nodded, then turned her attention to the two mothers with prams trying to maneuver their way into the tight space around the door. I went into the back and took a look at the kitchen and restrooms—both dated—snapped some more pictures, then headed back next door, thanking Sue on my way out.

'Well?' demanded Mrs. Banns the second I was through the door. 'What do you think?'

I froze for a split second, then said brightly, 'I like it!' Because what else could I say?

'Great! I knew you would. It needs a bit of TLC, but that's a good thing—means you can put your own stamp on the place. It's got solid bones, and there are apartments above. The leases run for another year or so, so you'd need to honor those, but after that you could do what you wanted with them. Lots of potential, I'm sure you agree. And *such* a nice area. We've seen it just get better and better during the years we've been here.'

'That's great!' I said, turning my attention to Paul and sending him an, *it's time to go* look. 'Thank you so much for letting me come by so quickly.'

'We want it to go to someone nice,' said Mrs. Banns, leaning across the counter and slapping it with her palm.

The image of a wigwam filled my mind as Paul ushered me towards the exit. 'Thank you!' I called as we left.

Paul showed me the apartments upstairs, which also needed modernizing, and then he ushered me back to his ludicrously tiny car. 'I've got to rush off, I'm afraid. Any immediate questions before I go?'

'Um ...' My mind whirled. There were probably a million things I should ask him, but I couldn't think of a single one.

'Everything you need is in that pack,' he said, motioning to the folder he'd handed me earlier. 'But be quick because it won't hang around for long.'

'Right, thanks,' I said, glad this intense situation was drawing to a close. 'I'll let you know ASAP.'

He waved his hand in acknowledgement, then slid into his car in a slick, well-practiced movement and sped off, leaving me feeling wrung out and disappointed, although I wasn't sure why, exactly.

I hurried down the street, just to put distance between me and the salon. I'd planned to get a taxi back to work, but walking felt wonderful, the stress falling away with each deep inhale and passing step, so I kept going on foot. It was only a couple of miles, so wouldn't take too long.

I let my mind wander as I walked, my eyes scanning the pretty Victorian terraces lining each side of the street, then tracing the curves of the river as it came into view. It was only when I pulled out my phone to snap a picture for Instagram that I realized I still hadn't read the message from Andrew.

I opened it immediately, and a breathy laugh broke free as I read his words.

Andrew 14:19: Did you just run away from me?

A giddy feeling flooded through me and I had to resist the impulse to clutch the phone to my chest, my steps suddenly light and breezy as I typed my reply.

Miri 15:02: No.

His reply came instantly.

Andrew 15:02: Liar.

I huffed out a delighted giggle.

Miri 15:02: You're not as polite as everyone thinks you are.

Andrew 15:03: Yeah, well, that's on them.

Miri 15:03: And now I see why they think you're intimidating.

Andrew 15:03: Which is it? Polite or intimidating?

Miri 15:04: You're such a man.

Andrew 15:04: I'm glad you noticed.

I'm glad you noticed? A cloud of butterflies took off in my chest, their wings so powerful, I was surprised to find my feet still on the ground. *What the hell?*

Andrew 15:05: How was the viewing?

I stared at the river, telling myself not to get my hopes up, but then my phone vibrated, and I was shocked to see an incoming call from Andrew. We never spoke on the phone. Or at least, not unless there was something transactional or time sensitive to discuss. There was no reason for him to call me now.

'Hey?' I said, holding my breath as I answered.

'Easier to chat. How was it?'

I went mute for a moment, rendered dumbstruck by this foreign experience. 'Uh,' I said, so he would know I was still there. 'The woman who owns the salon is a lot. In a good way. Kind of.' Why was I telling him about her? I was rambling. This was not the answer to his question. 'It was a great space or ... it could be. It would need a full refurb.'

'How do you feel about that?'

'Hmm ... I'm not sure I'm up for one that big,' I said, not realizing that was what I thought until the words came out.

'Why not?' he asked, sounding genuinely curious.

'It would be expensive, and I wouldn't be able to open until it was done, which would be a while, so the financial risk would be high. And I've got two other businesses to look after and no one I can rely on to run those, so, I ... I think it might be too much.'

'We could help,' said Andrew. 'Noah could do the refit, and I could help him. And I'm sure your crew would pitch in, too.'

Discomfort had me biting the inside of my cheek. 'Andrew, it's a business, not a charity. I can't expect my friends to give up their free time.'

'Yeah, but we're more like family.'

No. Even just the idea made me awkward and ... 'Would you ask them to help you with *your* business?' I asked, and he went silent. 'Everyone has their own stuff going on.'

'Do we though? Really? We go to work, row, and sleep. We spend every weekend together. Most of us are single. What exactly is it you imagine us doing with our time?'

'That's not the point.'

'Miri, what if we *want* to help you? What if people want to *earn* their ten percent discount?'

I froze next to the steps to my apartment, something in his tone making my insides turn to mush. 'I would feel bad. And anyway, I'm not sure it's the place for me. I need to think about it.'

'Well, if you need us, we're here. Got to go, I've got a meeting, but I'll see you tomorrow at club night?'

'Uh ... Yeah, I'll be there.'

Confused didn't even begin to express my feelings as I hung up. For long moments I just stood and stared at the picture of Andrew and me on my phone. He'd *called* me. To *chat.* And before that he'd flirted via text. What was this? What was going on?

I hurried up the stairs and pulled on my running tights. I had some newfound energy to burn, and it was a bright, beautiful day for a run by the river.

Chapter 13

E very Thursday after training during the summer, we had club nights. We hung out, complained about how hard our sessions had been, and different members cooked each week.

Usually, it was my favorite social event because it was effortless, everyone there without the hassle of having to make plans, and it was so cheap everyone always hung around. We all chipped in to cover the food costs, and any money raised in addition went to the club, so it was a glorious win win win, and I loved it. Apart from today because, Andrew.

The knots in my stomach pulled tighter with every step towards the clubhouse, anxiety gnawing at me as I worried about what I should do and say when I saw him. This morning he'd sent me a text with a picture of a coffee cup, the message saying it wasn't a patch on the coffee in my café, and my heart had swelled as I'd typed out my reply.

Miri 08:12: You might have a Miri's in your neighborhood soon …

Andrew 08:12: I hope so.

I hadn't yet decided if I wanted the salon and cafe, something worrying at my guts, something not feeling quite right, but I was rarely gung-ho about anything, always too aware of the risks, so maybe I should just go for it. In any case, I would have to decide soon or it would be gone, as Paul had reminded me in his email that morning, and then again in a text this afternoon.

Urgh. One problem at a time. And tonight's problem was that the eyes of the club would be on Andrew and me. *Again.* My crew had been asking probing questions since my family reunion, but it had been easy to deflect by text. Not so simple in the flesh.

I reached the clubhouse to find Hazel approaching the door carrying an enormous saucepan, the lid perched on top at a precarious angle—she and Ottie were on food duty—and I hurried forward to hold open the door.

'You look nice,' said Hazel, cocking an eyebrow.

Wigwam. Urgh! I didn't. Not really. I was wearing jeans and a shirt, but I'd blow-dried my hair, and seeing as almost everyone else would be clad in sweaty workout clothes, by comparison, I was all dolled up. I'd even considered wearing makeup, but had quickly cast that idea aside as ridiculous. Everyone would take the piss if I did.

'You too,' I said, because Hazel was wearing a cute, floaty summer dress and not her usual spandex. I remembered Andrew's remark about Noah and Hazel and wondered if something *was* going on between them. 'Anyone you're trying to impress?' I added, then watched her like a hawk.

She laughed as she passed through the open bar hatch and made for the kitchen, her back to me so I couldn't see her expression. *Damnations; I should have planned that better.* 'I wish,' she said, heaving the pot onto the stove.

'Now, Miss Catering Genius, how much rice do I need to go with this chili?'

I helped her put the rice on, and then Ottie showed up with a veggie chili and a ton of garlic bread. I vacated the kitchen because it was too small for three, and Ottie was stressing about whether all the garlic bread would fit in the oven.

I bought a gin and tonic from the veteran rower on duty behind the bar, then joined Belle and Livia on the patio, Livia lying on the ground, panting hard, and Belle leaning back in her chair, her flushed face turned towards the sky.

'Good run?' I asked, dropping into the seat beside Belle.

'I. Hate. Running,' gasped Livia. 'I'm a rower, not a runner. I'm not built for this shit.'

Belle chuckled. 'We threw in a few hill sprints just for fun.'

'I don't mind those,' Livia wheezed. 'Sprinting's fine, it's the rest of it I could do without.'

'Feels good though,' said Belle.

'If you say so,' Livia said skeptically.

We chatted as crews came in off the water, soaking up the sun as the clubhouse filled with novices, veterans, and coaches, but no sign yet of Andrew.

The appearance of each new boat coming into land made my heart give a hopeful little leap, but after many false alarms, I'd almost given up, wondering if the men's first crew were even out on the water tonight. But then they finally appeared, floating gracefully alongside the pontoon, and my eyes took in Andrew's sweaty, disheveled hair and pumped up shoulder muscles.

They got out and removed their blades with swift, practiced movements, their boat back on its rack only a minute or two later. Hannah, their cox, carried their blades up the ramp, and Pete and Noah helped her put them away.

'Hi gals!' said an exuberant male voice, as Seb, the fifth member of the men's senior squad, lowered himself into the chair by my side. He'd been out on the water in a single scull while the others trained in the four, as he didn't currently have a permanent seat in the boat.

'Coincidence you turned up just as that lot are strutting about?' said Livia, giving him a knowing smile as she peeled herself off the floor and dropped into a chair.

'Don't be gross,' said Seb. 'They're like brothers to me.'

'Uh huh,' said Livia, skeptically. '*All* of them?' She squeezed his arm, but he swatted her away.

'Do not put those dirty paws on my clean shirt. Some of us have showered.' He gave her a pointed look.

Livia rolled her eyes. 'You are not in the majority.'

'Miri looks nice,' said Seb, side eyeing me.

'Miri hasn't been training,' countered Livia.

'Hmmm,' Seb narrowed his eyes at me, then asked in a suggestive tone, 'what is it Miri has been doing, then?'

'Um ...' I was pretty sure the enquiry related to Andrew, but luckily, before I'd floundered for too long, Ottie yelled, 'Food's ready!' from inside. Seeing as not much could keep rowers from food—or at least, not the heavyweights—a crowd surged for the bar.

'Thank goodness,' said Livia. 'My stomach was starting to eat itself. Belle and I will get the food. You guys guard the seats.' She didn't wait for us to agree to her plan, instead launching herself through the open doors and sending Belle a *hurry up* look when she took too long to follow.

Belle dutifully got to her feet, although she threw in an eyeroll.

'Soooo,' said Seb, the moment we were alone.

'Such lovely weather we're having, don't you think? Hopefully it holds for the regatta this weekend.'

He gave me a shark-like smile. 'Nice try, Miri, if a little amateurish. Now spill: what's going on between you and Andrew?'

I fixed him with a long look. 'What's going on between you and Noah?' I countered.

Seb scowled and leaned back in his chair, casting his eyes towards where his crew were debriefing in front of the boathouse. 'Nothing. We ... well ... whatever might have happened didn't, and now it's over.'

'Why?' I pressed because Seb was an insensitive beast, and he could take it. To be fair, most of us lacked empathy and boundaries and restraint.

'Oh no, lovie. I told you mine, now you tell me yours.'

I sighed but relented; it was only fair. 'As of right now, there's nothing to tell.'

'But you want him?'

'You first.'

Seb tilted his head in defeat then turned his eyes to the river. 'I can't tell you details because Noah wouldn't want me to.'

'Oh,' I said. 'Does he like someone else?'

Seb visibly bristled.

'Sorry. That was ... sorry.'

'For that you get a double turn. Do you want to climb Andrew like a monkey?' His eyes flashed salaciously.

I gasp-laughed. 'Seb! You can't say things like that!'

He leaned forward and rested his chin on his fist, his features sporting a look that said, *spill*.

But I was saved by the return of Livia and Belle with our food. 'Yum, thank you!' I said, throwing Seb a triumphant smile, but Livia's hand slipped as she passed me my plate, and my garlic bread fell off the edge and landed in a patch of gritty, sandy stones.

'Instant karma,' Seb muttered as he accepted his own plate from Belle.

'Oh, shit, sorry.' Livia put her plate on her seat. 'I'll get you another one.'

'No need,' said a voice from behind us. A deep, commanding voice that made my stomach clench. 'I'm going to get food; I'll get some.'

'Thanks, Andrew,' said Livia, flashing me a knowing smile as she returned to her seat.

Seb leaned towards me. 'I think I can take the color of your cheeks as confirmation.'

I scowled, then accepted the cutlery Belle held out for me and turned my attention to my plate. But my appetite had fled, so after a few bites, I just pushed it around, waiting in dreadful anticipation for the moment Andrew would return. Everyone would watch us. Would they make jokes? Where was Andrew going to sit?

'Give it to me!' Theo's voice through the open doors sounded pissed, and we all turned as one to find out what was going on.

'No,' Andrew replied calmly, holding whatever Theo wanted away from him.

'You've already got one!'

'So have you.'

'Mine's an end piece. You've got two middle pieces. Come on, man, there's none left!'

'No,' Andrew repeated, then shoulder barged Theo out of the way when he refused to let Andrew past.

'You are such a dick,' said Theo, following Andrew out onto the patio.

Andrew dropped the second piece of garlic bread onto my plate then took the chair beside Belle, seeming not to have heard Theo's insult.

'Thanks,' I murmured, not able to look anyone in the eye.

'Oh for fuck's sake!' Theo whirled and stormed back inside. 'You're so whipped.'

Andrew chuckled as Belle said, 'Classic male posturing.' Then she turned to me. 'Are you hitting peak fertility?'

Livia barked a laugh as my mouth dropped open, and Andrew's fork stopped in midair.

'Yes, Miri, do tell,' said Seb, turning to me with mischievous delight shining in his eyes.

'Move over!' said Ottie, approaching us with a chair in one hand and a plate in the other. Hazel was only a step behind with a chair of her own. And then Noah, Pete, and Hannah were joining us, too, leading to a full seating reshuffle. I took Belle's plate as she helped rearrange, and by the time we were all settled in a circle, everyone had mercifully forgotten about the state of my fertility.

'How's the search for a premises?' Ottie asked from her seat opposite mine.

'Okay,' I said. 'I saw a place yesterday in Portico, but I'm not sure it's quite right.'

'Good!' said Livia. 'Selfishly, I want it to be here by the river.'

I laughed. 'Me too! So if you could boot one of the other shop owners out and make them sell to me for a reasonable price, that would be awesome.'

Livia turned to Seb. 'Don't you know anyone? You're a property agent.'

'A *residential* property agent,' he replied with a long-suffering forehead furrow, 'but I can ask around.'

'Thanks,' I said, 'that would be great.'

He shrugged as though it were nothing, while somehow simultaneously suggesting I should worship him until the end of time.

'Why don't you like the Portico one?' asked Hazel. 'It's a great area.'

'I know,' I said slowly, 'but it's a big project, and I'm worried about the financial projections. I've been modelling different scenarios, but I'm not sure it's quite right ... I feel like I might be missing something.'

'I can help,' said Andrew, lounging back in his chair, his legs spread a little, the defined ridges of his torso visible through his tee. He looked good enough to eat.

I couldn't decipher the expression on his face as everyone's eyes turned to him, and then to me, a loaded silence stretching as they waited for my answer.

'He is pretty much the spreadsheet king,' said Livia, waggling her eyebrows, her tone conveying so much more than her words.

'Uhhhh, yeah, thanks, that would be great. If you're sure you don't mind?' I looked past his left shoulder, my face burning.

'I want to help,' he said, taking me aback with ... was that irritation in his tone? My eyes flicked to his, which contained some emotion I couldn't name. 'We all do.'

'Ooo, yes!' sang Ottie. 'I'd love to get my paint brush out. Just say the word!'

'And I can help with the refit,' said Noah.

I narrowed my eyes at Andrew, whose face contained a smug, devilish look I hadn't seen on him before. 'Come over tomorrow night and I can take a look then.'

My heart stuttered as the entire group looked at me with expressions that I'm sure would have been comical if I hadn't been the one on the receiving end. 'Uh, sure, thanks,' I said with a tight smile. 'Sounds good.'

Chapter 14

I was practically shaking by the time I arrived at Andrew's apartment building, not far from the hair salon and café in Portico. His was one of five or six units in a small, tastefully constructed block, so although modern, it blended in among the older buildings all around.

I'd offered to bring dinner, but he'd told me not to, saying he had stuff he wanted to use up, so all I'd brought was a bottle of homemade kombucha we served in the café and my laptop, and it didn't feel like nearly enough.

I took a deep breath as I stood by the swanky glass door to the building, then pushed the button to his apartment. He buzzed me in almost instantly, saying, 'Hey, top floor.'

I took the stairs, hoping the climb to the third floor would calm my nerves, but it didn't. All it did was make me a little breathless on top.

I didn't even have time to compose myself because Andrew swung the door open as I approached, wearing sweatpants and a t-shirt that hugged his very large muscles in all the right ways. 'Hi,' he said, flashing me a smile that said I'd been well and truly caught checking him out.

'Uh ... hey,' I replied, my mouth dry as I held out the kombucha. He looked like a cozy Sunday morning, and I wanted to wrap myself in him.

'Thanks, I love this stuff.'

'I know.'

He went still for a beat, then stood back to let me in. 'Make yourself at home. I'm just finishing up in the kitchen. Do you want a drink? Some kombucha?'

'Sure, thanks,' I said absently, my eyes already busy roaming around the space.

The entrance led into a large, open plan kitchen-din-ing-living room, which was filled with light from the enormous windows. It was spacious but homely, with an oat-colored deep-pile rug that begged to be walked on in bare feet, shelves lined with well-worn books, and contem-porary artwork in warm, muted colors.

'Here you go,' said Andrew, handing me a tumbler, then he returned to the light granite counter tops and grey-blue units of his kitchen.

'Thanks. Do you live here alone?'

He looked up from chopping lettuce. 'I do now. I used to have a flat mate, but then things picked up at work and I didn't need the rent, and I like having my own space.'

'Me too. Can I look around?' I asked sheepishly, point-ing at the doors I assumed led to the bedrooms. One was slightly ajar, the walls a soft blue, with plush, cream carpet.

'Of course. Spare room's the far one, mine's the clos-est.' He smiled knowingly as I disappeared into the spare bedroom, glad for the moment alone to collect myself. This was perfectly normal. I was looking around a friend's apartment, just like I would with anyone. Nothing out of the ordinary here at all.

The bedroom was neat and tidy, with green walls and wooden furniture I recognized as Noah's work, including a wardrobe, chest of drawers, and bedside tables with tall lamps on either side of the king-sized bed.

There wasn't much else to see, so I moved to Andrew's room, briefly meeting his penetrating gaze before I ducked inside. His expression made my lungs feel half their normal size, and as I pulled in a deep breath, the smell of him engulfed me. It was all I could do to keep myself from racing to his pillow and burying my nose in it or rolling around in his sheets like an errant dog, trying to cover myself in his scent. A tight sensation spread out across my chest as I scanned the enormous bed, thoughts of Andrew lying naked under the sheets flashing unbidden across my mind.

I forced myself to focus on my surroundings, on the beautifully crafted wooden furniture, the tasteful ensuite bathroom off to the right, and a wall of wardrobes with sliding mirrored doors. But then Andrew appeared in the mirror behind me, and our eyes met in the glass. Beats of silence stretched out between us. 'Dinner's ready,' he said eventually, his voice husky, and by the time I turned around, he'd retreated to the living room.

I followed, needing to stay close to him, and I wondered if Belle was right. Maybe I was at peak fertility because my lips felt unusually sensitive as I ran my tongue across them.

'Help yourself,' said Andrew, pointing to the table in front of the kitchen island, or more accurately, to an enormous bowl of lettuce topped with seared lamb steaks, artichoke hearts, palm hearts, pickled beetroot, avocado, cherry tomatoes, olives, and a sprinkling of toasted seeds and nuts.

'Oh my God, Andrew. That looks and smells divine.'

He added a stick of French bread and a square of salted butter as I helped myself to the salad, my mouth watering in anticipation. Andrew sat beside me at the head of the table and loaded his own plate. It put us close, but was less intense than staring at each other from opposite sides.

'Any more thoughts about the salon?' he asked, topping up my kombucha.

I chewed and swallowed. 'No. This is delicious by the way.'

He smiled as he ripped off a chunk of bread and offered it to me. 'Glad you like it.'

'But I'm not convinced these ingredients needed to be used up,' I said, accepting the bread. The salad was crisp and fresh, the tomatoes firm, and the other stuff had come from tins or jars.

'I may have told a tiny white lie. But I hate how everyone expects you to bring food all the time, and I'm perfectly capable of cooking.'

'And when you say things like that, I wonder how anyone could ever think you scary.'

He smirked. 'Who are these people?'

'I'm afraid I can't reveal my sources. Although, scary probably isn't the actual word they'd use.'

'No?'

I shook my head.

'Then what?'

'Oh, I don't know.' I raised an eyebrow. 'Intimidating?'

He huffed out a half laugh, then said in a low voice, 'And what word would you use?'

The breath hitched in my throat as I met his gaze, his eyes so intense it sent a shiver down my spine. 'I think you're many things.'

'Such as?'

'You've always been kind to me.'

Heat burned hot in his eyes, which flicked briefly to my lips, then he said slowly, 'That's because I like you.'

Oh, holy mother of God. 'Well, that's lucky because I like you, too,' I said, looking up at him from under my lashes. 'It would be hard to be friends otherwise.'

He flinched, then looked away, and I instantly regretted my words. Why had I done that? Why had I said that?

Andrew stood, whatever had been building between us lying shattered all around. I wanted to take back the word *friends*. Or add something. I searched for anything to say, but before I succeeded, Andrew picked up my laptop and opened the lid.

'Show me,' he said, holding it out so I could unlock it with my fingerprint. I hesitated, trying to convey with my eyes that I was an idiot, that I didn't mean it, but he refused to look at me, his eyes on the screen. I unlocked the laptop and my spreadsheet appeared. He sat, first making a copy, then scanning the columns and rows, getting to know the lay of the land.

I decided watching over his shoulder was awkward for both of us, so I picked up my plate and carried it to the other end of the room, looking around as I finished my food. He didn't have much in the way of personal items, but there were a couple of photos of him and his parents, and one of him and his sisters. They looked so happy together, and I wished for the millionth time that I had a sibling.

I scanned his bookshelf, which were mostly filled with autobiographies and cookbooks with some very intimidating data science texts thrown in for good measure. I selected a book on barbeque, which had tabs sticking out of the side, discarded my now empty plate on the coffee table, and lay face down on the fabric sofa while I flicked through the pages, intrigued to see which recipes he'd picked out.

It was a history of barbeque, but with technical explanations on the different setups and cooking methods and with recipes, too. The tabs were numerous, and I wondered which things he'd already tried and which he planned to test out next.

I shifted, and Andrew's gaze flicked up at the movement. We locked eyes for a beat, but then he went back to his work, neither of us saying a thing, and my heart squeezed.

I exhaled a long breath, then pushed to my feet. 'Tea?'

'Please,' he said, but didn't offer anything further, seemingly consumed by his work.

I rummaged for cups and teabags, then watched as Andrew's fingers flew over the keyboard, using functions I didn't even know existed, shortcutting some of my steps. My chest lurched with a weird primal pride, like my body was telling me to mate with him so we could pass his superior spreadsheeting genes to our children. Or perhaps I'd been spending too much time with Belle ... either way, I had to fix this. I had to take control of my life.

I placed Andrew's tea on the table, then slipped into the chair beside him.

'Thanks,' he said absently, but he didn't look up.

'You're welcome.' I rested my elbow on the table, then leaned my chin on my palm, watching his every move like a creep. He was so sexy when he was concentrating.

He stilled, then slowly lifted his head, his eyes big and black as we appraised each other for a beat.

'Miri ...'

'Yes?'

'Why are you looking at me like that?'

'Like what?' I breathed, my heart stuttering as I silently prayed to every god that he wouldn't reject me again.

'Like ... that.' His leg found mine under the table, and I dropped my hand onto his thigh, gently squeezing the muscle just above his knee.

His mouth fell open, and the air turned heavy, but then my phone buzzed, and I had to fight a groan as I pulled it out to see an incoming call from Paul. 'It's the property agent,' I said, getting to my feet as I picked up. 'Hi, Paul.'

'Hi, Miri. I'm afraid I have bad news.'

'The salon's gone?' There was no other bad news he could be calling about.

'We've had a few viewings, and someone put in an offer earlier today. It's off the market.'

I inhaled deeply then held my breath. 'Okay. Thanks for letting me know.'

'Don't you worry, I'll keep searching for the perfect place.'

'Thanks, Paul.' I hung up and looked over at Andrew. 'That makes the financial projections less urgent.'

'Are you disappointed?' he asked, picking up his tea.

I concentrated for a moment on my emotions, trying to determine how I felt. 'Yes and no. It would have been okay, probably, but I wasn't totally comfortable with the financial risks.'

'Your spreadsheet looks good to me. I short-cut a few steps and run another couple of scenarios, but I think you can be confident with the projections you have. I mean, I'm no expert in hospitality, but your cashflows from the bar and café are awesome.'

'Yeah,' I agreed. 'Maybe I shouldn't be so nervous.'

Andrew shrugged. 'It says something that you're not devastated about losing the salon.'

'It never grabbed me, you know? But maybe nothing ever will.' Silence fell as he watched me, and I suddenly worried that maybe I was outstaying my welcome. We'd eaten, he'd looked at the spreadsheet, and there was no other reason for me to hang around. 'I should probably get going. I don't want to steal any more of your evening.'

His eyes widened a little, almost as though he was disappointed. 'Because I have something better to do than hang out with you?' Another beat of silence stretched between us, this one heavy, full of possibility.

'You could have a hot date for all I know,' I said, my tone low and flirtatious, but as he shut my laptop and got to his feet, I seemed to have said the wrong thing yet again.

'You're more likely to have one of those than me.'

'Andrew ...'

He rested his hands on the island, his face angled away, but then he turned back, seeming resolved. 'Stay and watch a film.'

I faltered.

'I have popcorn ...'

'I don't like popcorn.' But I also didn't like the idea of leaving.

'Chocolate, then.'

'Hmmm. Do I get to pick? Because if your plan is to make me sit through some gory action film ...'

The corner of his mouth twitched up. 'You can pick, but no rom coms.'

I scowled. 'You know plenty of men enjoy rom coms? It's just that society says you're not allowed to, so you tell yourself they're offensive.'

'You've been spending too much time with Belle.'

'Or maybe you haven't been spending enough time with her.'

'You want to watch a rom com?' he said in a way that suggested he might relent, and my insides melted.

'I want to watch a classic. Maybe—'

'Avatar?'

'That's not a classic.'

He scoffed, but didn't dwell. 'Equilibrium?'

'That is a classic, but ...' I thought for a moment, and then it came to me. 'Good Will Hunting.'

'Yes!' said Andrew. He pulled an expensive-looking box of chocolates out of a cupboard. 'You're right, that is a classic.'

I put the barbeque book back on the shelf, then sat on the end of the sofa farthest from the kitchen. It was a big three-seater, and when Andrew took the other end, there was clear space between us, which I was both happy and sad about. Although, he filled the space with the chocolates, which wasn't a bad consolation prize.

Andrew found a streaming service with the film, clicked play, then eased back, getting comfortable, spreading his legs a little, and I swallowed hard, then busied myself with pulling my legs up under me and taking a sip of tea.

'Chocolate?' said Andrew, holding up the box. They were the kind you bought from a counter where you selected each individual one, and I studied them, only half listening to the film's opening scene on the big flatscreen as I carefully made my selection.

'Did you buy these?'

'A present from my sister; Claire made them.'

'Oh, right, the woman from your work party?'

'Yeah. She's totally brilliant.'

I tried to suppress the irrational pang of jealousy that stabbed through me at him complimenting another woman. 'They look delicious.' I finally picked, and when I bit into it, found it was ginger coated in dark chocolate. 'Mmmmm, oh my God. That *is* delicious.'

Andrew's eyes were on me when I glanced up at him, his shoulders tense, lips slightly parted.

'Try one!' I demanded, then leaned forward and batted away his fingers so I could choose another one first. He pulled the whole box out from under my hand, and I whined like a brat. 'Andrew!'

'If they're good enough for you to have an orgasm over, I'm rationing them.'

'Why should orgasms be rationed?' I asked, stretching out and poking his thigh with my toe.

He covered my foot with his free hand, then dropped the chocolates next to my leg, selecting one at random and popping it in his mouth.

'Oh,' he said, 'that *is* amazing.'

I snatched them up before he could take them again and shuffled down and leaned my head against the arm of the sofa. Andrew put a cushion across his lap, then lifted the foot in his hand and placed it on top. He patted the embroidered fabric, and I rested my other foot beside the first, my chest lurching at the intimacy.

I selected another chocolate, then put the box down. It was probably rude to eat the whole lot, especially seeing as they'd been a gift from his sister. I tried to concentrate on the screen and not the feel of Andrew's thumb sliding along my arch, but the pressure was just right, hard enough to feel it *everywhere*, and every time he stroked, I had to stifle a hum of pleasure.

Eventually, I gave up any pretense of watching the film and tipped my head back, closing my eyes as he massaged with both hands. 'Where did you learn to do that?' I asked on an exhale.

'Does someone have to learn?'

I half opened my eyes. 'To do it like that you do.'

He pressed into my arch with his knuckle, and an involuntary moan escaped my lips, my back arching a little. 'Do that again,' I begged, and he repeated the movement. I moaned again, and he shifted, my eyes flying open, worried he was about to get up. 'Don't stop!'

'I'm not,' he said in a choked voice. 'I'm just ... getting more comfortable.'

He slid his thumb up the center of my sole, our eyes still locked, and desire trickled to my core. 'Oh my God, Andrew,' I said, biting my lip. He pulled each of my toes in turn, and I nearly combusted, my nipples so hard he could probably see them through my clothes.

I wanted to feel his fingers higher, to feel them all over me, and I had to resist the temptation to crawl forward and straddle him. But then I wondered *why* I had to. He was single, I was single, and we couldn't keep going round in these agonizing circles forever. I looked at him with hooded eyes, doing nothing to hide my lust, and he looked back, his features dark and full of promise.

And then he shifted, casting the cushion aside and prowling over me, up on his knees, looking down at me from above. He paused for a torturous heartbeat, then took my face in both hands, sliding his thumbs across my cheek bones. I savored the feel of his skin on mine, the anticipation, and then he tugged me upwards and covered my mouth with his, kissing me like a man starved.

My hands slid to his back, grasping onto him, needing purchase, seeing as I wasn't quite sure which way was up. He sucked on my lower lip, and I gasped, sliding my hand into his hair and grabbing hold, arching my back as he did it again.

He groaned, then moved one hand from my face, tracing his thumb down the column of my neck, over my collarbone, then farther south, pulling open the v-neck collar of my tee and pressing into the dip between each rib until he reached the swell of flesh at the top of my breast. He pulled his mouth from mine, then followed the same journey with his lips, kissing his way down my throat, gently sucking my pulse point, licking the hollow above my collarbone.

'Andrew,' I moaned, my hands on his muscular neck as I thrust my breasts up towards him, urging his lips lower.

He cupped my breast through my clothes, swiping his thumb back and forth across my rock-hard nipple, then nuzzled the naked flesh at the top, nipping and sucking and making me writhe against him. He rested his forehead against mine, breathing heavily as he cradled me like I was the most precious thing in the world. 'It's not enough,' he murmured. 'I need so much more.'

'Me too,' I moaned, burying my nose in his neck and inhaling deeply. 'You smell ... *fuck*.' I closed my lips over his neck and sucked and licked and bit, savoring him, but forced myself to pull away before I left a mark. He drew my lips back to his, and then my back hit the sofa, and his weight settled on top of me, and I surrendered entirely as he explored me, his hands stroking my hair and cheeks and neck while the thick ridge of his arousal pressed between my thighs.

We made out like teenagers, kissing and kissing as though there was nothing else in the world to do, and anytime we pulled apart, we came almost immediately back together, some fundamental law of attraction demanding it to be so.

I vaguely noticed that the film had ended, and that it was dark outside, but I would have happily kissed him all night, making up for all the time we should have been doing exactly that. But my phone rang, the tone telling me it was the bar, and my stomach dipped because no one ever called me to tell me anything good.

'Hey?' I said, answering the call while still on my back, Andrew propped up on his elbow beside me, his free hand stroking my stomach.

'I'm so sorry to disturb you,' said Julia, my French bartender, 'but Ange's mum just called. They have an emergency and Ange had to go. I could close up alone, but ...'

'No. No one closes alone,' I said adamantly, even though no part of me wanted to leave Andrew. 'I'll be there in ten.'

'Okay, thanks Miri. Sorry to ruin your evening.'

'Don't worry about it,' I said, then hung up.

Andrew kissed me the second the call was over, but pulled away all too quickly, standing and helping me to my feet. 'Do you need a lift?' he asked. If he was disappointed the evening had been cut short, he hid it well.

'No, it's fine. I drove.'

'I'll walk you down.'

I gathered my things and slid on my shoes, then met Andrew by the door. 'You really don't have to,' I said as he followed me out. 'I'm parked just along the street.'

He gave me a look that said not to argue, then locked his door behind us. 'If you get mugged outside my building, I'll never live it down.'

I snorted. 'I'm glad to know it's a selfless act.'

'Purely protecting my own interests,' he agreed, a step behind me on the stairs.

I pushed through the glass door onto the street, and the cool night air raised gooseflesh on my bare arms. I turned right, my van fifty meters down, and rummaged in my bag for the keys as we walked.

'Thanks for dinner,' I said, still rummaging, 'and for checking over my spreadsheet.' I found my keys just as we reached the van. 'And for the chocolates, and ... the foot rub.'

He stepped into my space, so close I had to tilt my head to meet his eyes, my pulse spiking as he slid a large, strong hand into my hair, cupping my nape. And then he lowered his lips and gently brushed them against mine.

My lips tingled as fresh desire coursed through me. 'More,' I breathed. I should have been embarrassed by the desperate plea laced into the word, but I felt nothing but pure, carnal need, so I didn't care.

He did as I asked, and we deepened the kiss, but then he pulled away, running his thumb across my bottom lip as he gave me a tender smile. 'See you tomorrow, M. Drive safe.'

Part of me wanted to stamp my foot, to demand he kiss me again, but I had to get back to the bar, and I didn't trust myself not to ruin everything by saying something stupid. So I got in my van and drove away.

It was a wonder I didn't crash as I headed home. The expression *love drunk* was a thing, but what about *lust drunk*? If it existed, I was definitely that, my brain showing me flashbacks when it should have been focusing on the road.

I sailed through closing the bar like I was in a dream, repeatedly finding myself paused mid-task wondering what it was I was supposed to be doing, and then the image of Andrew's green eyes and full lips would fill my mind once more, and I'd forget all over again.

I had no idea what was going on between us now, but the kissing hadn't felt fake. It had felt like Andrew had wanted it at least as much as I did. And I wanted it a lot.

More than anything else I could think of. I considered driving back to his after we finished closing, but that would look desperate, wouldn't it? Then again, if we were truly dating, that might be a thing I would do. *Holy shit*, was this real now? The thought was stunning, impossible, but it had been real kissing, I was sure of it, so did that mean we were actually dating? If only my brain would think straight …

'Are you okay?' asked Julia, my server, eyeing me suspiciously.

'Yeah, sorry,' I said. 'Just a bit distracted.'

'Good distracted, or bad distracted?' she asked in her thick French accent.

I smiled, and she cocked an eyebrow.

'It's the tall one, isn't it?'

'I don't know what you mean,' I said, walking ahead of her to the door.

'Mmm-hmm. Enjoy that feeling. It's something you cannot buy.'

Chapter 15

'Next stroke, easy there,' said Ottie from her position in the bow. We finished the stroke, then let our blades skim across the water as we drifted under the bridge into the small marina that housed the boat club. Livia had needed to stay late at work, so I was sitting in.

'Whole crew, backstops, ready, go! said Ottie. We pushed our hands down and moved gently up the slide, rolling the handles in our fingers so our blades squared, ready for the catch.

'Miri!' called an animated voice from the pontoon. 'I have a property for you!' I took the stroke, then turned my head to see Seb waving his arms, Andrew beside him, watching from the top of the ramp that led to the floating pontoon.

'Awesome!' I shouted. It was great and all, but I couldn't see the need for quite this level of urgency.

We passed the pontoon, and Ottie said, 'Next stroke, easy.' We dropped our blades onto the water, and this time dug them in, slowing our speed. We didn't need an order from Ottie to start turning the boat, chopping our blades back and forth as we'd done so many times before.

'You have to come now!' shouted Seb. 'The owner said he'd hang around until eight, which is in,'—he checked his watch—'seven minutes! And if you don't show, the listing will go live first thing tomorrow.'

'Oh shit,' said Ottie, looking at the line of two novice boats waiting to use the pontoon in front of us. 'Coming through!' she shouted, then she and Hazel started maneuvering us up the line.

'Sorry,' I said to the curious faces in the other boats.

'It's an emergency!' cried Seb.

Having successfully queue-jumped, we quickly undid our blades and launched ourselves onto the pontoon.

'No time,' said Seb, as I put my hands on the boat, ready to lift it out.

'Hey, you guys!' called Ottie, motioning to a novice crew at the top of the ramp, 'we have somewhere to be in five and a half minutes. It's an emergency. Can you deal with our boat?' Apparently, my crew was coming too.

'Sure!' they chimed as though delighted to be of assistance.

We pulled on our trainers, then rushed up the ramp, yelling, 'Thank you!' to the novice crew as we passed.

'Where are we going?' I asked, but Seb and Andrew had taken off at a sprint, so we had no choice but to follow them, no clue where we were headed.

'It's up the hill from your café,' Seb shouted over his shoulder as we raced across the open plaza, heading for my home.

No freaking way!

It must have looked hilarious, the six of us running as though our lives depended on it, but none of us cared. I was just glad I was wearing trainers, and not the flip flops I'd almost selected.

We raced past my café, then up the hill the other side that led towards town, which was lined with high end home renovation shops, restaurants, and hair salons. A gift shop and deli would be the perfect addition, especially as we were headed for the top end, so it would get footfall from the busier main shopping street, too.

'Wait!' Seb yelled as we competed to see who could make it to the top first. Of course Andrew won, followed by Seb, who had spotted what the rest of us hadn't, an older gentleman in a tweed jacket getting into a grey BMW parked in a loading bay on the pedestrianized street. 'Mr. Hollis!'

The man looked up at the sound of his name, and the rest of us screeched to a halt beside him.

'I'm so sorry we're late,' said Seb, panting hard. 'Miri was out on the water until approximately two and a half minutes ago.'

Mr. Hollis chuckled. 'I see,' he said, casting an appraising sweep of his eyes across our red-faced, sweaty group. 'Well, I'd better show you around then.'

'Thank you so much,' I gushed, breathing hard as I followed him up the worn stone step into his shop, which was filled with kitchen units and tile samples.

The building had been built into the hill, so the front was on a slope, all higgledy-piggledy and full of old-world charm, but inside, it was ... 'Oh wow,' I said, stepping into the space, which resembled the kind of kitchen you'd find in a lifestyle magazine.

It had soft lighting, big old slabs of stone on the floor, bespoke kitchen units lining the walls, and a marble-topped island in the middle. We all looked around open-mouthed as Mr. Hollis told us his backstory.

'My dad owned this shop,' he said, leading us down three steps at the back of the shop to a wide corridor where half the roof was sloping glass, with sliding doors to the right leading out onto a small patio. He had the section decked out with expensive looking granite, marble, and limestone tile samples, but it would also be the perfect space to show off gifts, and the patio would be a wonderful place for people to sit in the summer.

'I had hoped to pass it onto my son,' Mr. Hollis continued, 'but he isn't interested. Too much like hard work for him. Not that I blame him; this life's not for everyone. But Seb here said you already own the café and bar down by the river?'

I turned a warm smile on the grey-haired, kindly-faced man. 'Yes. I've had them for a few years and am looking for a new challenge.'

'You've made a great success of them from what I can tell. Everyone talks about coffee these days, but I'm most impressed by your tea selection. I do love a good Darjeeling.'

'Yes!' said Seb. 'Thank you. Finally, some support in this fight!' It was an ongoing argument between Livia and Seb.

'Hey!' said Ottie, swatting him. 'I like tea, too.'

'But the deli couldn't go back here,' said Belle, her finger tapping the side of her cheek. 'Too much heat from all the direct sunlight. It would have to go at the front.'

'That's better, anyway,' said Ottie. 'So then people won't have to walk so far if they're just popping in for food.'

'And even better, if they want to eat the food here,' said Hazel, 'they'll have to walk past the gifts on their way to the patio, and then again on their way out.'

'Impulse purchases will abound!' Ottie gleefully agreed.

'It would need a refit, of course,' said Belle.

'But nothing big,' countered Seb. 'Not like the other place you looked at.'

'No,' I agreed. 'Is there space out the back?' I asked Mr. Hollis. 'Anything I could use as a kitchen? Although, it's so close to the café, we could always do prep there and bring stuff up.'

'There's a small storeroom down here,' he said, going right to the back and opening a door, 'and a small WC, and there's the whole of upstairs, too. I've never done anything with it, really. My son lived up there for a bit, and over the years I've offered it to friends when they've needed a temporary place to stay, but now I just use it as extra storage.'

'Oh my God,' I breathed, bounding up the stairs to find two further rooms: a small kitchenette, and a large bathroom. 'This is amazing! I can change the bathroom into customer restrooms, and there's still plenty of space for a kitchen, and a storeroom, and more gifts if I find I need the space.'

'Or you could rent it out,' said Hazel. 'Either as studio space, or as a quirky meeting venue.'

'Ooo, for wellness gatherings,' said Ottie. 'I'm always seeing those on Insta.'

'Or flower arranging workshops,' said Hazel. 'They're all the rage for hen-dos.'

'It's got great light,' said Belle. 'And it feels nice. It would be a lovely venue.'

'Oh my ... guys!' I said, turning in a slow circle to take in every detail. My heart was racing, and it was like I was both there and not there, having an out of body experience while everyone around me was chattering excitedly and making further suggestions about how I could use the space.

This was it. Nothing could possibly be better, and especially not in this location. This was a do or do not moment, and if I didn't do it, I would probably regret it forever because much as I loved my café and bar, they were in a new, purpose-built unit. This place was quirky, full of personality and charm and history. The windows had shutters, and the floorboards looked original, and there wasn't a single straight line in the place.

It was the kind of shop you'd go to as a kid and remember forever, both because of the delicious treat you convinced your parents to buy, but also because it felt like an adventure merely by virtue of its myriad quirks.

I looked up to see Andrew watching me from across the room, his lips curved into an almost smile, his eyes intense and inquisitive. A swell of happiness filled me because not only was this the one, unquestionably, but because I was here with my friends. With those who loved me and wanted to see me succeed. With Andrew.

'Well?' said Seb. 'We really shouldn't keep Mr. Hollis any longer.'

'Oh, don't worry about that. I'm just glad the old place might be going to someone who cares. Not a big chain or soulless businessman.'

'I love it!' I heard myself saying. 'Please sell to me. I mean, I don't even know how much it's listed for, and this is definitely not the best way to start a negotiation. I should probably seem at least a tiny bit aloof and pretend I'm not head over heels. But I am head over heels, so please let me buy it from you.'

A squeal went up from Ottie, and the others all laughed, and I realized having them here was a brilliant asset because if Mr. Hollis said *no*, he'd be disappointing six people, not the customary one or two. Six people who were high on life and exercise endorphins. Who could possibly be so cruel as to bring us all down?

Mr. Hollis smiled a warm, fatherly smile. 'I'd love to sell to you. Seb here has the details, and we can hash something out in the morning. Right now, I have a hot date.'

I laughed, then clapped a hand over my mouth in disbelief. 'Wow. Thank you! Oh my ... Thank you so much!' And then I found myself being bundled into the middle of an enormous group hug.

'Out!' Seb called. 'Mr. Hollis has to go!'

Mr. Hollis chuckled as he watched us, then followed as we skipped down the stairs and out of the front door. 'I can't think of a better person to pass the baton onto,' he said, locking up. 'Or maybe a better group!'

We all laughed, then he drove away, and my crew bundled me again, everyone speaking at once.

'It's AMAZING!'

'Ahhhhh! Miri!'

'This is the most exciting thing that's happened in FOREVER.'

'We've got a new shop!'

'I'm going to phone my friend. She does pottery. Her stuff is *gorgeous*.'

We somehow headed back down the hill without discussion, presumably heading for my bar, and I was so excited, I bounce walked all the way, skipping a couple of times for good measure.

The others were still chatting, talking over each other, squealing, deciding they would be the first to tell Livia, and our coach, and everyone else we knew.

By the time we reached my bar, they still hadn't let up, and I was so elated and relieved and filled with nervous excitement, I called, 'Dinner's on me!' as I held open the door.

They all cheered as they headed inside, all except Andrew, who tugged the door from my hand, then stilled, looking down at me as he released it and waited for it to swing shut. Suddenly we were in our own little bubble, and the atmosphere, which had been fast and frantic slowed to a near stop, my senses heightened, taking in every tiny detail. The set of his shoulders, the intensity of his gaze, his musky scent mixed with the lavender from the planters.

'Congratulations, M,' he said, moving closer, his voice low and husky as he crowded me against the wall.

I bit my lip, exhilarated and happy and full of so many endorphins I thought I might burst. His eyes followed the movement, staring for a second, and then he kissed me, his lips eager yet gentle, and for a moment I let myself be consumed by him, his hand on my hip, the other in my hair, until his tongue caressed mine, and I worried that if I let him continue, we would never make it inside. Not to mention, I didn't want either my servers or our friends to see us making out like this.

I broke the kiss and urged him back a step, and he obediently moved away, his eyes angled down, his chest rising and falling in staccato. I squeezed his hand, then made to follow the others inside, but he blocked my path, lifting his arm and pressing his hand to the door. Anxiety flared in my chest as he leaned in because surely by now the others had realized we were missing. What if they came looking for us? 'Andrew—'

'You're amazing, Miri,' he growled, 'but you're not paying for my dinner.'

Chapter 16

The next few weeks flew by, and by the time I got the keys to the shop, I'd already formulated a full refit plan with Noah, and had visited countless artisan makers and local artists and farmers.

To start, we would only convert downstairs, prioritizing opening quickly, especially as I still hadn't fully decided how to utilize the upstairs space, although I loved the idea of using it for small events and workshops.

'The books will go over here,' I said to Noah, running through the plan. It was a Saturday, the day after I'd got the keys, and when I'd suggested we meet on Monday, he'd been the one to insist on getting started right away, which had made my heart swell. 'Shelves over here and in the middle. The deli counter will go to the right, and the checkout will be over here by the door.'

I wanted to open in a month, tops, so I'd catch the last summer tourists, and so my feet would be firmly under the table before the run up to the holiday season. It was ambitious, but that made it exciting, and Noah seemed up for the challenge, although he needed to fit working on the shop around his existing commitments, and some of his regular customers could be demanding.

The shop door swung inward, and I was surprised to see Ottie's excited face appear, followed by the rest of my crew, all sweaty after their outing on the river. They'd been at regattas for the last three weekends, so I hadn't seen much of them.

'Uh, hi?' I said.

'Oh, don't mind us,' said Ottie. 'We're just here to give you this.'

Hazel handed over a bottle of champagne. 'We were going to get you a card, but Belle vetoed it.'

Belle scowled. 'Cards are completely pointless. Most of them get thrown away almost immediately, which makes them a waste of money and resources.'

Livia threw up her hands, but to be honest, I was on Belle's side. I'd never seen much point in greetings cards, at least, not for moments like this, but, 'Oh, the gift cards will go over here,' I said to Noah, 'and I was thinking a small stand by the till, too.'

Noah nodded, making a note on his plan.

'Okay,' said Hazel. 'What can we do?'

Noah looked up and met Hazel's gaze. He seemed surprised and a little wary.

'Yes!' said Ottie. 'Put us to work. Ripping the old stuff out's gotta be the fun bit, right?'

'Well ...' Noah said hesitantly, 'you could help us move the old display units upstairs?'

'Are you keeping them?' asked Livia. 'If not, I'm sure Hazel could sell them for you, what with her Etsy habit.'

I chuckled as Hazel shoved Livia. 'I'm going to keep them for now. We might end up using them upstairs.'

'Right,' said Livia. 'Come on then, let's get going.'

An hour later, the men's crew showed up—all except for Theo—and Andrew squeezed my arm as he passed me, racing to help lift the ridiculously heavy marble countertop. My stomach dipped because it was the first time I'd seen him in weeks.

We'd exchanged messages back and forth, and he'd even called a couple of times, but we'd both been so busy, we'd had no time to see each other in the flesh. Which was probably for the best because neither of us could afford to take our eyes off the ball. I had to focus on the shop, on making it a success, and Andrew was in the middle of his acquisition.

But I was so confused. Neither of us had brought up what all the kissing meant, and although we weren't dating for real—not officially—we were also way past friends. I wanted him like I'd never wanted anyone before, my eyes snagging on the flex and strain of his muscles as he lifted a cabinet single-handed, biting the edge of my lip as my insides turned to goo. He looked up, his eyes finding mine, and a knowing smile spread across his lips as he caught me staring. I returned his smile with an accompanying embarrassed eye roll and shake of my head, then moved to the nearest cabinet, trying in vain to suppress my smile and ignore the giddy squeeze in my chest.

With the help of the men's crew, we had the old stuff upstairs in no time, and finally got a proper sense of the space we were working with.

'Wow,' said Seb. 'It's big.'

Livia turned in a full circle. 'It feels great,' she sighed. 'The feng shui in this place must be amazing.'

Belle tutted skeptically.

'Hey!' said Livia. 'They've proven it with science. Or, at least, I think I read that somewhere.'

'Did you read it on Instagram?' teased Ottie.

Belle laughed as Livia scowled. 'I don't know. Maybe. But to bring us back to the point, this place is divine.'

'It really is,' I agreed, with a delighted grin.

Ottie made an impatient ticking noise. 'Okay, what next? We're wasting time.'

I hugged her, unable to believe my luck that I'd ended up with such amazing friends. 'First, I'll get the café to make us coffee and cake,' I said, 'then we do whatever Noah says.'

Over the next two weeks, my crew painted the walls, ceilings, and woodwork, Noah worked like a person possessed on the shelving and stands and counters, a friend of Seb's helped with the electrical work, and one of the novice rowers was a plumber who squeezed fitting a new restroom downstairs into his busy schedule.

Belle and Hazel organized the patio, filling the planters with flowers and arranging the plant pots just so, and I found a load of mismatched metal furniture at a reclamation yard that looked perfect in the rustic, aged space outside.

As the days ticked by, my helpers diminished, until only Ottie and Noah remained, but I was just so grateful for everything all my friends had done, as it meant I'd be able to open on time and on budget.

Alongside the refit, I ordered new shop signs, set up a till and inventory system, decided on return and exchange policies, recruited staff, and bought stock. The days and nights blurred together, and the weeks blended into one, servers from the café or bar often having to call to remind me I was supposed to be working a shift.

After one such phone call, Ottie approached me, her body held awkwardly, squirming as though embarrassed.

'What is it?' I asked, my attention snapping to her and away from loading inventory into the system.

'Well ...' said Ottie, looking away.

Concern clamped around my insides. 'Otts, what's wrong?'

'Oh, nothing,' she said. 'It's just ... well ... I know you're recruiting staff for the shop, and ... I ... well, I was wondering if you would consider employing me?' She held up her hands as she rushed to continue. 'I know you don't usually like to employ friends, and I totally get that. I know it's a weird dynamic, but I promise I would never question your authority or take liberties or expect perks your other employees don't get. And the thing is, I could really do with the money. Especially if you would let me fit my hours around rowing and my PhD. Because otherwise I think I'm going to have to take a break from the club for a while, you know? Not that you should let that affect your decision. And I'm sure you have more qualified people applying, and anyway, just in case it was something you might be willing to consider.'

She looked hopeful and ... desperate, and I prolonged her misery by taking a moment to process her words, feeling bad but needing the time.

She was right, I didn't usually employ friends because the one time I had, it had got messy. I'd had to fire her, and we'd never spoken again. And that was a friend who wasn't part of the club. It would be a million times worse if it happened with someone there.

'Or, you know, just think about it?' said Ottie, crestfallen as she turned towards the door.

'Wait!' Ottie had worked tirelessly on the shop refit, and all for free, and now I felt guilty about that, accepting help from her when she could have been working for money all that time. And she was sensible and diligent and clever. I would be lucky to have her as my employee, but, 'It might be weird,' I said tentatively, 'and if it is, we need to agree that we'll just put an end to it with no hard feelings on either side.'

A hopeful gleam shone in her eyes.

'I really appreciate all you've done to get this place ready for opening—so much more than anyone else—and I need to pay you for that time, too. You've been such an enormous help, and ... Yes! Okay. Let's give it a go.'

She squealed and leapt forward, hugging me. 'Thank you! Thank you! Thank you!'

'Seriously, Ottie, we have to see how it goes, and if it doesn't work out, it doesn't work out.'

She pulled back, holding my arms and looking me dead in the eye. 'I understand.' Then she squealed again. 'But I promise it will!'

The scramble to be ready for opening was still intense, despite the help from my friends, because no matter how well-planned things might be, there's always stuff you just can't do until the last minute, like filling the fridges with perishable food and stocking the shelves.

Ottie had been an absolute trooper, and since I'd put her on payroll, she'd stepped things up to a whole new level. She was smart and organized and had a great attitude, and I was feeling confident things would work out. She'd taken a load off my shoulders already, which meant I'd even been able to get back to training properly alongside work.

She was in the stockroom, writing signs to put outside in the morning—our opening day—and Noah was fixing the final shelves into place as I unpacked tins of tea. Noah stood back to check his work, scowling hard, but the shelf looked perfect to me.

'Is everything okay, Noah?' I asked.

'Huh?' He turned to face me, his blue eyes crinkling the smallest fraction. He was good-looking, objectively speaking, in a hair-a-little-too-long, surfer-dude kinda way. He pushed his sandy colored locks out of his eyes as he waited for me to speak.

'You seem a little ... preoccupied today?' Had been for a few days, actually.

'Oh, yeah, it's nothing.' He turned back to the shelves, dismissing the topic, but for some reason I couldn't let it go.

'Is it Seb? You know he and Livia are just friends, right? I mean, I know they flirt, but ...'

Noah laughed as he turned back to face me. 'Seb and Livia? You know Seb is gay, right? Like never been even a tiny bit attracted to a woman, no interest in boobs, all about the cock?'

'Noah!'

'Yes?' He tilted his head in a laid-back challenge, but I wasn't in the mood for letting it go. I'd been starved of real conversation for weeks, and I craved it.

'Then what is it?' I pressed.

'Nothing.'

'Yeah, right ...'

He put down his screwdriver and crossed his arms. 'If we're going there, what about you and Andrew?'

I crossed my arms, too. 'What about us?' The words sounded defensive because it made my heart hurt to think about him.

'You're giving us all whiplash.'

I scowled.

'Well? Are you together? Do you like him? He's obviously crazy about you.'

'Why would you think that?' I said too quickly, then held my breath as I waited for the answer.

Noah smirked. 'Because whenever you're around he can't take his eyes off you.'

Really? I wanted to ask, to dig for more, but somehow managed to stop myself. I looked at the greeting cards by the till, then at the tins of tea, anywhere but into Noah's eyes because I was terrified he would see the truth, that yes, of course I liked him, but some dysfunctional part of me found it hard to admit that to anyone but myself.

Rarely did minutes tick by when I didn't find myself distracted by thoughts of him, of sharing his tent and playing croquet and kissing on his sofa. At the supermarket, I'd bought a tin of artichoke hearts just because it reminded me of the salad he'd made. When I was serving drinks in the bar, I would freeze midway through getting the card machine, remembering something Andrew had said or a look he'd given me, and whenever I caught sight of someone wearing club colors, my heart leapt, hoping it was him.

'Helloooo?' said Noah, and I realized I'd done it again, checked out of real life to the place in my head where only Andrew and I existed.

'It's not that simple.'

He tutted. 'It's exactly that simple.'

'Really?' I challenged, cocking my head, silently threatening to return to the topic of Seb.

'Well, okay, maybe not exactly, but you obviously like him, and we know he likes you, so what's holding you back?'

It was a good question, but I didn't have a good answer. 'I've been busy. And we've been friends for such a long time, and—'

'Just talk to him, will you? You have this whole quiet, mysterious vibe that's really hard to break through. Maybe he's confused.'

'I am *not* quiet and mysterious. And what if *I'm* confused? Besides, weren't you just telling me it was obvious I liked him?'

'So you *do* like him?' Noah raised a triumphant eyebrow.

'Would I be dating him if I didn't?'

'You're dating again?'

I scowled, crossing my arms more tightly, my shoulders rising. 'Well ...'

'See, this is your problem. You're overthinking it. Just tell him you like him!'

'He knows I like him.'

'Does he? Really? As I said, you're hard to read.'

'You know who *is* hard to read?'

He narrowed his eyes but allowed my blatant deflection. 'Hazel.'

Noah exhaled a laugh, then started packing up his tools. 'Nah, she's kind, that motivates everything she does. You? You're Miss Poker Face. No one has a good read on you.'

'That is not true!' Surely my crew didn't feel that way? I mean, I was kind of introverted, but it was best to be that way, not to stick out for the wrong reasons, to keep my head down and let my ergo times do the talking. I'd learned that the hard way, after the debacle with my coach, and it had served me well. I'd stayed out of the boat club drama and had flown largely beneath the radar. At least until Andrew. Which was good. Wasn't it?

'Why would anyone care, anyway? I'm not that interesting.' I pulled the tape off the cardboard box that had held the tins of tea.

'Why would you say that?' His eyebrows pinched in concern. 'You're probably the most interesting one of us all.'

I laughed. 'Don't be ridiculous. You take old bits of wood and turn them into masterpieces.'

Noah turned bashful at that.

'And all the others have high flying jobs, or academic careers, or founded a billion-dollar freaking company with their ex.' That was Belle, although she didn't like to talk about it because she'd left him before it got really big. 'I started a café and bar; it's nothing special.'

'You own two successful businesses. Soon to be three. And you've held the best women's 2k ergo score for over a decade.'

I smiled pityingly at him. 'And that, my friend, is my greatest achievement. Who cares?'

'We're rowers, and you have the best 2k ergo score,' he joked. 'You're a freaking celebrity in these parts. Just being close to an ergo score like yours gives me a reflected glow.' I shoved him, and he laughed, then turned serious. 'People care because they like you, Miri.'

I pursed my lips, giving him a cynical pout. 'They like discounts. Most of them don't even know me.'

'Yeah, you're right about some of those arseholes, but my crew and your crew, they do know you, and they care. Why do you think they've been helping with all this?' He held up his hand and circled it in the air.

'Because you're hoping for gossip about me and Andrew, apparently?'

This time he didn't let my deflection stand. 'Miri ...' He gave me a look worthy of a cool headmaster, and I looked at my feet, uncomfortable under his scrutiny.

I exhaled a long breath, feeling guilty, not wanting him to think I took him or his work for granted. 'I know you care. I didn't mean ... I really appreciate everything you've done on the refit. You know that, right?'

'I know, Miri,' he said in a gentle tone, 'but maybe let yourself be appreciated by everyone else, too ... especially Andrew.'

'Noah!' I threw a ball of scrunched up packing tape at him.

He chuckled as he caught it easily and tossed it into the trash can. 'And maybe hold the thanks until you've seen my bill ...' A mischievous gleam lit up his eyes, and I swatted him with the cardboard.

He plucked it from my hands and tossed it onto the growing pile of flattened boxes. 'So? Are you going to talk to him?'

'I would hate to lose my mystery ...'

'Come on, Miri. If you like him, just tell him. He's been so freaking mopey lately; he didn't even bring his barbeque to the last regatta.'

I gave him a long look, my mind whirling. Was that true? Was his acquisition going badly? Maybe I should call him ... but he was always the one to call me.

'Well?' he pressed.

'I like him,' I said, my voice little more than a whisper.

'Then tell him.'

'He knows, Noah. He knows and I've barely heard from him in weeks.'

'But ...' He seemed confused.

'Do you know who I'm worried about?' I asked, my tone jokey, an attempt to lighten the mood.

'Who?' He replied distractedly, still puzzling over my words.

'Hazel.'

His eyes turned sharp. 'Why?'

'She just hasn't seemed herself recently, and despite your read of her, she doesn't open up to us. I think she might need a friend.'

He went silent for a long time, seeming to be fighting some internal battle. 'I know what you're implying, Miri, but I can't be that person for her.'

'Why?'

He closed his eyes for a beat, and when he opened them, hurt radiated out, chilling me to my core. 'Because I'm totally in love with someone else.'

'Seb?' I breathed.

He gave a small nod. 'But it's not going to happen.'

'Why?'

'We're just not ... compatible.'

The raw emotion in his voice had me biting my lips together, and I didn't press him for more, my heart breaking twice, once for Noah, and once for Hazel—if Andrew's suspicions about her feelings for Noah were true. I gave a resigned little nod, then said quietly, 'Noah, how do I tell Andrew I'm totally in love with him, too?'

Chapter 17

My launch celebration party was in full swing, and I stood behind the bar, surveying the room filled both with my dearest friends and my mother and Aunt Bea, who were having a delightful time holding a bunch of novices hostage at a table on the deck.

Opening day had been a rip-roaring success, with a glut of customers, more sales than I could have dreamed of, and Ottie's organizational skills keeping everything running smoothly so I didn't even break a sweat. Meaning I'd had time to cobble together a last-minute celebration in the bar for everyone who'd helped make the shop a reality.

I poured myself a Moscow Mule—my first alcoholic drink of the night—then took my glass and the pitcher and rounded the bar, joining my friends at the large table they'd commandeered along the inside wall.

I deposited the pitcher in front of Ottie, then slid onto the upholstered bench seat next to Hazel, who immediately shoved me back to my feet, saying, 'I need to pee!' But I wasn't sure if I believed her because when I sat back down, I found myself scooting in next to Andrew, who smiled broadly as he wrapped an arm around me and gave me a side hug, then softly kissed my temple.

'Congratulations, Miri,' he said, squeezing my arm before releasing me. 'Sounds like it went well?'

Ottie half launched herself across the table, grabbing my hand, forcing me to hastily abandon my drink so it didn't slosh everywhere. 'It was the BEST!'

'*You* were the best,' I said, smiling warmly. 'I am so glad you were there.'

'Oh, stop,' she said, pulling back, then leaning her chin on her fist in a way that clearly said something more like, *please continue to say nice things.*

I laughed, wondering how many drinks she'd already consumed. 'I honestly couldn't have done it without you.'

Ottie's answering grin was full of pride. 'I told you I wouldn't let you down.'

'I couldn't have done it without all of you, actually.' I lifted my drink and scanned my eyes around the table, then nodded to Noah. 'Especially you.'

'And me!' Seb called indignantly from the other end of the table, where he and Livia sat huddled together, thick as thieves.

'And you,' I agreed. 'I am eternally grateful to you for finding me the perfect premises.'

Seb inclined his head and raised one shoulder in a wildly flamboyant gesture. 'You're welcome.'

'To all of you,' I said. 'Thank you for everything.'

'To Miri!' Livia called, lifting her glass.

'To Miri!' everyone parroted, and then Livia giggled and said something in a low voice to Seb, and the table's attention shattered into side conversations about regattas and terrible bosses and whether Hannah was pregnant and if two of the novice men were after the same novice woman.

It all washed over me because Andrew slid his hand into mine on the seat between us, his touch short-circuiting my brain.

And then Hazel reappeared and made me shuffle farther along the bench, so our legs pressed together, and our hands rested on top of his thigh. I had no words, barely daring to breathe, every one of my senses trained on him as he slid his thumb slowly back and forth over mine, the air between us sparking with electric energy.

And then he nudged my leg with his, and I couldn't help but turn my head, his face so much closer than I'd realized, his eyes boring into mine. 'It went well?' he murmured, leaning in so I could hear his low rumbling voice over the music and chatter.

'Really well,' I gushed, then told him about all the tiny little insignificant details. How the florist three doors up had brought me a welcome plant. How Mr. Hollis—the previous owner—had popped in and bought enough cheese to keep him going for a month. What a marvel Ottie had been. How much it meant that so many club members had come by.

'I'm sorry I couldn't make it,' he said, his eyes apologetic. 'I had an all-day meeting about the acquisition, and then my sister had a run in with ... well ...'

'It's fine,' I breathed, his woodsy scent making me light-headed. 'You would have come if you could.' And he'd sent a good luck text, which I'd re-read whenever I'd had a spare second throughout the day.

Andrew 07:03: Break a leg today, sweetheart. I know you'll kill it. I can't wait to hear every detail. Xx

How had he meant *sweetheart*? Ironically? Sincerely? Was it a typo? A famous quote from a film I couldn't remember? And the kisses ...What did two kisses mean, exactly?

Andrew squeezed my hand, his expression regretful, and my heart plummeted. 'I have to go. I'm still supposed to be at the meeting. I told the team I had an emergency, that I'd be back later.'

'Andrew! You didn't have to do that ...' But despite my gently chastising tone, elation bubbled through my chest.

'I wanted to.'

My eyes got stuck on his and I wished more than anything that we were alone.

'Hey, Miri?' called Livia.

I reluctantly pulled myself out of my Andrew shaped bubble. 'Yeah?'

'I meant to check in about the Founding Day party. Are you still good to organize, or do we need to rope in someone else?'

Shit. I'd completely forgotten I'd volunteered to organize this year's party. It was our biggest event of the year and always took place around the day the club was founded, ninety something years ago.

'Of course! I'm completely on top of it.'

Everyone laughed because I was a terrible liar.

'Okay, well, I will be.' I pulled out my phone and typed a quick message in the events channel of the club's Discord server, asking for volunteers.

A few phones pinged around the table, and then mine vibrated. I looked down to find two novices had already offered their time. 'See! Everything is totally under control.'

I exited out of the app and felt Andrew tense beside me. I turned my head and found his eyes on my phone. Or more accurately, on the photo of us that still covered my background. I'd changed the lock screen, but hadn't been able to bring myself to change them both.

'Oh ... uh ...' I hid my phone, a flush of embarrassment no doubt turning my face an unflattering shade of scarlet. *Great.* Now he would think I was some kind of stalker.

But he squeezed my thigh, drawing my attention back to him and making every muscle in my lower body pull tight. 'Walk me out?'

My heart lurched as I gave a small nod, my mind conjuring images of all kinds of things we might do outside, away from the scrutiny of our friends.

I led the way to the door, not looking back, feeling the eyes of everyone who knew us tracking our movements, ready to spring into gossiping action as soon as we were outside. I called to the bartenders, asking if they needed more ice, trying to convince them, at least, there was nothing interesting going on. They nodded, but it was a mistake to attract their attention because now their curious eyes followed us, too.

I practically ran through the door and down the stairs, not able to breathe until I reached the empty parking lot, and then Andrew snagged my hand and pulled me to his chest, and I couldn't breathe at all.

'You still have our photo as your background,' he growled, moving his hand to my neck and running his nose down mine.

He slid his thumb across my pulse, and my eyes fluttered closed. 'You called me *sweetheart* in your text,' I whispered.

His answer was a kiss. A sweet, exploratory press, and I exhaled a sigh as my lips parted. His touch was tender yet firm, worshipful yet insistent, and I melted into him, molding my body to his as he deepened the kiss.

He pulled away, panting, and rested his forehead against mine. I wanted to whine at the loss of him, wanted to demand that he return his lips to mine, but it wouldn't be fair, he had to work, and hadn't he done the same for me that night in his apartment ... let me go without complaint? I slid my hands to his hips, grabbing hold for a moment, steeling myself to say goodbye.

'I'm sorry things have been weird between us,' he murmured.

I shook my head, still reeling from the immensity of the kiss. 'Me too.'

'I don't want it to be like that any longer.' He slid his hands down my arms, and I nodded, all I could manage, apparently having lost the power of speech. He pulled me towards his truck, opening the door and reaching inside.

'Happy opening day, M,' he said, handing me a chocolate box tied in a bow.

'Andrew!' I looked down at the familiar plush packaging of Claire's chocolates, then returned my gaze to his. 'Thank you.'

He kissed me again, this one brief but mighty, like when a wave pulls back and moves the sand. He released me with a frustrated grunt, but I held onto him, pressing my forehead to his chest, my mind needing a moment to work out which way was up.

I let him go, and he reluctantly climbed into his truck and drove away, a strange feeling settling in my chest as we waved goodbye, like maybe he'd taken some part of me with him.

I felt so light and giddy and full of possibility that I might have been floating on air, my chest pulling me up as though filled with helium. I opened the box Andrew had given me and gasped because inside were little chocolate Ms, and a note that said, *Congratulations, M. I'm so proud of you. A x*

'He's leaving?' The unexpected male voice made me jump, and I slammed the box closed and whirled to find Theo standing behind me, so close I wondered how I hadn't noticed him already.

'He has to work,' I said, folding my arms against a sudden chill and clutching Andrew's gift to my chest.

Theo rolled his eyes. 'Figures. Work always comes first for that one.'

I should have walked away, should have known better, yet the spawn of Theo's accusation had been growing in my mind. It had become a caterpillar, and it had finally munched through my resolve, which was why I found myself asking, 'Why did you call him a liar?'

A coy smile curled the corner of his lip. 'Because he is one. But you already know that, don't you?'

My heart rate kicked up at least ten beats. 'What do you mean?'

He chuckled. 'Oh, come on! He has a whole other life nobody at the club even knows about.'

I scowled. 'Nobody but you?'

He raised his eyebrows in a short, quick lift, then turned his head away, suddenly mute.

'Cat got your tongue, Theo?' I goaded, tired of whatever game he was playing. 'Or maybe you're just full of shit like usual ...'

He turned his head slowly back to face me, but still seemed to be fighting with himself, his jaw working back and forth.

I scoffed, then made to leave. 'Night, Th—'

'I used to work for him.'

I froze. 'You used to ... what?'

He huffed out a sneer. 'It's not me that's full of shit.'

I held my breath. It was easy enough to check if it was true, and something like regret shone in Theo's eyes, making me believe him. 'What happened?'

He looked away again. 'Andrew's an arsehole, that's what happened.'

A bolt of dread hit me square in the chest, and I told myself to ignore it, to ignore him. But I couldn't. 'What do you mean?' I said, the words small and vulnerable.

'I can't tell you.'

What the actual ... 'Excuse me?' Irritation boiled my blood. Why did Theo always have to be like this? Not that long ago, I'd found it in some way alluring, but now ... 'Why not?' I demanded, wanting nothing more than to shove him in the river.

'He slapped a gag order on me.'

'A ... what ...?' My anger sputtered out. 'Why?' It sounded bad, like the kind of thing maniacal bosses did to poor, defenseless employees, but there had to be a perfectly reasonable explanation. Andrew wasn't like that. Andrew was good and kind and had left his meeting to see me. He'd bought me chocolate Ms!

Theo's features pulled into a tight, pained line, although some hint of victory lurked beneath. 'You know what a gag order means, right?'

'But—'

'I can't tell you shit, but if I were you, I'd ask him. Always good to know who you're getting into bed with.' Theo turned on his heel and headed for the bar, and the air whooshed out of me like a deflating balloon.

I stood and numbly watched until he turned the corner, then finally took a breath. It was probably just Theo being Theo. He was a petulant child, a player, and he didn't like that Andrew had ruined his game when it came to toying with me.

But even with my pep talk to myself, I couldn't dislodge the empty, shaken feeling that squeezed my mind, so I ditched the party, feeling a little bad about the ice and abandoning my friends, but not bad enough to go back.

Andrew wasn't a liar.

But he hadn't told me about his business, and we'd been friends for years.

Because he just wants to be a data scientist ...

Although he seemed to enjoy being the boss at his work party, and when giselle-legs had fawned over him.

No. I was being unfair. I shouldn't let Theo get to me. I would ask Andrew about it, and he would explain everything. But despite my attempt at reasoning with myself, the caterpillar in my mind was spinning silk around its fat little body, wrapping the worry away for later, and I didn't dare to think what it would look like when it emerged.

I closed the door to my apartment and pulled out my buzzing phone, finding a reply from Andrew to my message on Discord. A reply the whole club could see.

Andrew 20:21: Count me in, baby.

And then my phone exploded with messages from my crew, and I quickly turned it off.

Chapter 18

Ottie working in the shop meant she had near-endless opportunities to question me about Andrew, so, much to her chagrin, I'd taken to allocating her tasks for the club's Founding Day party any time she uttered his name.

Which meant party planning was in great shape. Pete had agreed to run the barbeque along with several novices, everyone would bring a bottle, and we would make big vats of punch using the money from the very low entry fee.

Through extensive group messaging—mainly to keep everyone off the topic of Andrew and I—we decided on a *Light the Night* theme. I wasn't totally sold, but Ottie and Livia were all in on the concept, and had already sourced disco lights and projectors from a friend who worked in events, so who was I to stand in the way of their formidable abilities to get things done?

It was all coming together, and aside from adding the additional food items to my next catering order, which I was doing now, and the actual set-up, which would happen tomorrow, we were done.

I hadn't seen Andrew all week and had heard little from him, with only a few brief texts, his time completely consumed by his acquisition. I tried not to let it affect my mood, but between Theo's bullshit and the radio silence, I couldn't entirely put aside the idea that maybe I didn't know Andrew at all ...

The bell in the shop dinked just as I finished the food order, and I looked up to see who was there. 'Hey!' I said, recognizing the first woman as Beth, Andrew's little sister. 'How's it going?'

'Good, thank you,' she said with an exuberant smile, holding the door for the tall, voluptuous black woman behind her. 'How about you?'

'Just finishing up the party planning.'

'Oh ... for the boat club? Is now a bad time?'

I stifled a laugh. 'No! I generally like it when people come into my shop.'

'Oh, right. Sorry ...'

I chuckled at her bashfulness as I rounded the counter. 'Anything in particular bring you in?'

'Andrew sent us!' she said, beaming. 'And he sent us with this!' She held up a credit card that presumably belonged to her brother.

'Oh ...' My eyes flicked to the second woman, wondering who she was.

'We're here for twelve gift baskets,' Beth continued, 'for the DrewDox team working on the acquisition.'

'It's taken over their lives,' the second woman added in a light, gentle voice. She gave a little shake of her head and exhaled a warm laugh. 'We haven't seen any of them in days. I'm Claire, by the way.'

Claire ... Why did that name ... Oh, the chocolatier. I appraised her with fresh eyes, immediately wondering if she and Andrew had ever had a thing; she was certainly beautiful, and accomplished, and his family seemed to treat her like one of their own. 'It's nice to meet you,' I said with an amiable smile.

'Andrew *loves* Claire!' gushed Beth, snaking her arm through the other woman's. 'We all do!' She grinned and raised her shoulders.

Claire nudged the younger woman, then turned to me, a knowing smile on her lips. 'Did you enjoy your chocolates?'

I faltered for a moment, trying to work out what she meant.

'The ones Andrew bought you,' she pressed.

I flushed crimson. 'I ... uh ... the Ms?'

She nodded. 'He was very particular about that order.'

'Oh, they ...' This was all so very disorienting. 'They were divine.'

The door dinked again, and I'd never been happier to see Ottie appearing through it. It was one thing for my crew to dig for information about my relationship with Andrew, but quite another to be ambushed by his sister and their close family friend.

'Ottie, this is Claire and Beth,' I said. 'Beth's Andrew's sister. He sent them for gift baskets.' Which was a very generous thing for him to do, and my chest swelled with a strange, tight feeling.

'I'm the sister!' Beth said exuberantly.

'Oh, hi!' sang Ottie, her eyes lighting up, then she said in a hushed, conspiratorial voice, 'Is your brother as hopelessly in love with this one as we all think he is?'

'Ottie!' I snapped in warning.

The others laughed. 'I have heard a lot about you,' replied Beth.

'Gift baskets ...' I said, trying to divert them.

'I'd hoped he'd drop by so I could observe them,' said Ottie, continuing as though I hadn't opened my mouth. 'But Andrew hasn't even been at the club all week.'

'He's got a big work thing going on,' said Beth. 'It's so important that if anyone even dares to step outside the office, they'll be summarily fired.'

Fired. The conversation with Theo came rushing back.

'Or worse,' Beth continued dramatically, 'they might not get their precious bonus!' She clutched her hand to her chest, and Claire rolled her eyes. 'I shouldn't make fun; Andrew's very generous.'

He really is, I didn't say. *And tall and handsome and kind, but with a bit of a sullen, brooding thing going on that keeps everyone away. And he's so secretive it makes me nervous, like there's something bad lurking beneath, something like sacking his employees, who are also his crew members, and putting gag orders on them so they can't tell anyone about it.*

My phone rang—one of my suppliers—and I excused myself, asking Ottie to help Beth and Claire, and heading out onto the patio to take the call. By the time I returned, the two women were finishing up their enormous purchase, and I could hardly believe how quickly Ottie had pulled it all together.

'Find some things you like?'

'Yes!' squealed Beth. 'SO many things. This place is going to be top of my Christmas shopping list!'

My face split into a broad smile because it never got old, people telling me they liked the shop. 'Great!'

The bell dinked yet again, and Theo entered, a prickling sensation creeping across my skin as his eyes scanned the four of us. What the hell did he want? He did a double take when it came to Beth, then froze, their eyes locking across the room.

'I'll come back later,' he muttered, then left, and my face creased in confusion. *What the hell?*

Beth flushed scarlet, and Claire was looking at her with a curious expression on her face.

'He's pretty to look at, but an absolute arsehole,' said Ottie. 'Don't waste your time on men like that.' Then she threw me a meaningful look, and I scowled hard.

'It was so nice to see you again, Miri,' Beth breathed, her voice smaller than before, her smile half the wattage, then she added with a cheeky smile and a knowing glance at Ottie, 'I'll hope to see you at a family dinner soon!'

'Beth!' Claire chastised, then turned to Ottie, suddenly all business. 'You'll courier the gift baskets?'

'Of course! I'll do that now.'

Claire followed Beth out of the shop, and I rounded on my friend the second they were gone. 'What the fuck, Ottie?'

She stifled a laugh. 'She is SO sweet. I want her as *my* sister-in-law.'

'Ottie, seriously, can you knock it off?'

The wind disappeared from Ottie's sails, and her features dropped as she realized I wasn't fooling around. 'Oh, sorry, Miri. I ... is everything okay? You know I'm only joking, right?'

I sighed deeply. 'I know, but sometimes it gets a bit much.' I rubbed my face with my hands. 'Trying to figure out a relationship is hard, and it's ten times harder when the whole club is watching our every move.'

'I'm sorry,' she said again. 'I'll tone it down. But ... you like him, right?'

I hissed out a frustrated breath. 'Ottie, you literally just said—'

'No ... I know ... I just mean,' she lifted her hands to placate me, 'if you don't want him, then for God's sake put him out of his misery. His sister just came in to buy up half the shop!'

I scowled hard. 'He needed gift baskets for—'

'Whatever. Look, the point is, the man's obviously besotted, and I think you are, too! He practically declared his love for you on the club's Discord server, and you left him hanging! Why don't you just get out of your own way and give it a go?'

'Or alternatively, everyone could just fuck off and leave my love life alone.'

I grabbed my bag, and Ottie's eyes flew wide. 'Hey, Miri, I'm sorry, I ...'

But I didn't want to hear it. Instead, I yanked open the door and stormed all the way home.

I couldn't sleep, Ottie's words circling round and round in my head. *Besotted*. She was so dramatic. But also, was he? Was *I*? Was there anything real between us at all? I hadn't seen or heard from him in days. He'd sent his sister to the shop, yes, but that wasn't the same as a declaration of, well, anything. It was a purely economic arrangement, and for all I knew, he could have been using it as a way to get his sister to spend more time with Claire, who he *loved* so much ...

Ottie had messaged to apologize, and I'd messaged back saying it was fine, but that had done nothing to ease the hive of aggravated bees buzzing around my mind.

Urgh. At five in the morning, I threw the covers off and went down to the café, helping the staff on the early shift get pastries in the oven, and making the first batch of sandwiches for the counter.

After an hour, it was clear there were too many cooks in the kitchen, so I left them to it, heading to the boat club and grabbing a single scull from the racks. A few other scullers were already out, and it was a gorgeous, still day, with barely a ripple dancing across the water—the kind of conditions we rowers dreamed of.

But the farther I travelled, the more frustrated I became, the gentle rhythmic splashes of my blades failing to lull me as I'd hoped. The flight of my boat across the water seemed mocking, no matter how hard I pushed, the beating sun glaring, the birdsong shrill. The idea of him being *besotted* turned sour in my mind, and I wondered why he hadn't called, had barely messaged, hadn't set foot inside the shop.

The word *besotted* seemed increasingly ridiculous, in fact. Men like Andrew did not become besotted, especially with women like me. Maybe with women in smart suits to match his sharp mind, who drove fast cars and yelled things like, *Sell, now!* into their phones.

And yes, I owned three businesses, but they were trivial compared to his. No big acquisitions requiring complex modelling. No multi-million-dollar investments. Nothing difficult at all. I was no one special, and Andrew ... well, he was.

The idea of him being besotted with me? Absolutely not. But if everyone thought I was head over heels for him ... Was I really that transparent? It was embarrassing. Mortifying, actually. The thought made me want to crawl into a hole and hide, and I had no idea what to do about it.

By the time I made it back to the boat club, the place was a flurry of activity. Crews coming in and out, a crowd of novices milling about, waiting to be told what to do, veterans sitting on the patio in the early morning sun, watching proceedings with a critical eye.

I put my boat away, then headed home. I showered, changed, and when I got back to the boat club, a small group of party volunteers lounged in front of the clubhouse waiting for me. Not that I felt much like a party.

I managed a few lackluster instructions, and then Ottie and Livia took over, putting everyone to work in their usual efficient way. Hazel periodically reassured everyone that they were doing a great job—despite the impression Livia might be giving them—while Belle merrily got on with whatever she wanted, ignoring the directives entirely.

We bustled about, moving boats out of the boathouse—where we would hold the party, seeing as it was bigger than the clubhouse—then lifting furniture and lighting in. I was so preoccupied I didn't even notice the men's first crew until they'd already put their boat on the trailer and were hanging their blades on the racks. My heart leapt as I looked around for Andrew, and when I spotted him, he was on one end of a sofa, carrying it into the boathouse.

He smiled as he passed, and I smiled back, ruing the butterflies fluttering in my chest, then I gathered a couple of volunteers and headed for my café to retrieve the ingredients that had just arrived. I spent the next couple of hours in the clubhouse kitchen, making salads and dressings, then mixing up big vats of punch behind the bar.

It was midafternoon before I resurfaced, finding the work all but done, and most people had headed home to change. The boathouse had been transformed, with brightly colored fabric hanging from the racks, seating placed down each side, and a cozy circle of sofas and armchairs at the back.

'Perfect!' said Livia, making me jump as she materialized from under a swathe of fabric, standing back to admire her work.

'And these projectors will look amazing when it gets dark!' Ottie shouted excitedly from the top of a nearby ladder.

'Wow!' said Hazel, appearing at my shoulder. 'That came together quicker than expected!'

'Many hands make light work,' said Belle, one step behind Hazel.

'Although, Theo is such a dick!' huffed Ottie, climbing down the last few rungs of the ladder and coming to join us. 'I asked him to do one single thing, and he laughed, then took off.'

'We'll be limiting his free punch, then,' I said, and the others snickered.

Ottie pursed her lips. 'I might take a stint on the barbeque just to spit in his burger.'

'Seems like a lot of hassle for not much reward,' said Belle. 'We can do better.'

'Ooo, if Belle's getting involved, I'm scared for him,' I said on a laugh.

'We could turn his pee blue?' Belle suggested.

'Or tell all the novice women he's got an STD,' said Livia.

Ottie cackled. 'That would hit him where it hurts.'

I looked around for Andrew but couldn't see him, and refused to ask the others where he'd gone, so we locked up the boathouse and headed to mine to get ready. We only had a couple of hours before the party started, and most of us didn't put make-up on very often, so it would take some time.

We sat back on the sofas in my apartment and finally opened the bottle of prosecco we'd been talking about pouring for the last hour and a half. Livia and Belle handed round the glasses, and we chinked before savoring our first mouthfuls, the bubbles so vigorous, they made my jaw ache.

We were dressed in ridiculous outfits in all the colors of the rainbow, with a hefty helping of neon thrown in for good measure. Our makeup was bright and loud and shimmery, and we all wore some variation of chunky bling jewelry that would reflect the disco lights, as would the sequins on my body-hugging dress, along with my clumpy silver platform shoes.

I blew out a long breath and looked at the ceiling, willing the prosecco to hurry into my blood, hoping it would improve my mood in a way both exercise and the distraction of party set-up had failed to. 'My outing this morning was so frustrating,' I blurted, some part of me needing to share my Andrew worries, even if I had to do it in a roundabout way.

'Really?' said Hazel, turning curious eyes on me.

'Ours was so good!' said Ottie, adding, 'What?' when Hazel scowled at her.

'We know why Miri's outing was bad,' joked Livia.

'Guys,' snapped Hazel, ditching her usual mild-manners, something that seemed to be becoming more common for her of late. 'Can you please try to be supportive?'

'*I* am,' Belle chirped proudly, like an overachieving school kid.

'It's tough love,' said Livia. 'And as ever, we're merely jealous that Miri has a love interest and we do not.'

'Two, if you count Theo,' Ottie added.

'Which we don't,' Hazel said sternly.

'You've got to pony up and tell him how you feel!' said Livia. 'It's the only way.'

Ottie visibly backed off, looking apologetic and a little sheepish.

'They do have a point,' said Belle. 'Although, if you're not sure if you want him, you shouldn't feel any pressure from us. You should take your time.' But then she looked expectantly at me, clearly waiting for an answer.

'Crew selection for Nationals is next week, isn't it?' I said, trying to run away from the topic I'd so clumsily brought up, but when Ottie, Livia, and Belle went tense, I wished I hadn't. 'So it's great you guys had a good outing!' I added lamely.

'Yeah,' said Livia. 'I mean, it would probably make sense for the crew to stay as it is, given how much time we've spent in the boat together.' She wasn't being a bitch, she was just saying it as it was, but my competitive side raised its head anyway, and I couldn't let it go.

'I've been training,' I said, a little too sharply.

'We know, but you haven't been in the boat with us,' said Livia, never one to back down.

'Well, anyway, it's up to Cassandra,' said Hazel, giving us an escape route, which we grabbed with matching shrugs.

I smiled gratefully at Hazel, although honestly, Livia had a point. My ergo scores were still the best, but I hadn't been out in the boat with them much, and if they were gelling as a crew, I didn't want to upset their hard work. But I'd never not gone to Nationals, not since I'd first been in a senior crew, and it would hurt to stand on the sidelines and watch.

Chapter 19

'I think I'm going to dump my boyfriend,' said Belle, whose words were a little slurred after many rounds of punch.

It was goodness only knew what time, dark outside, the lights flashing in all their glory, the DJ long gone, and two veterans were now fighting over the playlist like a couple of children.

We'd commandeered the comfortable seats at the back of the boathouse, and it was so good to hang out and get drunk with my friends and forget about crew selection, and work, and stupid boys.

'Why?' said Livia, tipping her head to one side. 'Why in God's name would you pass up regular sex when it's available to you?'

'Well,' said Belle, leaning forward as though the point she was about to make was of great significance, 'that's just the thing. I hit peak fertility last week, and I didn't even bother calling him. Not a good sign.'

Livia cocked an eyebrow. 'Might that have something to do with a certain ex of yours who just opened a new office in town?'

Belle snorted. 'That ship has well and truly sailed.'

'Well, just think carefully before you pull the trigger,' said Livia, 'because it's bleak out here. I mean, a desert. Nothing lives. So much so that I woke up the other morning and realized I'd been dreaming about a work colleague who's basically the anti-Christ.'

'Mmm-hmm,' said Ottie, rolling over from where she lay belly-down on a sofa and looking at Livia suspiciously. Ottie was drunk enough that I was beginning to worry about her.

'Don't give me that face,' Livia trilled. 'He's trying to steal my project. He's my nemesis. The enemy.'

'I really want more punch,' I said because the thought popped into my head, 'but I'm comfy.'

The men's crew joined us, and my chest swelled as I smiled up at Andrew from under my lashes. I wondered if he'd sit by me, hoped he would, but then a woman I didn't know caught Andrew's arm and drew him into conversation. I scowled but couldn't look for long because he was standing right behind me, and I couldn't listen because Theo plonked himself down beside me, then leaned in, too close.

'It's okay,' he said, his eyes fuzzy, lids droopy.

'What is?' I demanded, the alcohol fog in my brain clearing a little on account of my alarm.

'You can admit it.'

'Admit—'

He bumped my shoulder with his. 'You love me really, don't you? The way you look at me with your puppy dog eyes ...' He smiled as though he'd said something clever.

Oh. At first, embarrassment threatened, but that made me angry. 'Yes, Theo, I *love* you,' I deadpanned. 'I love you.

I can't help myself when I'm around you because you're just so ... desirable.'

I looked up to find Andrew watching with an unreadable expression, and my stomach dropped. *No! Please, God, tell me he heard my scorn.*

'I knew it!' said Theo, his eyes flicking around to see what kind of audience we had. 'We have chemistry.'

'You're an idiot,' I said, moving to get up, needing to find Andrew, who'd disappeared.

Theo caught my hand. 'We were dating, and then all of a sudden, you were with Drew? Pft! Like that would ever last.'

I yanked my hand out of his grasp, and only just resisted the temptation to slap him. 'Theo,' I hissed, fury firing hot in my veins, 'you are a man whore. You cheat on every woman you date. You don't like me. The only reason you want me is because you can't have me, and Andrew is ten times the man you are.'

He sat back as though I *had* slapped him. 'But you just said you loved me!'

'It was sarcasm, dipshit. Now leave me alone.'

I climbed unsteadily onto my platformed feet and raced outside into the cool night air, one single thought in my mind. *Andrew.* I had to find him and tell him the truth. I couldn't let him think I'd lied to him, that I liked Theo. That I *loved* Theo. But Andrew would have known I was being sarcastic, wouldn't he? He would know me well enough to—

I collided with a solid wall of muscle as I flew out of the boathouse, looking up to find Andrew, a blank expression on his face. He held out a paper cup filled with punch, and for a second, I just stood there, open-mouthed, my brain putting two and two together and coming up with something that might or might not have been four. But I didn't take the drink. Instead, I slipped between his outstretched arms and wrapped myself around him, holding him tight and breathing him in. He hugged me awkwardly because he had a drink in each hand, and when I pulled back, I could have sworn he was going to kiss me, right there in front of everyone.

'Oh my God, Miri!' said Ottie's slurred voice. She barreled into me on one side and Livia on the other.

'That was sensational!' said Livia, as they dragged me between them towards the locker rooms.

'I'll be right back, Andrew.'

'Because she lurrrrves you,' Ottie sang.

'Ottie!' I hissed.

'Oh, Jesus,' said Ottie, shaking us off and taking off at a run. 'I'm going to be sick.'

Livia and I tossed each other a dismayed look, then ran after her, getting to the locker room just in time to hold her hair and rub her back. 'Maybe next time you should eat something alongside the drinking,' I joked as she washed her mouth out.

'I've only had *four*,' Ottie protested. 'And it's cheaper not to eat.'

Livia and I shared another look, and the air turned thick and heavy. 'Do you ... need money?' Livia asked, putting a hand on Ottie's arm.

Ottie batted her off. 'No!'

'We can help, Ottie,' said Livia, undeterred.

'I do not need your ... I'm fine!'

'I can give you an advance on your paycheck?' I suggested. Ottie was an amazing employee, and I hated to think of her struggling financially. Why hadn't she said anything?

Ottie screwed up her face. 'Hmmm. Would be weird. But ... maybe?'

I got out my phone and fired off a quick email to my accountant, noticing at least two mistakes as soon as I pressed send, but deciding not to worry about that for the moment. 'Done,' I announced, and Ottie smiled and closed her eyes, then launched herself at me, hugging me in a death grip.

'You're the best,' she slurred.

'Uh ... thanks.' Footsteps sounded through the door, and I turned to face them, Ottie still attached.

'I'm going to go,' Hazel said as soon as she appeared, her features black and brooding. 'I'll take Ottie home.'

'Uh ... everything okay?' I asked, wondering what on Earth could have happened in the two minutes we'd been away.

'Fine.'

Silence settled, more looks darting between me and Livia, while Ottie was half-dozing against me.

'What happened?' Livia asked gently.

'Nothing.'

'Hazel ...' I said.

'Just leave it,' she hissed, in a completely un-Hazel-like manner.

'Sorry,' I breathed, so surprised at her tone that I flinched back a pace.

She softened a little. 'I just need to go home, and so does she.' Hazel prized Ottie off me, then bundled her out of the door, while Livia and I waved them dumbly goodbye.

'What the fuck was that about?' said Livia.

I shrugged. 'Beats me, but she hasn't been herself for a while. Andrew thinks she likes Noah ... I wonder if it's related.'

'Oh,' said Livia, as we made our way back to the party. 'I thought Noah liked—' She clamped her lips shut and her eyes went wide and guilty, as though remembering she wasn't supposed to tell anyone.

I giggled. 'Seb? Does he like Noah?'

Livia drew her finger and thumb across her lips, miming zipping her mouth closed while shrugging.

I winked at her. 'Mum's the word.'

Andrew was, unsurprisingly, no longer where I'd left him, so we returned to the horseshoe of seats at the back of the boathouse, my heart fluttering up a few notches when my eyes found him lounging on a two-seater sofa. Belle and Noah had taken the opposite sofa, while Seb was in the armchair between them.

'Everything okay?' asked Belle, her brow slightly furrowed. 'Where are the others?'

'They left,' I said, perching on the arm of Andrew's sofa.

Livia shoved me as she passed, hard enough that I had no hope of staying upright. I fell backwards, my head landing on Andrew's solid thigh. He only just managed to lift his arm in time and get his drink out of the way.

'Livia!' I exclaimed.

'You're welcome,' she sang, dropping down to sit across Seb's lap.

Seb high-fived her, and I rolled my eyes, making to sit up so my head wasn't so close to Andrew's crotch, but he grabbed me and held me in place as a novice woman appeared by his side.

'Andrew!' she cooed. 'Come dance!'

'Uh ...' he said, wrapping his arm more firmly across my torso. 'No.'

'Oh, come on!' she pressed. 'You *promised* me a dance.'

'Dude, take a hint,' snapped Livia. 'He's with his girl-friend.'

I tensed at the word, but didn't correct her, and the novice narrowed her eyes as she looked poutily down at me and then at Andrew. But he wasn't looking at her, and I smiled up at him, forgetting everyone around us, his leg comfortable, his warmth making me drowsy.

The novice stormed off, but none of us gave her a second thought. We were all drunk and ridiculous and I wouldn't hold it against her; Andrew was the catchiest catch of them all, after all.

All, after all. I chuckled to myself as I let the music and conversation wash through me, only vaguely aware of Seb asking what had got into Hazel to make her leave so soon. Noah leaving. Livia punching Seb and telling him not to be so insensitive.

And then Andrew's fingers were caressing my forehead, and I closed my eyes, savoring the utter perfection. He combed his nails gently through my hair, traced the line of my nose, squeezed my earlobe, and the lead weight that had been inside me all day finally lifted, dissolved by the feel and smell and rightness of him.

I became aware of the world slowly, something warm and soft but also firm under my face. Andrew's torso, I realized as my brain began to focus. Both his arms were around me, and I was lying half on top of him in the near-silent boathouse, nothing but the muted chatter of birds outside filling the air, the musty boathouse smell mingling with the musky scent of Andrew.

The doors were closed, slivers of light from the small slits around the sliding wooden panels the only illumination, but even that was too bright, so I closed my eyes again, listening to the sound of Andrew's heart as my face moved up and down in time with his breaths. It was blissful and simple and I thought how happy I would be for every day to start like this, waking up naturally with the sun and the sound of birdsong, Andrew wrapped around me.

He stirred, tightening his grip as he shifted a little.

'Don't move,' I mumbled groggily. 'I'm comfy.'

He huffed a laugh into my hair then pulled the blanket more firmly around me. Where he'd got it, I had no idea.

I tilted my head to look up at him as he lounged back with his perfectly mussed hair, one leg on the ground, one under me. He watched me with hooded eyes, his fingers gently stroking my back, and I shifted up and forward, brushing my lips softly against his without giving myself time to think.

He exhaled, and when I opened my eyes, I found his closed, so I kissed him again, this time pressing harder. His lips parted, and I gave a little sigh, happy chemicals firing through me.

'We shouldn't, Miri,' he breathed, and my heart plummeted. But he kissed me again with light, exploratory movements, so I didn't stop, sucking his bottom lip and sliding my hand under his shirt.

'Miri ...' But as he pulled his lips away, he rubbed his cheek against mine, and the hard bulge under my hip spoke volumes.

'What?' I pressed, moving my lips to his neck. Maybe Ottie was right, and all the others. Maybe I should just tell him what I wanted.

He wound his hand around my ponytail and tugged me back, the almost rough treatment sending a zing of awareness to my core. 'Do you really want this?'

'What?' I breathed. How could he ask that?

'I ... After all that stuff with your coach,' he said, his free hand moving to my cheek, 'you said you didn't want to date anyone at the club.'

It was true, I had said that, but that had been years ago, a decade, maybe.

'But then when you and Theo ...'

'Andrew—'

'I know you don't want him, but if you don't want anyone at the club, I'll understand.'

'I said that ten years ago, and I never even meant it! I regretted the words as soon as they were out of my mouth, but I couldn't find a way to take them back.' And it had served me well ... But, was that truly what had been holding him back all this time?

His eyes bored into mine, a muscle ticking in his jaw.

'And you never made a move, so I assumed you didn't see me like that. You friend-zoned me.'

'You friend zoned me!' he protested. 'I didn't make a move because you told me not to!'

'But then you rejected me!' I said, half sitting. 'When we kissed in the parking lot, you pulled away, and then in the tent, you left ...'

He slid his hand to my neck and pressed his forehead to mine. 'I left because otherwise I would've taken it too far. I would have made you moan so everyone knew exactly what we were doing, so everyone would have known you were mine.'

Fuck. That was—

'And then you ended it,' he said quietly.

'I didn't!'

'You—'

'Well, you dumped me right back.'

'Miri, fuck ... Just tell me what you want!' He'd pulled back a little, his features tortured.

'I want you,' I said huskily, then kissed his neck. 'Maybe I've always wanted you. It was too hard having you but not having you, and I didn't want it to be fake.'

Andrew stilled beneath me, all aside from his fingers sliding up my back, and I met his eyes. 'I wanted it to be real, too.'

'But the woman at your work ... I wondered if maybe that was why you took me to the party.'

His eyes searched mine, and he seemed confused. 'Who?'

I looked away, my cheeks flushing with embarrassment. 'Or Claire? Everyone keeps telling me how much you *love* her.'

He pulled my eyes back to his, and my heart practically burst at the tender look he gave me. 'Claire's dating my sister, Miri.'

'Oh.'

'I don't want anyone but you.'

Our lips met in a tender caress, and this time when I opened my mouth to him, he didn't pull away. He licked my tongue, and I stifled a moan.

He pulled me more firmly on top of him, and bliss coursed through my whole being as his arousal pressed between my legs, as though every nerve in my body were delighted by him. I grabbed handfuls of his hair, terrified it would end, that he would pull away like he had before. But he didn't. He just kissed me with slow, sensual movements and explored me with strong, confident hands.

I had no idea where my body ended and his began or where we were or which day it was or my name, and when he broke the kiss, I clutched at him. 'Don't go,' I begged, my voice a desperate plea.

'I'm not going anywhere.' He rolled his hips. 'But we can't do this here.' He pulled me up as he sat, and I straddled him, wrapping my arms around his head, needing to stay pressed against him for just a little longer.

'Miri,' he coaxed, but I clung harder. 'Baby.'

'No pet names,' I breathed, but really the word lit me up inside.

He slid his hands up and down my back, squeezed my ass, skirted the sides of my breasts. 'Miri, we need to get out of here or I'm going to lose my fucking mind.'

I started to pry myself off him, but somehow our lips met again, our need burning hot. I ground my hips, seeking friction, and he groaned, just as the pedestrian door to the clubhouse banged open.

'Oh, for fuck's sake!' sneered Theo, pulling out the pins holding the enormous doors in place, then sliding one half to the side.

Neither Andrew nor I moved, too dazed, and then Belle came into view on the far side of the opening, along with five or so others, and I sprang to action, climbing off Andrew and racing out ahead of him, my face burning hot enough to light a fire.

'Your funeral,' Theo said under his breath as I passed him. 'Don't come crying to me when it all blows up in your face.'

'Fuck off, Theo.' Very little could have made me think badly of Andrew in that moment, and certainly nothing from Theo's lips.

My mind spun with the lingering sensation of Andrew's touch as I surveyed the mess left over from the party, which, all things considered, wasn't too bad. Realizing there was no quick escape, I reluctantly joined the clean-up effort, grabbing a chair and carrying it towards the clubhouse.

'Fun night?' asked Belle, her tone light and suggestive as she picked up a chair and fell in beside me.

'Yes, thank you. You?'

'I doubt as good as yours.'

I smirked as we dumped the chairs, then headed back outside. 'Why are you here so bright and early?'

'Couldn't sleep,' she said, sliding a load of paper plates into a recycling box.

'Why?' I asked, taking a moment to really look at her, and finding her features drawn, deep worry lines creasing the corners of her eyes.

'Oh, I don't know.' But she chewed on her bottom lip, looking like she might say more. 'Just—'

'Move!' called a voice behind us, and two veterans almost barreled into us as they carried an enormous speaker towards the storage room inside.

'Shit!' I said, pulling Belle out of the way. 'Careful!'

They ignored me, then two more came through with a second, and by the time they'd gone, the moment had passed, and Belle had moved away. *Damn.*

Livia appeared at my elbow and nudged me with her arm. 'Fun night?' she asked, in an exact replica of Belle's question from barely two minutes before.

'Yes, thank you. I slept like a baby.'

'I bet you did ...' Livia waggled her eyebrows. 'But what was with that novice trying to pry Andrew from your grabby little hands?'

'It was bad,' Belle agreed, 'and she can't even blame peak fertility.'

'Huh?' Livia and I said together, spinning to face her.

Belle shrugged. 'I heard her talking in the locker room the other day. She's on the pill. Scrambles your hormones so you barely even want to have sex.'

'Oh, right ...'

Belle had told our crew of this magic several years ago, and most of us had ditched the pill in favor of a coil. I'd been skeptical, but she was right. Of course she was right. It was Belle, and science. I'd learned to never doubt her.

Not a quarter of an hour later, the place was almost spotless, proving the adage that many hands make light work, and although the boats were still on the trailers and the lights were still up, it was good enough that when Andrew came up behind me, snagged my hand, and pulled me away, I didn't even pretend to put up a fight.

Belle and Livia shared meaningful looks, then called something after us, but I didn't hear their words, too pre-occupied by Andrew.

'We're going to mine,' he said, bundling me into his truck.

'We are?'

'The whole club will go to your café, and I don't want to share you.'

'They will?'

'They're hungover, of course they will.'

'And what if I want breakfast?' I said with a mock pout.

'I have eggs. I'll cook.'

I melted, and he kissed me, then pulled away and shut the door, and suddenly I was alone, the silence too loud. Was this really happening? Truly? The world inside my head became a haze and I couldn't focus on anything. Snippets of sounds and color and motion registered, but the swell in my chest kept taking over, expanding up my spinal cord and short circuiting my brain until I could sense nothing but extreme elation and a smattering of nerves.

Andrew yanked open his door and jumped in, and I regained some ability to function, but then the swell surged again, and somehow we were halfway to his apartment and I couldn't breathe, didn't know what to do or say or think.

And then we were pulling into his underground parking garage, and he held out his hand and led me to the elevator.

And then we were in his apartment, and he was wrapped around me, telling me how long he'd wanted me, and we were kissing and gasping, our hands exploring every inch they could reach. I pulled Andrew's polo shirt over his head, revealing the most perfect expanse of tanned skin and sculpted abs, and as he pushed me backwards into his bedroom, the divine smell of him wrapped around me like a blanket, causing my every nerve and sense to come alive, what had been pastel suddenly technicolor.

'I can't believe this is happening,' I breathed, my eyes roaming over his broad, muscular physique, tousled hair, and kiss-swollen lips.

'Believe it, Miri,' he said, then turned me in his arms so we both faced the wall of mirrors and ran his nose up and down my neck. 'It's real.'

My eyes fluttered closed as he kissed and nibbled and sucked, and my hand snaked into his hair, arching so my breasts thrust forward into his palm.

I opened my eyes to find an intense, dark look on Andrew's face, and he dropped a hand to my leg, playing with the hem of my dress, then sliding the fabric up my thighs, caressing my skin as he went. He stopped only when the stretchy fabric was rucked up around my hips, then slid a finger down the crease at the edge of my underwear and drew circles on the sensitive skin of my inner thigh. I moved my legs apart, giving him better access, and willed him higher.

It was as though I'd said the words out loud because his fingers edged upwards, and I tipped my head back against his shoulder, using his neck for purchase. 'Higher,' I breathed, needy and impatient. He huffed a laugh into my neck, but obeyed, and my eyes rolled back in my head as he reached the apex of my thighs, pushing aside the fabric of my underwear and skirting me with a light touch.

'Andrew,' I moaned, pressing my hips back into him.

He nipped my ear. 'Watch,' he murmured, and I did as he bade, opening my eyes to find him watching me, too.

Our eyes met in the glass, and I whimpered as he stroked me. It felt illicit, like we were watching someone else, and I squirmed against him, already so close to the brink.

I pulled his lips back to my neck, and he moved his other hand to my breast, palming me through my clothes. My bra was thin and lacy, and it rasped against my hard nipples as Andrew squeezed and massaged.

'Oh my God,' I breathed. 'Yes ...'

My moans became louder, the movements of my hips against his hand more frantic. 'You're so fucking sexy,' he whispered, his eyes back on mine in the glass as he curled a single finger inside me and stroked. I cried out as my body convulsed, my legs buckling as the most intense pleasure I'd ever experienced pulsed through me.

He held me through it, still stroking, wringing out every last bit of pleasure and whispering how beautiful I was, how he was so glad I was finally his, and when I'd recovered enough to open my eyes, I found him still watching me in the mirror, his features stormy and seductive.

I turned in his arms and smiled up at him, taller than usual in my platform shoes.

'You're so perfect,' he said, stroking back my hair.

I shook my head. 'No one's perfect.'

'You are,' he murmured, then kissed me slowly, reverently, until I was greedy for so much more.

'I want you inside me,' I breathed, and after the briefest of moments, where his jaw flexed, and he looked at me with a nipple-tightening expression I'd never seen on him before, he pushed the dress straps off my shoulders and tugged at the fabric until it dropped to the floor, lying in a sorry roll of elasticated material around my shoes.

He looked down at my breasts, my nipples visible through the lace of my bra, then ducked his head and sucked me through the fabric, his mouth hot and wet and demanding. I arched and held his head, gasping as he nipped me, then stepped forward so my legs were on either side of his muscular thigh and rubbed myself against him. His hand wrapped around me, supporting me as I moved my hips and squeezed my legs together, and I moaned, impatient for so much more, knowing nothing would be as good as the hard, enticing bulge in his jeans.

I moved back and my hands flew to his fly, making quick work of the fastening, then yanking the fabric apart. I slid my hand inside his briefs, and he hissed a sharp exhale, then groaned as I ran my hand up and down. I looked up into his eyes as I did it again, then pushed both his jeans and briefs down to his ankles, dropping to my knees before him and tapping on his feet until he helped me take them off.

I sat back on my heels and looked up at him, and his eyes turned feral. I ran my hands up the backs of his calves as I went up on my knees, and he slid a hand into my hair, then turned to look at us in the mirror. I took his shaft in my hand, angling my head to watch as I ran his tip down my cheek.

'Fuck, Miri,' he breathed, and I looked into his eyes as I licked the tip, slowly lapping at the underside. 'Jesus.'

I sucked lightly, then took him deep enough to hit the back of my throat. He made unintelligible noises, then swore, then fisted his hand in my hair and gently moved his hips in time with my mouth. And then he pulled me off him and dropped to his knees, kissing me so our tongues mated in deep, rhythmic pulses as he guided me onto his lap.

I climbed onto him without breaking our connection, pushed my flimsy underwear aside, and sank onto his length, using his neck for purchase as I moved, gasping into his mouth at the delicious stretch.

'Like this?' I said, moving slowly up and down.

He groaned. 'Yeah, like that, Miri. Fuck ... yes.'

I moaned into his neck as I worked my hips, spreading my legs wide as he grabbed my ass and urged me faster.

'You feel so fucking amazing ...' he groaned.

I ground harder against him, rocking my pelvis against his in little pulsing movements, tension building tighter inside me with each stroke. 'Yes,' I breathed, biting his ear. 'I'm so close, I'm ... Andrew ...'

'Me too, fuck ... yes ...' And then he froze.

'Don't stop! Andrew!' I desperately tried to keep moving, but he held me still.

'Miri, are you on birth control? We haven't ...'

Fuck. I lifted myself off him. Never in my life had I forgotten to have that conversation. I stood, my mind reeling, even if my body screamed at me to sit back down and finish the job. 'I have a coil,' I said. 'I'm clean. I ...' What the fuck had I been thinking?

Andrew grabbed hold of my thighs to stop my retreat. 'I'm sorry,' he said. 'I'm clean, but I shouldn't have—'

'It's okay,' I said quickly, the shock abating a little.

He got to his feet and wrapped his arms around me. 'I'm sorry. We don't have to do this. I can make breakfast. We can wait.'

I leaned into him. 'No, I ...' I needed his mouth on mine, to feel the reassurance of his touch, so I pulled him down to me and our lips fused in a tender yet searing kiss that banished any thoughts of stopping. 'I need you back inside me.'

He hesitated. 'Miri ...'

I ran my hands over his sinfully hot body, then took his cock in my hand.

'We don't have to,' he said in a strained voice, like he barely had himself under control.

But I didn't want him under control. 'Inside me,' I repeated, squeezing.

'Miri ...'

'I want to, Andrew.'

'I have condoms.'

I shook my head. 'I trust you.'

'And I trust you,' he said, looking down into my eyes, 'but—'

'It won't feel the same.'

He closed his eyes and pressed his forehead against mine.

'I want you like just now. Nothing else will do.' I pushed him backwards until his legs hit the bed, and then he sat, watching me with dark eyes as I stood before him in my underwear.

Intensity crashed back over us, and I ran my hands over his chest and across his shoulders, not able to get enough of him to satisfy my fingers. He pulled down my underwear, kissing my hip bone as he leaned forward.

'You smell so fucking good,' he said, pressing his face into my ribs as I straddled him.

'You too,' I moaned, sinking onto him once more.

He grunted as I took him all the way inside me.

'And you feel—' I rolled my hips and pulled my shoulders back.

'Fuck.' He discarded my bra, then palmed my breasts, sucking a nipple into his mouth, and I stilled for a moment, my insides pulsing around him as I savored the slide of his tongue against my sensitive skin.

I rocked, and he released my breast with a gasp, his hands flying to my hips, fingers digging into my ass.

'Fuck,' he breathed as I kept rocking.

'You said that already,' I teased, pulling our bodies flush and wrapping my arms around his neck, already close to the brink.

I made a series of garbled noises as I moved my hips, meeting his thrusts as best I could but fast losing the ability to do anything at all. And then he slid his fingers between us, and as soon as he touched me, I exploded around him, whimpering as deep, shuddering pulses of pleasure wracked my body.

It went on and on, and then Andrew stood, lifting me as though I weighed nothing at all and lying me on the bed, spooning me, an arm over my hips as he pushed back inside, sending a fresh wave of delicious aftershocks skittering through me. He slid his fingers down across my belly, then gently caressed my swollen flesh, and I bucked, an unintelligible sound spilling from my lips as the pleasure intensified.

'You're so perfect,' Andrew whispered, and this time, I didn't bother to contradict him. 'You're mine.'

'Yes,' I moaned, both on account of his territorial words and the way his fingers were still playing me like an instrument. 'Mmm, yes. Don't stop.' I lost track of everything as he kept me in that heightened state of pleasure, kissing my skin and playing with my breast until eventually he pinched my nipple and bit my neck, and a fresh wave of pleasure radiated out from his touch. He thrust a few final times, grunting a series of words I couldn't make out, and then we collapsed together, languid and happy and spent.

Snuggling with Andrew on his sofa, basking in the late morning light, having just eaten a bacon and egg sandwich made for me by him, while wearing a robe that smelled of his dark, sweet scent, will forever be my most perfect way to spend a Sunday. Even better if you throw in nuzzling, which Andrew very much was.

'You're so beautiful,' he murmured, burying his face in my neck. 'You smell like summer.'

I slid my hand into his hair and sighed as he sucked my skin, then moaned softly as he pushed my legs apart and settled between my thighs.

I leaned my head back and let my eyelids fall closed, my body pliant, happy to be at his mercy, to let him lavish attention on me like this forevermore. But then he stopped, and some of his weight lifted, and I opened my eyes to find him looking down at me as though I was a feast he was preparing to devour.

'You're so fucking hot,' he groaned, tracing his finger down the v of my robe, which had fallen open enough to reveal most of my breasts, his light touch making me shiver with anticipation.

I closed my eyes again and sank into the sensation, his fingers ghosting across my nipple, making me moan and tip my hips. He lifted his hand. 'More,' I whispered, wanting it again, harder, but he teased me with another featherlight caress. I arched my back, trying to press into his touch, but he removed his hand, then flicked me gently, making my hips lift and my eyes roll back in my head.

He pulled apart my robe and traced the ridges of my ribs in firm strokes that sent sensation skittering to my core, then cupped both sides, just under my breasts, applying pressure with his big, powerful hands, while his thumbs swiped back and forth.

He slid his hands down across my abdomen until his palms pressed gently into the base of my belly, and I moaned as my body turned liquid. Then his cock was nudging at my entrance, and his thumbs were pressing ever lower, making me mewl like a happy kitten as they reached my core.

I bucked my hips, and he lowered himself over me, one arm supporting his weight while a hand remained between us, pushing me apart so he could slide inside.

I made a garbled, 'Mmmm,' noise and lifted my feet, wrapping my legs around his hips as he moved in and out with long, slow, delicious slides, still caressing me with his thumb. I couldn't believe this was finally happening, or that we could have been doing this all along. So much wasted time ...

He stilled. 'You okay, sweetheart?' he asked, pulling me back to him.

'Ye-ss,' I moaned, as he rolled his hips. He smirked, then did it again, and I turned to putty in his hands, dropping my feet to the cushions and letting my knees fall open, and he kissed me as he moved, so deep and primal that my body became nothing but a ball of pleasurable sensation, winding tighter with each drive of his hips.

His movements grew steadily faster, more urgent, harder, and I made whimpering, gasping, moaning noises that I couldn't quite believe were coming from my lips. 'Let go, M,' he murmured, something uncontrolled and wild in his tone that snapped the winding thread inside me, and we came together on one last shuddering thrust.

Not too long later, we swung by my apartment and grabbed my running gear because we both needed to exercise off the low-level hangovers that had kicked in just before lunchtime. After considerably more kissing, we finally made it out, careful to avoid the members of the rowing club still downstairs in my café, eating off their own hangovers.

We headed up the river, and the buildings soon fell away, replaced by tall reeds and steep riverbanks, willows and herons, the faint smell of cut grass in the air.

We jogged at a leisurely pace, chatting about our families and holiday plans—or lack of them—the party, our friends, and what had gotten into Ottie: *who knew*, and Hazel: *Noah?*

We paused when we came to a road crossing the river, drinking some water from the backpack Andrew had filled with lunch and a picnic blanket, but the smell of fried meat and onions had me looking longingly over the bridge, to where a food truck was parked up on the edge of a parking lot. My stomach gurgled and I turned puppy dog eyes on Andrew.

'Oh no,' he said, catching my drift. 'No.'

'Just look at it,' I moaned like a candy-starved kid in a sweet shop.

'No, Miri ...' He looked horrified that I would even suggest such a thing. 'It's—'

'Delicious,' I finished for him.

'Not okay two weeks before Nationals.'

'Pleeeeeease,' I begged, only half-joking. When had I last had a kebab? And one little nutritional slip wouldn't hurt, especially to cure a hangover. It was practically medicinal.

'You'll get food poisoning.'

'I will not!'

'The bad kind that lives inside of you for years.'

He ushered me across the road and down a tiny path on the other side. 'But Andrew ...' I whined.

'We just need to get out of smelling distance,' he said, sliding his fingers through mine. 'Then you'll see reason.'

We followed the footpath signs to where a kissing gate barred our way into a field. 'Urgh, you're such—' He pressed me up against the wood and, well, kissed me.

'I'm such ...?' He asked between presses of his lips.

I shrugged because I couldn't remember what I'd planned to accuse him of. 'Such.' *Kiss.* 'A good.' *Kiss.* 'Kisser?'

He huffed a laugh and pulled away, sliding his hand back into mine, then awkwardly pulling me through the swinging gate, refusing to release me.

'But what about the kebab?' I asked, looking longingly over my shoulder.

'You can have all the kebabs your heart desires after Nationals. Just a few more weeks ...'

'But I'm probably not even going, anyway, and it won't hurt.'

He pulled me back into a jog, and we ran to the other side of the field, to where a smaller stream fed into the river, creating a small, sandy beach on our side that was perfect for paddling.

I raced the last bit, squealing with delight. 'I haven't been here in years! I'd almost forgotten it existed.'

'I used to bring my sister here. Before ... well ...' He trailed off, busying himself with spreading out the picnic blanket.

'Before what?' I asked, kicking off my shoes and socks and lying on the blanket, accepting my pot of pasta salad with a slightly pouty smile.

He sat beside me, not meeting my eyes as he said, 'She was a teenager. There was this ... boy. It didn't end well.'

The topic seemed painful, so I didn't push, instead filling my mouth with pasta and letting the rushing of the water fill the silence.

To my surprise, he continued, and I listened intently as I chewed. 'It was hard for Beth when my dad died. Hard for us all, of course, but ...' He exhaled heavily. 'It was somehow different for her. She was so young and ...' He shook his head. 'Well, you know what it's like.'

I gave a small nod. 'Everyone's experience is different,' I said quietly. My dad died when I was in my twenties, but we'd never been all that close. 'And my coach was more like a father to me. At least until ...'

'He was an arsehole,' Andrew said venomously.

'Not to start—'

'He was an arsehole. End of story.'

I frowned. 'Only at the end. Before that, he was strict, yes, but that made me disciplined ... kept me humble.'

'He undermined you,' Andrew spat, then closed his eyes and exhaled a long breath. 'Sorry, I ...' When he looked at me again, his eyes were pained. 'I didn't realize how deeply he'd buried his poison, but when you said you were nothing special, that anyone could do what you've done ...' He clenched his fists. 'Even if he hadn't lied about—' He stopped himself. 'It makes me want to punch the motherfucker.'

I sat up, scooting close and putting my hand on his arm. 'I choose to remember the good bits. When he was doing his job, trying to get the best out of me.'

He shook his head again. 'He should have been fighting for you, building you up, not tearing you down. And thank fuck he got found out when he did.'

'But ...' I stilled as Andrew's words sank in. I'd never thought of it that way.

'He was a fucking liar, Miri.'

'I know that!' It was why he'd been kicked out of the club. Was probably the reason I found it hard to trust people in general, keeping everyone a little at arm's length.

Andrew slid his hand to my neck and looked deep into my eyes. 'You're fucking amazing, Miri, and I want to rip his head off for ever making you think otherwise.'

'Not that amazing,' I quipped, averting my gaze, the intensity of his deep green eyes too much. 'Diminishing in my old age, in fact ... I probably won't even make it to Nationals!' I tried to keep my words light, to make it sound like I didn't care.

'They'd be idiots not to take you.'

I scoffed. 'I've hardly been in the boat in weeks. They most likely won't.'

'I would.'

I shook my head. 'Well, you will be in the selection meeting, so ...'

'I know,' he said, then pushed me back and crawled over me, my head resting on the blanket as I looked up at him on hands and knees above me, 'and I'll always fight for you.'

My stomach clenched, my heartrate rocketing. 'Andrew, you can't. You're Men's Captain! You have to be fair.'

He tipped his head indulgently. 'And I will be. You're the best we have.'

Tears filled my eyes. I'd never had anyone to fight for me. My parents had been too preoccupied by fighting with each other. Then Dad died and all Mum cared about was me becoming an Olympian, then telling everyone what a disappointment it was that I hadn't made it. I didn't have any siblings, and although my aunt, Bea, had been a lifeline in some ways, there had always been limits to her love.

Andrew cupped my face, stroking my cheek as he looked from one of my eyes to the other. 'You're family, M, and there's nothing more important to me.'

My heart clenched so hard I thought it might have stopped working, my throat closing over so all I could do was choke on my tears. We'd only just got together, and it was all too much, too intense, too perfect. Why me? Why now, after so so long? 'But you hide them,' I said, 'your family.'

The words were as shocking to me as they seemed to be to him because he flinched, then moved off me, lying by my side and taking a long moment before saying slowly, 'I don't hide them. I just prefer to keep my private life to myself.'

'Why?' I breathed, knowing I probably shouldn't, that I should preserve the flawless day for as long as I could, but some self-destructive part of me pushed me on.

His shoulders sagged. 'It's easier that way.'

'Why?' I pressed.

He broke eye contact and turned his head away, and panic hit like a bolt of lightning in my chest. I pushed up onto an arm. 'I'm sorry, Andrew. I didn't mean ... I just ... I'm really bad at this ... at ... well ... relationships.'

The melancholy slid half off his shoulders as he returned his gaze to me, a tentative smile on his lips. 'Relationships?'

Oh, shit. My cheeks heated because we hadn't had that conversation. He'd called me *his*, the memory sending a fresh bout of tightness through my chest, but we hadn't labeled anything ... Then again, he had just called me family, although he hadn't specified if he meant the house-and-two-kids kind.

He was still watching me closely, seeming to expect an answer. 'Is that what you want, Miri?'

I couldn't look at him. Didn't he want that? 'Well ... um ...' I swallowed hard, willing my mind to find words. I should just tell him. Be honest ...

'Because I already told Beth you're my girlfriend.'

My eyes flew wide and I swiped him. 'Andrew!'

He caught my hand. 'And she told Dox and my mother, and they want you to come over for dinner so they can dote on you and tell you embarrassing stories about me and—'

I kissed him, and he made a rumbling growling noise in his chest that sent desire skittering through my blood. I jumped up and raced for the water. 'Come on!' I called, needing to move, my heart threatening to burst with joy. He launched to his feet, and I shrieked with glee as he chased me.

Chapter 20

The next few days passed in a blur of scrumptiousness. Every day we woke up together, trained and showered together, and then we had breakfast in my café together, where I finally managed to stop him from paying, but only because I gave strict instructions to the staff not to take his money, much to his chagrin.

'I'll just buy you a ridiculously expensive present,' he said as he kissed me goodbye, 'and buy gift baskets for my favorite clients in your shop, and hold all future work parties in your bar ...'

'Andrew, no,' I said in the sternest voice I could manage, which wasn't overly stern, seeing as how he was crowding me against his truck, my back pressed to the cold metal as he lavished me with love.

It was so good between us, our lives were like a honeymoon. Each morning after he left, I daydreamed about him until lunch, at which point he would return, we'd put our lunchbreaks to good use in my apartment, and then we'd while away the evenings after training, chatting or reading or working side by side until we fell into bed and wrapped ourselves up in each other's arms again.

It was too good to be true, and a little voice inside my head kept telling me to enjoy it, to make the most of it because, how could anything so perfect possibly last?

Thursday evening rolled around at breakneck speed, and I was about to head upstairs for a quick five-minute break when my phone pinged with a text.

Seb 18:07: Forgot to ask ... can we borrow a big pot tonight? And can u drop to club? Livia n me cooking. No time to swing by. Don't tell her I forgot to ask! [Grateful hands emoji]

I sent off a quick reply, reassuring Seb that I'd drop one to the club, and that I wouldn't tell Livia about his lapse, then grabbed a pot from the kitchen and hurried it over, telling my staff I'd be back as soon as I could. The bar was already rammed given the balmy weather, which meant no club night for me.

I raced across the piazza and through the gate, but paused by the wide open doors to the clubhouse, where Livia's raised voice stopped me in my tracks. 'She hasn't been in the boat!'

'Yes,' Cassandra—our coach—calmly replied, 'but her ergo scores are—'

'Ergo scores don't always float. You know that!' Livia insisted. 'And the boat's been going well. We're really gelling.'

My stomach dropped as I realized they were talking abut me. Crew selection for Nationals. *Shit.* I shouldn't be eavesdropping. This was bad. I would leave the pot somewhere else and—

'Andrew?' said Cassandra.

Livia tsked.

A long pause filled the air, and I wondered if I'd some-how missed his answer. 'It's not my decision,' he eventual-ly said in his deep, rumbling voice, and my heart stuttered as I waited for him to go on. For a *but*. For anything!

'Very well,' Cassandra concluded in a crisp, clipped tone. 'Miri will sit this one out.'

Fuck.

I whirled around, my head racing, stomach churning. I wasn't going to Nationals ... For the first time in ... *Fuck!* And Andrew hadn't said anything! Hadn't even—

'I tried to warn you,' said a quiet voice. I jumped, then found Theo watching smugly from the entrance to the locker rooms behind me. 'But no one ever listens to me.'

'What do you ... What?' I whispered, not wanting the group inside to hear. I frowned, trying to decipher his words amid my turmoil.

'Andrew!' said Theo. 'I told you he's a liar, and now he's stabbed you in the back just like he did to me.'

I shook my head a little. 'What the fuck are you talking about?'

Theo took a step forwards, a sly smile on his lips. 'He convinced you that you were important to him, didn't he? But when push came to shove, what did he do? Did he stand up for you? Did he take your side?'

My head spun. 'What?'

'He did the same thing to me.' He shrugged. 'It's his MO, I guess. Convinces you that you matter, makes you feel important, and then ...' He held up his hand and gestured in the direction of the open doors.

'But ...'

'At least he didn't put a gag order on you like he did to me. The fucker paid me off, too. Used my situation against me. I tried to warn you, but ...' He held up both hands in an almost comical expression. 'No one ever listens to me.'

I felt sick. What was even happening? Was this even real? But the rushing and churning and blackness at the edges of my vision seemed real enough.

'He's a liar,' said Theo. 'And not the first time you've fallen for one of those if rumors are to be believed. Did you really shag him, by the way? He was your coach, wasn't he? Old enough to be your fath—'

It was very hard to breathe, and I'd bent forward to counteract the wooziness threatening to floor me, which was why it took me a moment to realize that Andrew had appeared seemingly from nowhere, slammed Theo against the wall, released him, and was now blocking his exit.

'You bastard. Move!' Theo ground out, trying to shove Andrew out of his way, but his attempts were ineffectual.

'Is it true he used to work for you?' I asked, my words a whisper.

Andrew's head whipped around to look at me, his eyes wide. 'Who told you that?'

'I did,' Theo said proudly, pulling Andrew's attention back to him.

'You signed a contract,' Andrew spat.

'Then it's true?' I breathed. 'You put a gag order on him?'

Andrew paled. 'I can explain.'

Theo laughed and folded his arms as though knowing something I didn't. 'This should be good,' he said haughtily.

'Go fuck yourself,' Andrew bit out.

'I'd rather fuck your mum ... Or maybe your sister ...'

Andrew shoved him against the wall again, and this time held him there, one hand on his throat.

Theo laughed. 'Go on, Andrew,' he choked, 'tell her the truth.' Andrew said nothing, and Theo flicked his eyes to me. 'You think you know a guy ...'

'Andrew?' I said, my voice shrill.

Andrew slammed Theo against the wall one more time, then grabbed his shirt and hurled him towards the gate. Theo stumbled but stayed on his feet. 'Get the fuck out of here,' Andrew growled.

Theo laughed as he sauntered through the gate, and I couldn't make sense of any of it.

'*Shit! Miri!* Are you okay?' Livia's hands were suddenly pulling me upright, then she was hugging me, while Cassandra watched on from the doorway, stoically flicking her eyes from Andrew to me and back again, assessing us with clinical features.

'I'm fine.' I said mechanically, my eyes on Andrew, who was watching me with a pained expression. 'I just ... I need to ...' My phone vibrated, and I knew it would be the bar. They were short-staffed. Needed me. I didn't have time to deal with this right now. 'I ... um ... I have to go.'

I half-yanked myself from Livia's grasp and turned to leave.

'Miri, wait, I can explain.' Andrew stepped closer, and I looked at him but didn't really see him, my mind and body numb. 'Please.'

I shook my head, trying to clear the fog, but it wouldn't budge. *Did you really shag him?* Theo's hateful words filled my mind, playing over and over. How did he even know? Theo hadn't been at the club for long, only two or three years, and I'd thought everyone had forgotten, that they'd finally moved on. There hadn't been one single joke when I'd started dating Theo or Andrew, but it would never truly be over, would it? It would always be there, hanging over me.

'Just let me explain, please ...' said Andrew, close enough to touch me. But he didn't.

'What happened with Theo?' I asked, vaguely aware of Cassandra and Livia still watching from the doorway. 'At your work?'

Andrew closed his eyes and swallowed hard, and when he looked at me again, I'd never seen regret quite like it. 'I can't tell you,' he said quietly. 'I'm not allowed to tell you.'

Tears stung my eyes as Cassandra and Livia headed back inside, leaving us to fight alone.

Andrew ran a hand through his hair. 'I wish Theo would just get the fuck out of my life ... Leave me and my family alone.'

'But you row in the same crew! You can't hate him that much.'

'He makes the boat go faster. I'm the men's captain. What would you have me do? Put my personal preferences above the wellbeing of the club?'

'You should have told me you used to work together. Was that what this whole thing between us was about? Getting back at Theo?'

He reared back as though I'd punched him. 'No! Of course not. Miri ... I couldn't tell you. I can't ... Just ... Come with me, I'll explain everything. I'll find a way to—'

'They need me at the bar.'

He dipped his head, the gesture forlorn. 'Then I'll come over later?'

'I don't think that's a good idea.'

'I heard what Theo said,' Andrew said carefully, 'about your coach. I ... Are you okay?'

Maybe I'd been right all along. Dating anyone at the club would always dredge up the past, what had happened, the lies my coach had told about me and him. The things we'd supposedly done ... Just the thought of it made me want to be sick. 'I'm fine.'

'I don't want you to be alone. Let me come over.'

I shook my head. 'In relationships, you're supposed to tell each other everything, aren't you?'

'Miri ...' He reached for me, but I pulled away.

'I can't do this. The lying. I can't be with someone who isn't honest, who hides things.'

He watched me with desolation in his eyes as tears flooded down my cheeks. He swayed towards me, looking like he might reach for me again, so I inhaled a shuddery breath and steeled myself. 'I have to go.'

He froze, a deep frown on his forehead, his body rigid. But somehow as I made to leave, I passed close enough that my hand brushed against his, and then my forehead pressed to his chest, and then my lips found his, and we were kissing through my sobs.

'I'm not lying, Miri,' he breathed into my ear. 'I'll fix this. I promise.'

That time when I pulled away, I made sure to put distance between us, then refused to look at him as I wiped away my tears and went to work.

Chapter 21

I worked every shift available over the next few days, ignoring anything on my phone but calls from suppliers and messages from my staff. I silenced the notifications from everyone at the club and refused to look at how many new messages had been added to the group chats every day.

I had too much to process, didn't know what I thought about it all, and was still in shock from Theo's words. *Did you really shag him?*

Each night I dreamt about Theo and my coach and Andrew, their faces swimming together and becoming nightmares. Untrustworthy, all of them. I'd thought it was finally behind me, the stuff with my coach, how he'd made everyone believe we were sleeping together to bolster his own ego. None of this would have happened if I'd just stuck to my own simple rule and not dated anyone at the club.

And on top of the lies and dredging up my past, it hurt that I hadn't been selected for Nationals. I knew it was unreasonable and childish, but I'd never not made it. I was the best in the club, and even if my rational mind knew they'd made the right choice, my heart cracked in two every time I remembered Andrew's words. *It's not my decision.*

That's all he'd said. He'd told me he would fight for me, but he hadn't! He hadn't even tried.

But even knowing that, knowing he was a liar, I still wanted him, and that hurt even more, knowing I could never have him again, that I would never feel his strong, protective arms around me. I loved him. Had loved him forever but had called it friendship and put it in a safe little box to protect myself. Turns out I'd been right to. I'd watched him date other people, and that had been unpleasant, but he'd always been there, buying me drinks, squeezing my arm, watching out for me, and somehow that had been enough. But now I knew what it was like to truly have him and I wasn't sure I'd ever recover from the loss.

What was it about me that attracted liars and cheats? Why was it so hard to find a nice guy? How would I ever find anyone who made me feel even a fraction of what I felt for Andrew? But I couldn't be with someone I didn't trust, so even if I had to endure the most cavernous, grinding heartache, I would do it because in the long run it was the right decision, and I was a rower, I knew how to dig deep, to take the pain, to ignore my body when it told me it could take no more.

But he hadn't even called …

Fresh tears poured down my face. It was surprising I even had tears left to cry, my eyes constantly red and puffy, and my sleep-deprived, heart-broken brain supplied a torturous, low-level thumping beat everywhere I went, a dire, relentless soundtrack to my life.

The piercing trill of my doorbell sounded all around me, but I ignored it; I couldn't face a delivery person in this state. Unfortunately, it wasn't a delivery person, and the bell came again and again, followed by a determined rap on my door, followed by Livia's voice through the letterbox.

'Miri! I know you're in there!' *Bang. Bang. Bang. Trrrr-riiiiiilllllll.* 'Miri! We're worried about you!'

I was surprised my crew hadn't ambushed me at the bar or café already, to be honest. I'd been avoiding the shop any time Ottie was on shift, and their restraint was more than I'd thought them capable of.

'MIRI! I'm not going away until you answer this door!' She pressed the bell for what must have been thirty whole seconds before I finally gave in, peeling myself off the sofa and wiping my eyes.

I pulled the door open, unconcerned about my appearance, and Livia faltered, then threw her arms around me. 'You look God-awful!' she said, showing no signs of letting me go. 'We've been so worried about you. And Andrew, for that matter. He looks like shit, too.'

My heart squeezed to the point of pain, and I pulled myself out of her grip. 'Why are you here?' I snapped, because if Livia thought she was on some kind of mission to get me and Andrew back together—

Livia turned uncharacteristically sheepish, looking down at her hands. 'I just wanted to say I'm sorry, really.' She stepped inside and shut the door, and I retreated to the sofa. 'I don't know how much of the selection meeting you heard, but—'

'Enough to know you didn't want me in the crew, and that Andrew couldn't care less,' I blurted, and it felt good to finally get it out.

'Oh. Right ...' said Livia, stopping a few paces from the sofa and narrowing her eyes as though reassessing what to say next. 'Well, that's not quite what happened.'

I scowled, and she held up placating hands. 'You're right about me. I argued not to have you in the boat, and I'm sorry, it sucks, but I stand by that decision.'

I waved my hand impatiently. I didn't need a reminder of how I wasn't good enough, even though I knew she was only doing what was best for the crew.

'But Andrew ... He argued that you should be in the boat.'

I pinned her with a glare. 'I *heard* him say it wasn't his decision!'

'Yes,' she agreed, her tone tight, 'but before that, we had a long conversation, and all through it he argued that you should be in the crew. He said if it were his decision, it would be an easy choice. So it came down to Cassandra in the end. Like Andrew said, it was her decision to make.'

I sat back and hugged a cushion. 'Oh.' *Ohhhhh. He fought for me? He didn't lie! Well, maybe not about that, but he lied about other things.*

'And I've never seen Andrew so animated about crew selection. I mean, I know I haven't been Women's Captain long, but I don't think I've ever seen him so animated about anything, to be honest. He nearly swayed Cassandra, too.'

My stomach dropped. 'Oh,' I said again, not at my most articulate, but feeling lighter, some of the heartache having lifted.

'If you ask me, his feelings for you were clouding his judgement, but ...' Livia shrugged exaggeratedly, looking at me with a dry smile.

I hurled my cushion at her, and she squealed and threw herself aside, avoiding the projectile by a hair.

'That was mean.'

'Funny though ...' she said through a laugh. She scooped up the cushion, then dropped down onto the other side of my L-shaped sofa. 'Look, I know it's none of my business, but he really cares about you. And you've seemed so happy since you *finally* got together ...'

'He lied to me,' I said, mostly out of irritation.

'About what?'

'Did you know Theo used to work for Andrew?'

'As a data scientist?' she said slowly, her forehead pinched.

I shrugged, realizing I had no idea. 'I don't know.'

'But—'

'Look, the details don't matter. What matters is that he lied, just like my coach ...' I trailed off as tears threatened.

Livia stared at me for a long moment, and I turned my gaze away, not able to stand her pity.

'Somehow Theo knew ...' I said, my voice almost cracking on the words. 'He asked me if ...' I bit the insides of my lips as silent tears rolled down my face, 'if the lies my coach told were true.'

'Oh ... Miri,' Livia shifted closer and pulled me into a hug. 'I'm so sorry.'

'Does everyone still talk about it behind my back?' I asked through a sob.

She pulled away, appalled. 'No! Never! I don't think Ottie even knows.'

'Then how? How did Theo find out?'

Livia shrugged. 'It could have been anyone who was around back then, but my money would be on the veterans. They sit around and natter like a bunch of old biddies, drinking pints and reminiscing about the good old days. Some of them like Theo ... I think they're in awe of his womanizing ways.'

I closed my eyes and shook my head. 'But now he knows, everyone will talk about it again. Everyone will look at me and whisper and—'

'They won't.'

'You can't know that.'

'Hardly anyone at the club now even knows your old coach existed. And if any of us hear anything, we'll shut it down. And if anyone hears Theo talking about it, Andrew will legit punch him in the face. You should have seen the look Andrew gave him earlier just for walking into his eyeline. Andrew's fucking scary when he wants to be.'

More tears gushed from my eyes. 'But they're rowing together at Nationals!'

Livia laughed. 'Not any longer they're not. Andrew told Cassandra it was him or Theo, and of course she chose him.'

'Oh ...'

'Right?'

'Is everyone gossiping about why they're fighting?'

'Nope, no one knows. Well, no one aside from me and Seb. But we only gossip together. Out of earshot. And we only say how great it is that Theo's finally got what was coming to him. And most of the other women hate Theo, seeing as he's slept with half of them and then dumped them for the next one.'

I laughed through my sob, and Livia squeezed my arm. 'It's not like last time, Miri. Theo's not a pathological liar. He's angry and hurt and lashing out. I don't know why, or what happened between him and Andrew, but he's like a teenager, erratic and emotional. Your coach set up a sophisticated web of lies, and you were in your twenties and had no way to fight back. He was desperate to look like the big man and was losing his power over you and he couldn't handle it. That's not what's going on here.'

I sniffed, then bit my lip.

'My advice would be to talk to Andrew. Let him explain.'

'I tried. He said he can't te-ll me.' My voice broke fully this time.

Livia rubbed my arm. 'That's not good, I agree, but there must be a reason.'

'And what if there's not?'

'Then we cross that bridge when we get to it. But I've never seen anyone look as sad as Andrew does over a breakup. Something else is going on, and you'll never get closure unless you find out what.'

Nationals started today, but I was not there. I was working in the shop, trying not to feel sorry for myself, trying not to think about Andrew. Trying not to think about anything, really. At least the shop had been busy, thank goodness, meaning less time to wallow.

The bell dinked for the gazillionth time, and I looked up, plastering a fixed smile on my face, but when I saw who it was, I froze, forgetting to even say hello.

'Hi, Miri,' Andrew's younger sister, Beth, said quietly, awkwardly.

'Uh ... Hi?'

'Can we talk?' she asked. 'I don't mean to ambush you, but ... well ...'

'Did Andrew send you?' He'd sent me a few messages over the last couple of days, nothing heavy, just checking in to see if I was alright, but I hadn't replied. Instead, I'd stared at the picture of us kissing on my phone and cried myself to sleep because that somehow seemed like a better option than talking to him.

She looked anxious, like maybe I would throw her out. 'I came because there's something I want to tell you. Something I think you should know.'

My heart raced, adrenaline and dread mixing in my stomach. 'About Andrew?'

'No,' Beth said in a whisper, and her eyes kept darting sideways like a skittish horse, as though she might bolt at any moment. 'About, well ...'

'Do you want to sit?' I asked in a soothing tone, coming around the counter and trying to seem approachable.

She shook her head, but my attempts at reassuring her seemed to be working, at least a bit because she inhaled deeply and said, 'It's about Theo.'

I stopped in my tracks.

'Theo and ... me.'

Ohhhh. And even though I didn't say it out loud, my face must have given me away because she gave an embarrassed nod, then looked anywhere but at my face.

'Yeah, exactly,' she said, clasping her hands. 'Theo used to work for Andrew and Dox, and ...' She trailed off and didn't show any sign of continuing.

'You and Theo had a ... relationship?' I prompted, even though I probably shouldn't have. But I couldn't help myself. Theo, and Andrew's twenty-year-old sister?

Her face flushed. 'Well, I'm not sure ...' She pulled her sleeves over her hands and bunched her fingers into fists. 'I don't think you'd you call it that.'

'Youuuu slept together?' I said slowly, lowering my head, trying to show her she would get no judgement from me.

She nodded. 'On Andrew's desk. The night of my eighteenth birthday.'

My eyebrows flew up towards my hairline.

'Turns out he has cameras in his office.'

A startled bark of laughter came from my lips, and I clamped my hand over my mouth, appalled at myself. 'Sorry, I ...'

She gave a half-laugh. 'It's okay. It's bad, I know. But I was eighteen, and Theo's, well ... Theo. He was older than me, and *very* attractive, and he paid me all this attention, and my friends mooned over him any chance they got, and he had this arrogant bad boy thing going on, and a mysterious past and ...' She shrugged. 'Andrew warned me off him. Told me Theo had slept with half the company, but if anything, that just made him *more* attractive.' Her shoulders lifted towards her ears. 'I was an idiot.'

'Hey, we've all been there.'

She eyed me speculatively. 'Yeah, well, Andrew ... Dox messaged me to say something was wrong with him, that I should come home and patch things up between us. She thought it was me being away that was finally getting to him, on top of the acquisition and work, but turns out it wasn't me he was wound up about. It was you.'

I gave a disbelieving exhale, shaking my head. 'I, um ... I'm not ... I ...' I shook my head some more, impersonating one of those irritating nodding dogs. 'No. I ... don't think ...'

She watched me with astute eyes, eyes that reminded me of her brother, and I shrank into myself, not really sure what she was saying, just knowing that it was making me uncomfortable.

'Andrew came to see me last week,' said Beth, folding her arms across her chest. She paused, her face flaming, the words seeming difficult to find. 'When Andrew found out what happened between me and Theo, he sacked Theo for gross misconduct and told me never to see him again. I *hated* him for it. I cried and screamed and generally made a fool of myself. I told Andrew that it was my life, that I could do what I wanted, that Theo liked me ... wanted to date me ...' She gave a bitter laugh. 'I was young and naïve. Theo dropped me like a stone.'

'Sounds about right,' I said, wondering how freaked out I should be that Andrew's little sister and I had Theo in common.

'Theo started boasting, telling people at the company what had happened, but everyone who works at DrewDox loves my brother and sister, and someone told them. They didn't want Theo to have that power over me, so they offered him money in return for his silence.'

'The gag order ...' I said, half to myself.

She nodded. 'Andrew took the whole thing hard. He saw it as his fault because he'd welcomed Theo into the company and felt like he should have sacked him sooner. But Theo's background ... Andrew met Theo at this youth program he was sponsoring? Theo was volunteering too because he wanted to help kids who'd had a rough start like him. They got talking, and Theo's clever, so Andrew offered him a job ... I think Andrew didn't want to abandon him, you know? He felt responsible in some way. I think he still does.'

'That's why he rows with Theo?'

Beth shrugged. 'I don't know. Andrew's always kept his reasons to himself. He keeps most things to himself, actually, and he's got worse since the stuff with Theo. It's like he's gone into hyper-protective mode or something, but he would have told you all of it if he could have. He wanted to tell you himself, but he's bound by HR policy, same as Dox. If they tell anyone, Theo can sue them.'

Fuck.

Beth inhaled a long breath. 'I went travelling, needed to get away, and with time I've realized I should never have done any of it. Maybe I was rebelling, I don't know.'

Silence stretched between us as I let her words settle in. Andrew wasn't being secretive about Theo. He *couldn't* talk about it even if he wanted to. 'I'm sorry,' I said, my voice small as I worked through it all in my head.

She raised one shoulder, dismissing it. 'Andrew asked me to tell you. Begged me, actually. He tried to convince Dox to renegotiate with Theo, to offer to pay him again so Andrew could tell you the truth, but Dox wouldn't let him. So he came to me and asked me to tell you—I'm the only one not bound by some kind of contract. I said *no* to start, but then ... I've never seen Andrew like that—distraught, drawn, and exhausted. He's modest, so maybe you don't know how clever and hardworking he is, but he's won all these awards, and clients are clamoring to work with him, and people are desperate to work *for* him ... to learn from him. He has this vision, and he's just bought this massive company, and he really is a great guy. He cares about people, and especially about you, so much that honestly, it kind of scares me.'

'I ...' I floundered, no idea what to say to any of that.

'It would have been so much easier for him if I'd just told everyone the truth about Theo, but he never asked me to. Not once. Even when Theo joined the rowing club. Even when Theo tried to turn one of Andrew's clients against him. Everywhere Andrew goes, there's Theo, a thorn in his side, and Andrew's always just sucked it up, acting like he doesn't care, all to protect me. Until now. Until *you*.'

I leaned back against the counter and shook my head a little in disbelief. Andrew had been protecting his sister. And he'd offered to fake date me, to what? Save me from myself? 'Or maybe he's finally just had enough and wants to stick it to Theo,' I said weakly.

She narrowed her eyes, giving me an unimpressed look. 'He loves you, Miri. He's never been like this about anyone.'

'He doesn't ... um ...'

She raised an eyebrow. 'Have you seen him? He's a mess. He can't sleep. Dox says he hasn't been turning up to work. He took three days off last week. He's never done that. Ever! He's loved you for years, and he thinks it's over, that you'll never trust him again.'

I scoffed. 'Andrew hasn't loved me for years.' It was impossible. He'd had many other girlfriends, all of them beautiful and successful.

'No? Then why did he name a boat after you?' She crossed her arms as though she'd just pulled a check mate.

'He didn't!' I ran through the names. '*Dr. Dox.*'

'For Dox, obviously,' said Beth. '*Busy Livy* for me—my childhood nickname—and—'

'*Em*,' I said triumphantly. *Take that, Andrew's little sister. The name has nothing to do with me.*

She looked at me as though I was an idiot. 'Exactly. *Em.*'

I frowned. She did know my name, right? 'What do you—'

'And what does *Em* sound like?' she asked, tipping her head to one side.

'I don't know ... Emily?' Or at least, that's what I'd always thought when I saw it.

'It's never struck you that it sounds like the letter *M*? Like M for Miri?'

Oh. 'No,' I blurted, blushing hard.

She raised her eyebrows, a faint smile on her lips.

My head swam as I tried to make sense of it, as I tried to breathe. 'No ... it's not ... that's not ...'

She grinned. 'He loves you, Miri. Always has.'

I hastily wrote a sign saying the shop would be closed for the rest of the day, locked up, and ran for my van. It would take four hours to drive to Nationals, assuming a good run, but I had to go. Had to see Andrew. Had to apologize ... and find out if the boat was really named after me. Surely I hadn't been that blind?

I was lucky with the traffic, and made it in three hours and fifty seven minutes, swinging my van into the campsite we always stayed at and scanning the rows for Andrew's monstrous tent. It took a while because apparently these days, every second self-respecting camper had one at least as big, but eventually I found his and parked up.

I did a quick check of the tents, found no one home, then headed back towards the entrance on foot, my head down as I raced for the loudspeakers in the distance. Even after four hours to think on the drive, I had no clue what to say to him, and my mind focused on the task as I jogged.

Should I just tell him I love him? Maybe not the best opening line. But then again, it was the truth. Should I apologize for ever doubting him? For jumping to conclusions? For—

'Miri?' Hannah's high-pitched voice pierced my thoughts, and I careered to a stop and whipped my head around to see her and the whole men's crew drinking pints under a sun umbrella at a wooden picnic table.

Shit. 'You lost?' I asked, flicking my eyes around the table as I caught my breath. Pete, Seb, and Hannah on one side, and Andrew and Noah on the other.

None of them said anything, all of them looking expectantly at Andrew, and it turned out Beth hadn't been lying. He did look like shit. His jaw covered in stubble, dark circles under his eyes.

'We lost,' he confirmed, then got to his feet. 'I didn't think you were—'

'Can we talk?' I blurted, my eyes flicking sideways to our audience, my face burning.

He hesitated for a split second, and my heart nearly broke, the idea that he would reject me too much to bear. But then he strode to my side, saying quietly, 'The women's race is in an hour, so no one's at the tents, we can talk there.'

I nodded, then turned back the way I'd come, trying not to hear Hannah and Seb's excitable whispers. We walked side by side, but he didn't try to touch me, the air between us taut, the silence heavy.

'I'm sorry about your race,' I said eventually, as we finally entered his tent and could shut out the world.

He shrugged, then motioned to a camping chair, watching me with hawk-like eyes.

I didn't move. Couldn't. And after a long silence, said, 'Beth told me about Theo.'

He nodded. 'I know, she texted.'

'I'm so sorry. I had no idea. I ...'

'Why are you here, Miri?' he asked, taking a step closer, so he was only an arm's length away, so close I could smell his musky male scent.

'I ...' Why was I here, exactly? To apologize, yes, but I'd already done that. I'd probably have to do it a few more times before he forgave me ... if he ever forgave me. Right, yes, that was why I was here. To beg his forgiveness ... Wait, no, that wasn't quite right. I was here to tell him ... to tell him ... to ... *Fuck!* Why was this so hard?

'Miri?' he said gently, stepping even closer, so close I rested my forehead against his chest and breathed him in, my hands on his torso, steadying myself, grounding myself. Something about his presence made me calm, made me feel like wherever he was was exactly where I should be.

He pulled me away and cupped my cheek, then kissed me gently. 'Is this why you're here?' he asked, sounding so hopeful my heart broke.

I nodded, then kissed him again, opening my mouth to him, offering myself to him. The kiss was deep but unhurried, tender, and full of so much more than we could ever convey with words.

'I love you, Miri,' he whispered in my ear. 'I should have told you sooner, should have been honest ...'

'No, I'm sorry. For doubting you, for causing all this mess.'

We kissed again, and I gasped at the rightness of it, the feel of him under my fingers, the relief and safety and joy.

'Beth told me everything. About Theo, about his background ... I just ... I ... I never want to see him again. How can you stand it? Having to be around him every day at the club ... In your crew!'

Andrew held me against him, and I nearly cried, wrapping my arms around him, hugging him tight and closing my eyes. He didn't hate me. He still wanted to kiss me. He—

'I don't think about him at all,' he said, in a voice so benign, I believed him.

I pulled back and searched his deep, green eyes. 'You ... How?'

He smiled down at me and stroked my hair. 'If anything, I feel sorry for him. He's a lost kid from a troubled background who threw away the best opportunity he'll likely ever get when he slept with my sister. He has no qualifications, no friends, no family ... He has potential. I wouldn't have offered him a job if I didn't think so, but that's it. I used to feel sorry for him, but now the only time I give him a second thought is when he's hurting someone I care about. Why would I? I have more than enough to occupy my mind, everything I ever wanted.' He turned a little bashful. 'Or at least maybe now I do.'

'So that's why you wanted to fake date me? Because you thought he would hurt me?'

He stroked a hair behind my ear, and I shivered, gripping him tighter. 'I never wanted to fake date you, Miri. I've wanted to real date you for over a decade. But after what happened with your coach ... And then you said you would never date anyone at the club, and ...'

'I didn't even mean it,' I breathed. 'I was so upset about everything with my coach, and my dad had just died, and I felt so alone. That day, when I said it, I lashed out with the first thing that came into my head.'

'I know,' he said, stroking his thumb across my cheekbone. 'Or at least, I realize that now. Or maybe I did when you started dating Theo.'

I swallowed. 'I'm so sorry. That must have been ...'

He ducked his head and kissed me, then pulled back and captured me in the deep sea green of his gaze. 'I couldn't stand it. I went from never thinking about Theo to thinking about him all the time, obsessing over him, trying to work out how to tell you what an arsehole he was without breaking the stupid fucking HR rules. I thought about dragging him out into the street and beating him senseless, or warning him off you, or ...'

I half-laughed. 'I'm glad you didn't. I knew all along what he was like, it's just there was no one else, and desperate times call for ... well, anyway, I thought you and I would only ever be friends, and the longer it went on, the less hope there seemed to be, what with your endless parade of ridiculously accomplished and beautiful girlfriends.'

He chuckled. 'None of them meant anything next to you. Perhaps I was hoping you'd see them and get jealous.'

I barked a laugh. 'Don't worry, I was.'

He raised a coy eyebrow. 'Was that the purpose of your handsome-yet-not-overly-accomplished boyfriends?'

I punched his arm. 'Don't pretend you were jealous of any of them.'

He buried his hand in my hair and tugged gently. 'I was so fucking jealous. Why do you think I joined Pete's gym on top of rowing? I had to punch something.'

I preened but didn't fully believe him. 'You're lying.'

'I am not.'

'I love you.'

He kissed me until I was breathless. 'I love you, too.'

'But I still can't get my head around why you put up with Theo in your crew.'

Andrew shrugged. 'He makes the boat go faster.'

I exhaled a laugh and shook my head, but the weirdest part was that I totally understood. 'Fucking rowers.'

ell

Not long later, we stood with the men's crew and our coach near the finish line, Andrew hugging me from behind as we waited for my crew's race to start. It was strange, not having been through the pre-race routine, not carrying a boat to the water, not feeling the butterflies on the start line. Although I had butterflies for entirely different reasons ...

'I can't wait to get out of here,' Andrew murmured in my ear. I leaned into his touch as he kissed my temple. 'And there's no way we're sleeping in my tent.'

'Then where on Earth—'

'We're finding the swankiest, most luxurious hotel within a twenty-minute radius.'

'We can't!' I turned my head to look him in the eye, trying to work out if he was being serious.

'I assure you we can,' he countered, his expression telling me that he very much meant business.

'I can't abandon my crew ...' Although, a swanky hotel, just the two of us, didn't sound terrible.

'They didn't pick you,' he whispered. 'They're dead to me.' I gasp-laughed and swiped him, and he kissed my neck, making me squirm.

'Andrew ...' I breathed, chastising him but also, not. 'We can't leave,' I said, my eyes falling closed on account of the gentle sucking sensation. I had to wait for him to stop before I could find words to continue. 'Your tent is essentially the Ritz; we're already staying in luxury.'

'Too many people,' he said, moving his lips to my ear, which was better, less intimate, but still highly distracting. The race had started, yet I had no clue what was going on. Good thing it would take a few minutes for the eight crews racing side by side to get to our end of the lake. I could bask in Andrew's affections a while longer and not miss the finish.

'But it's after Nationals,' he whispered.

'Almost ...' I said slowly, not catching his drift.

'If we leave, I'll find you the most delectable, grease-filled kebab known to man.'

'You want our first real date to be a kebab?'

'God no! But maybe you do, and I'd endure far worse to get you on your own.'

My heart squeezed, and I turned my head and kissed him, momentarily forgetting where we were.

'Here they come!' squealed Seb, jumping up and down, pulling my attention back to the race, *Em*'s yellow hull now only five hundred meters away.

'Andrew,' I asked, turning in his arms so I could see all of his face. 'Did you name that boat after me?'

He paused, then smirked, then beamed, then dropped a peck on my lips. 'You finally worked it out.'

I scowled. 'I didn't, actually. Your sister told me.'

He shrugged as though that made more sense, and I pinched his arm, which only made him hug me tighter.

'You deserve it,' he whispered.

'Hmm,' I said, skeptically, but the boats were nearly on us, and everyone around us was screaming and clapping and chanting, and we let ourselves get swept up in the moment, jumping and shouting along with everyone else, the nerves somehow worse on the sidelines than on the water.

'Go on Dex!' we all screamed, the race too close to call, my crew—my friends—right in the middle of the fray. 'Go on! Go Dex!'

I was sad not to be out there, fighting for a medal, giving it everything I had, but with Andrew behind me, and my friends all around, I felt strangely content watching my crew fly across the water, screaming at the top of my lungs as they edged ahead of the pack, clasping my hands to my frantic heart as they put in their final furious push, especially because they were doing it in a boat named just for me.

I really hope you enjoyed Miri and Andrew's story, and if you did, I'd appreciate a rating or review on Amazon. If you're active on social media, sharing it on there would be greatly appreciated, too, especially on TikTok, where it's no exaggeration to say you could literally change an author's life.

READ NEXT: If you love paranormal romance as well as contemporaries, check out Nation of the Sun, where Amari has hated her soulmate, Caspar, for a hundred years, but in this life, he finds her before she remembers her past …

Author's Note

W rite what you know, they say. Well, my formative years were spent at a rowing club, training six days a week and competing at regattas all over the country. I was National Indoor Rowing Champion, and had the *second* fastest 2k ergo score in our club (bested by a pesky light-weight, no less, although she did get a silver medal at the World Indoor Championships, so how's anyone reasonably supposed to compete with that?).

Connect with Harri Beaumont

Find Harri on:

Instagram:
https://www.instagram.com/harribeaumont

TikTok:
https://www.tiktok.com/@harribeaumont

Pinterest:
https://www.pinterest.com/harribeaumont/

Titles

Titles by Harri Beaumont:
Love and the Lottery

Titles by HR Moore (Harri's fantasy romance pen):

The Ancient Souls series (complete):
Nation of the Sun
Nation of the Sword
Nation of the Stars

Shadow and Ash Duology (complete):
Kingdoms of Shadow and Ash
Dragons of Asred

Rules of Atlas Magic:
Celestl
Dromeda (coming soon)

https://hrmoore.com/

Printed in Great Britain
by Amazon

45542802R00169